*Praise for*

# TRACY PRICE-THOMPSON

## A Woman's Worth

"The exciting cast of characters in *A Woman's Worth* will keep you intrigued with their loves, lives and lies. There's plenty of suspense, family values and good ole loving. But what stands out most is how her male characters, as hard as they are, aren't afraid to really love the women in their lives."               —*upscale*

"*A Woman's Worth* is a masterfully written story where Price-Thompson not only demonstrates her writing talent with prose that makes you read a sentence twice because of its beauty, but she also provides a compelling not-happily-ever-after story that will keep you flipping the pages. . . . A novel that will have your heart pounding, your eyes tearing, and a story lingering in your mind long after you've read the last page."        —*Quarterly Black Review*

"This intriguing family drama will have you empathizing with the characters, and the ending of this captivating book will take you totally by surprise."               —*Romantic Times*

"Price-Thompson has a keen ear for spoken cadence for evoking a scene—its hues, humidity, pulse, and scents—all the while keeping the tension taut."               —*Ms.* magazine

"With *A Woman's Worth,* Price-Thompson explores cross-cultural issues relating to gender and sexual freedom and, most important, accentuates the core of Black identity—the enormous strength of family."               —*The Skanner* (Portland)

"[*A Woman's Worth*] leaves you wanting more."   —*Asbury Park Press*

# Black Coffee

"A racy tale of romance and ambition in the military."

—*The Washington* P[...]

"Price-Thompson has set this novel among a seldom-writte[...] about group, African Americans in the military. . . . [She does] a[...] excellent job of showcasing a lifestyle not often glamorized b[...] contemporary novelists."  —*Booklis*[...]

"[*Black Coffee*] puts a literal spin on the war between the sexes. . . . This is not a lighthearted, sweet-talking love story, but an energizing slice of ultra-contemporary romance."

—*Publishers Weekly*

# Chocolate Sangria

"A wonderfully written novel that demands attention from page one."  —ZANE, author of *The Heat Seekers*

"[A] heart-wrenching tale of love and family . . . a fable on the consequences of keeping secrets and betrayal."  —*USA Today*

"Vivid, striking prose, heartfelt and authentic. *Chocolate Sangria* is a thought-provoking book that examines sensitive issues among people of color."—MARCUS MAJOR, author of *4 Guys and Trouble*

# A Woman's Worth

# A
# WOMAN'S
# WORTH

A NOVEL

## TRACY PRICE-THOMPSON

 ONE WORLD | Ballantine Books | New York

6457

2005 One World Books Trade Paperback Edition

Copyright © 2004 by Tracy Price-Thompson
Reading group guide copyright © 2005 by Random House, Inc.

Published in the United States by One World Books, an imprint of The Random House Publishing Group, a division of Random House, Inc., New York.

ONE WORLD is a registered trademark and the One World colophon is a trademark of Random House, Inc.

Originally published in hardcover in the United States by One World Books, an imprint of The Random House Publishing Group, a division of Random House, Inc., in 2004.

Library of Congress Cataloging-in-Publication Data
Price-Thompson, Tracy.
A woman's worth: a novel / Tracy Price-Thompson.
p. cm.
ISBN 0-375-75778-3
1. African American men—Fiction. 2. Mothers and daughters—Fiction. 3. Female circumcision—Fiction. 4. Americans—Kenya—Fiction. 5. Women—Kenya—Fiction. 6. Alabama—Fiction. 7. Kenya—Fiction. I. Title.
PS3616.R53W66 2004
813'.6—dc22    2003063962

Printed in the United States of America

www.oneworldbooks.net

4   6   8   9   7   5   3

Text design by Jo Anne Metsch

*This work is dedicated to the good black men who've
touched my life, past and present.*

*Most important . . .*

*To my husband, Gregory C. Thompson,
who walks it like he talks it,
and personifies the true essence of a M-A-N,
while making me feel like a natural W-O-M-A-N;*

*And to my dear friend, Timmothy B. McCann,
whose dedication to his children is extraordinary,
and whose words of wisdom and cherished friendship are sorely missed;*

*And to the enduring memories of my father, brother, and brothers-in-love,*

*Edward Marcus Johnson III
Bland Jentry Carr, Jr.
Joseph Andrew Hansome III
George Carroll Thompson III*

*The world is a lonely place without you. . . .*

A Letter from Tracy . . .

Shortly after my first novel, *Black Coffee,* was released, an interviewer asked, "Tracy, what are your goals as a writer?" My answer then was the same as it is now. My goal as a writer is to respect my readership, and in order to accomplish this I must continually challenge myself to present you with stories that are unique and exciting. Of all the accolades a writer can receive, for me the ultimate thrill is to have a reader pick up a copy of my work and know they are about to take one hell of a ride. To understand that they will not get cheated out of something fresh, and will not be presented with a carefully veiled repetition of my last work. I am thrilled to have a reader flip to the opening pages of my current work and wonder with gleeful anticipation, "Ooooh, child! Where is this gal gonna take us this time?"

Of course, this means I owe it to you as my reader to be a creative writer and to pay attention to my writer's voice. I have to tap into my muse and think outside of the box. I must refrain from falling into the trap of, book after book, changing the title and the physical descriptions yet clinging to the same worn themes and stereotypical characters while praying that you, the reader, aren't astute enough to notice.

That said, you can be assured that *A Woman's Worth* was written with the ultimate respect, and with you in mind. Between these pages I test the realms of sexual promiscuity and explore cross-cultural issues relating to gender and sexual freedom. As such, I trust you will feel my characters' pain and live their joy as you travel with them along their perilous roads. And as always, I ask that you hang on tight and enjoy the ride.

# A Woman's Worth

# Wind

E vening in Paris oozed from her skin, embracing him in its sexy aroma. The gorgeous sister grinned and pulled a customer along behind her as Bishop stood watching from the foyer. He gave a low whistle as she sashayed past, high heels clicking against the hardwood floor, tantalizing ass swirling up a storm under her hot lemon skirt.

"Don't hurt nobody!" he called out, his eyes dancing in his fifteen-year-old face. The woman winked over her shoulder, and Bishop laughed as she reached back and squeezed the thigh of Birdtown's fire chief, then ran her fingers over his swollen crotch before nudging him past the security guards and up the flight of stairs that led to her second-floor bedroom.

A southerly wind charged through a hall window, whipping the paisley curtains into a twirl. Fresh from the gym and dressed in sweats and high-top Converses, Bishop adjusted the boxing gloves hanging over his shoulder and strode past the kitchen, where the smell of catfish and butter beans hung in the air.

A man could get a lot at Slim Willie's Place. It was a joint brimming with vice and good times, and each Friday when the eagle flew, dinner was on the house and came with a wedge of sweet-potato pie that had Alaga syrup baked into the crust.

The house was a rectangular wood-frame with a tar roof and high ceilings. There were six bedrooms on the third floor and four on the second. On the first floor there was an office, a kitchen, a dining room, and a large parlor, where Bishop now paused to enjoy the sights. The room was spacious and spilling over with work-hardened men who had lined up to sample the finest women Birdtown had to offer.

Nothing about his parents' lifestyle had been hidden from him. Bishop had known early on exactly what it was the beautiful women of his house were selling. Had left bug-eyed Sammy Smalls bruised and bloody in the third grade for calling Dimples a prostitute and Slim Willie a pimp. "Not true," Slim Willie had said, laughing. "Your mama was pure when I met her, and I ain't never touched a ho."

A popular tune filled the air, and Bishop watched as several couples took to the dance floor. Hard-shoed men swung their partners in a six-step hustle, their rough hands pressed into slender, arched backs. Threading through the crowd, Bishop approached a table where three women sat smoking cigarettes and sipping cold beer. House mothers, they'd been with Slim Willie from the early days and were considered family.

"Hey there, Big Gussie. Evening, Miz Leila. How do, Miz May? Anybody seen Dimples?"

Gussie answered. "Her and Boogalou gone to see about Janie. The poor thing done took sick again."

"Hmph!" May snorted. She tossed her corn-silk wig and smirked. "Dimples my ass! Bishop ain't studying his mama. Dimples can go to shit, if she wants to. Bishop's eye is on that new girl over there. Reenie, with her young, fine-ass self. Mama, hell. The boy ain't got nothing but poontang on his brain!"

Leila laughed. "Well, what you 'spect from a child who done

spent his whole life surrounded by titties and ass? Drowning in
fishnet drawers and lace garter belts." She stood and slunk toward
Bishop, peering through her lashes. "Yeah, I think it's time"—her
voice dropped a creamy octave—"for the boy to stop chokin' that
chicken and get his cherry busted by a real pro."

"Oh, *my* God!" Big Gussie threw up her hands and hollered.
"The baby boy is gonna get him some *pussy*! Look like just yesterday I was spanking his narrow ass and changing his funky diapers!"

"And that ass still ain't big as a bar of soap after a week's washing!"

Bishop tolerated the banter good-naturedly as the women
poked at his muscles and marveled at his perfect smile.

Laughing, Leila posed in her thigh-high boots and held one
hand in the air, demanding attention. Despite her forty-two years
she was firm everywhere and held her own against the younger
women of the house. She tilted her head and stared into Bishop's
eyes. "I think the boy is ready to get started right now." Her full
breasts jiggled and enveloped him in a cloud of Chanel No. 5.
Winking at the ladies, she grabbed his hand and guided it between her legs, then pulled it back and made a show of swirling
her pink tongue in and out between his fingers.

"Chile," Big Gussie said, snatching Bishop away as Leila tried
to give his thumb some head. "You must be smellin' yourself!
Leave the boy be! Your tired ass ain't worth half as much as you
think it is!"

"Sheeiit . . ." Leila laughed. "You gots to be kiddin'!" She
slapped her right flank, and her flesh rocked deliciously beneath
her pale pink swing skirt. "Do this ass look tired to you?"

▏▏▏▏▏▏▏▏

Bishop crossed the room to where two armed men stood block-
ing a narrow doorway.

"Roscoe. Jake."

"Boy."

Bishop waited while Roscoe unlocked the door, then loped

down the short flight of stairs and stepped into the dimly lit room where cutthroat games of poker and tonk went on twenty-four hours a day. He was greeted by the stink of whiskey, cigars, and dangerous men. The institutional gray walls were completely lined with soundproof paneling, and the atmosphere was almost tomb-like compared to the festivities going on upstairs.

In the center of the room a cluster of bulbs dangled by exposed wires. Beneath them a huddle of players were paired off around two palm-worn tables, their original colors rubbed away by the heavy, money-raking hands of gambling men. At the table on the left, Slim Willie sat dressed in all white, studying his cards. An ivory fedora was broken down over his brow, his thin legs were crossed at the knee, and a spiral of smoke coiled skyward from the Tiparillo he bit between his teeth. He was short, with a pale, ro-dentlike face. His nose twitched once, then he glanced up and nodded at his son.

On the far side of the room behind a vinyl-topped bar stood bull-chested Skeeter Powers, a killer with bloodshot eyes, a left hand that was short two fingers, and forearms as thick as tree trunks. He smiled as Bishop crossed the room.

"Chicken!" Skeeter pointed a cocked thumb and forefinger. "Whatchoo say now, boy? You ready to shoot them jabs and throw them hooks?"

"Chicken." Bishop shook his head, fist-dapping Lazy Jackson and Casper Wilson, who leaned on the bar, drinks in hand. "Man, when is everybody gonna stop calling me that?"

"Take it light, boy." Skeeter picked up a rag and wagged it over the countertop. "'Ere'body in here know you got your daddy's quick hands and strong heart. Ain't nuthin' yellow 'bout you but your skin."

Bishop sat on a stool next to Casper, while Lazy swigged from a bottle. "Sup?" He nudged Casper with his elbow. "Long time no see."

"Sure is." Casper drummed his fingers on the countertop. "You still holding that oh?" His blond hair was in a buzz cut, and his nails had been trimmed and filed.

Bishop nodded. "Yeah. Fourteen and oh. Doc says if I keep my chin tucked, I got a good chance of making the Gloves next year." He straddled his stool. "Heard you a big-time politician now. Slumming?"

"Nah."

"Then what brings a clean white boy like you into the bottoms tonight?"

"Your daddy. Finished up my time as an alderman, and I'm heading up to the governor's office. I reckon I have a decent chance of taking the elections next year. But first"—he angled his head toward Slim Willie—"I wanted to come and pay my respects to Slim, and let him see that all his hard work hadn't gone down a shit hole."

"Uhmm." Bishop nodded again. As bad a cat as Slim Willie was and as much as he hated white folks, he could be good that way. Casper was the son of Birdtown's mayor, and ten years earlier Slim had saved him from a cutting outside a gambling joint in neighboring Argle, a small mining community on the wrong side of the tracks. Casper had run up a sizable debt, and house rules demanded that payment be taken out of his ass. They had him on the ground with his pants around his ankles when Slim stepped in and did him a solid.

Bishop had always wondered why his father had stepped up for a white boy whose daddy fried brothers like they were whiting and porgies, but Slim had assured him, "Son, black or white, every man deserves to die with his dick on. Besides, the kid looked like he mighta been worth somethin' one day. Never know when we might need him."

Behind the bar, Skeeter wiped down bottles and spoke over his shoulder. "Who'd you leave on the back door?"

Lazy answered. "Junius and . . . Black Rabbit."

"Front?"

"Clyde . . . and Bigger." He paused. "Why?"

"Nuthin'," Skeeter growled. "Sumpthin' just ain't feelin' right, that's all."

Lazy's jaws creaked opened and he laughed, a sluggish, braying sound. "Well . . . what the fuck's poking . . . you in the ass? Don't tell me . . . somethin' got big bad Skeeter's dick . . . soft."

Casper laughed, and Skeeter spun around and slammed both hands down on the bar. The muscles in his forearms bulged as a blast of whiskey-fouled breath flew from his mouth. "Just what in the fuck you think is gonna spook me, you lazy-lipped son of a bitch? I fought with the best of them at Da Nang and got hit four times at Saigon. I was back out in the bush an hour after they patched me up, and that same night I took out half a platoon of Charlies by my goddamn self—some wit' my rifle, some up close wit' my bayonet, an' even more than that wit' "—he raised his palms and all three men flinched—"these here two hands!

"And"—Skeeter glared at Casper with killer eyes—"I kin tell you sumpthin' too, Mistah White Boy. Skeeter don't scare, and Slim Willie don't neither! Whatever you seent Slim do that night in Argle, you ain't seent shit. Slim might look light in the ass, but that there is a scrappy niggah if I ever seent one."

He motioned to Bishop. "What kinda man you think can live in a house wit' sixteen snatches an' don't play in but one? Chicken, I seent your daddy cut a niggah's ass too short to shit and too thin to win! And that time Mackie Moe and his boys ran a train on Black Sheila? Oh!" Skeeter shuddered. "It was a ugly thang! Everywhare Slim touched that motherfucker he bled. Crushed Mackie's gun hand in one fist. Took me, Roscoe, and Buttermilk to pull Slim offa them boys, and grabbing hold of him was like tryin' to hold tight to cold snakes."

He gazed at Bishop with something close to pride in his eyes, then said, "You shoulda seent them cats, Chicken Boy. Your daddy had 'em laid out like mashed-up doll babies. Skulls crushed and bones broke all the hell up." He frowned. "Much as I seent in the war and as many mens I done took out, you think I'd be used to it, but the way Slim carved them niggahs up was the most terrible thang. Only a damn fool would wanna get caught on the wrong end of your daddy's hand."

Bishop nodded and tore the plastic wrapper off a toothpick. "You got that shit right. Motherfuckers know Slim don't play. So chill, my man! Damn! Can a brother get a root beer?" He reached over and slapped Skeeter's thick shoulder, and it was like pounding concrete.

Skeeter grunted and looked under the bar for a glass. He took an A & W from a small refrigerator and pried the metal cap off with his back teeth. "Whatever, boy. Somewhere out in Birdtown, shit is gettin' stirred. My right eye ain't jumpin' for nuthin'."

"Goddamn, Skeet!" Bishop laughed. "Ain't nothin' out there to sweat. There ain't too many fools who wanna roll up in Slim Willie's Place to die. Remember," Bishop said, swigging the froth from his soda, then counting off on his fingers, "you don't tug on Superman's cape. You don't hock spit into the wind. You don't pull the mask off that old Lone Ranger, *and you don't fuck around with Slim!*"

Bishop manned the bar while Skeeter played twenty-one at the table opposite Slim. He was enjoying another cold root beer when he heard the door open above them.

"Hey, Slim!" Roscoe yelled from the top of the steps. "Buttermilk say Blind Joe upstairs fuckin' wit' Little Momma. Say he up there tossin' shit around her room 'cause she won't let him keep a pair of her dirty drawers! You want me to go throw his raggedy ass out? You know I'll do it!"

Slim flipped over his hole card, an ace, and raked in the pot. "Naw, man. Blind Joe don't mean no harm. He got a panty fetish, that's all. Plus, he be family." Slim grinned and pulled out his pearl-handled stiletto. He slid the sharp tip beneath his quarter-sized nail beds and began cleaning them. "You can't go around throwin' family outdoors. He likes Skeeter, though." Slim nodded. "Gone, Skeet. Gone up an' see about it."

Skeeter's cards hit the table. "Hell, naw!" He pointed at Lazy, who had a beer in one hand and a shot glass of bathtub brew in the other. "Send that slow niggah up! I'ma set my ass right down here tonight."

"Gone, Skeeter." Slim Willie waved. "Lazy's 'bout full. Go right up and come on back down. Don't fool wit' none a the ladies, just put Uncle Joe down in a empty room and come on back."

"But Slim—"

Slim cut him off with a raised palm. "Damn, Sergeant! This ain't 'Nam! Ain't nuthin' jumpin' off in the next three minutes you gone miss out on! Ere'body is in place tonight. The soldiers is on guard. Gone, now!"

Skeeter stood and moved slowly toward the steps, his footsteps heavy. Near the doorway he turned. "Don't yawl let nuthin' go down," he growled, letting his eyes touch every man in the room, "and live to talk about it. Or you'll hafta come see me."

⁂

It was after midnight, and Slim Willie's Place was jumping. The music could be heard from the parking area out back, and Dimples coughed and twisted her pretty face as she and Boogalou stepped out of Slim's white Cadillac, arms overflowing with garbage bags of soiled linen taken from Janie's apartment.

With a warm wind pushing at their backs, they struggled toward the house. Boogalou sneezed and shuddered, sending her platinum braids swirling around her head. "Girl, Janie gots to do something 'bout all them goddamn animals! House smelling like ten kinds of hell! She ain't gonna find but so many fools willing to go up in there stepping in cat shit and hacking up fur."

"I know." Dimples cringed at the stiff strands of cat hair covering her short white dress and matching bolero jacket. Her dark skin looked like velvet under the moonlight. "I don't like it neither, but that colon cancer ain't no joke. It's eating her ass up and there's no way I'ma let her lay up there by herself, filthy and hungry. Did you see what she was eating when we got there? Bald-headed macaroni? With no cheese?" She shook her head. "Lord, Janie ain't got nobody but us, Boog. Who else gonna go see about her?"

At the front of the house they climbed the three wide steps and stood on the slatted porch. With her knee braced against the door, Dimples adjusted her bags, hoisting them in her slender brown arms. Behind her, Boogalou sucked her teeth and complained. "Shit, it ain't that I mind helping out, 'cause I don't, but goddamn! How many mutherfuckin' cats do one pers—"

Boogalou gurgled, then pitched forward and hit the wooden porch with a thud. Dimples stared as her friend lay on the ground clutching her neck and writhing for air. Her braids fell around her face as a slit stretched across her throat like a crazy grin and a red puddle pooled on the wood beneath her head.

Cold steel chilled the back of Dimples's neck, and she gasped.

"Don't turn around, and don't say nothin'."

The man leaned into her, and she heard heavy footsteps scramble up the stairs as his partners joined him on the porch. "What—"

She was shoved forward, the odor of fear and wine thickening the air.

"Bitch, shut your black ass up! Slim must be slippin'. Thought he trained his ho's better'n that." He nudged her. "Get real close to the door, then knock hard and let 'em see who you is! Act a fool so I can put a hole in your neck."

Dimples dropped the plastic bags and tapped on the door with the toe of her shoe. She trembled as the cover plate of the peephole slid left, then right, and a series of locks were turned. Festive sounds rushed from the house as the wind pushed her through the door. With the barrel pressed into her neck, Dimples bit her lip against her fear. She stood in plain view of Bigger and Clyde, who had their weapons drawn before she saw their hands move.

Behind her, the gunman laughed. "Calm down, cowboys.

Wouldn't wanna make me blow this ho's head all over them fancy new suits."

"Motherfucker!" Clyde swore. "Pharaoh?"

Dimples sneezed.

Two short blasts exploded near her ear, and Clyde fell to the ground. Gun-deaf, she never heard the third shot, the one that took Bigger out.

Cringing, Dimples turned and saw four familiar men. Pharaoh and his boys. Junkies and lowlife thieves. And that Sammy no older than her Bishop.

They forced her past the dying men, down the foyer, and toward the crowded parlor. As they rounded the corner, a thunderous voice boomed out from the top of the stairs.

"I done *told* your blind ass! Panties is for pussies—what the fuck?"

Dimples looked up as Skeeter barreled down the stairs muscling Blind Joe ahead of him, his face a mask of rage and disbelief. A third shot rang out and a dark hole appeared on Blind Joe's forehead. The slug continued on, ripping through Skeeter's neck before lodging in the wall behind him. Skeeter sank to his knees clutching his throat, then tumbled headlong down the steps. He came to rest at Dimples's feet, his dead eyes wide and angry.

Biting back a scream, Dimples was forced onward, the cracking of firearms lost in the booming sounds of Parliament and Funkadelic. She stumbled and nearly went down near the entrance to the parlor, and the man behind her used his pistol to prod her along.

"Straighten up an' act naturally, gal. You wouldn't want my boys to open up on all a these payin' customers now, would you? Put Slim outta bizzniss real quick that'a way!" He pushed her forward. "Head on over to them big niggers near that side door. We gonna hit the basement first, then Slim can show us where the real money is."

Dimples's knees were rubber as she stepped into the room,

guided forcibly along the wall and toward the door where Roscoe and Jake stood watch. The men held her hostage, crouching behind her single-file, using her body as a shield.

As her heart pounded, she felt a strange breeze sweep along the floor and cloak her, and for the first time since Boogalou hit the porch Dimples smelled her own death. But the scent riding the wind was greedy. It snaked up her nostrils and etched a rancid trail down the back of her throat, and she tasted Slim Willie's blood.

And with Slim Willie gone, their son didn't stand a chance.

Staring straight ahead, Dimples met Roscoe's eyes. Understanding filled his gaze as he pulled his weapon and shot into the air. Patrons hugged the hardwood floors, and pistols and revolvers barked in short, uneven bursts. Dimples seized the advantage, and the shit hit the fan. She took a short step forward and slammed her foot down, grinding her heel into Pharaoh's instep. The gunman screamed, and Dimples swirled and kicked hard into his crotch. Grabbing his testicles, Pharaoh screamed again and threw up, splattering her legs and feet.

Rounds whizzed by and Dimples dropped to her knees. She crouched against the wall as couples fell, bullets passing through snuggling bodies and cashing in two marks for the price of one. Grown men crawled from the room on their hands and knees, and she watched in horror as bullets picked them off one by one.

She screamed and covered her face as Roscoe went down, firing his weapon until the light left his eyes. Junius slid down the wall, a grimace on his face and a small hole darkening the front of his shirt.

And then lightning seemed to strike as pain exploded on the top of her head. Dimples looked up as Pharaoh's fists rained upon her, hammering her nose, blackening her eyes, battering her cheeks. Trails of vomit still hung from his lips. No one except Lester Wilkes had ever beaten her this way, and something inside her snapped.

She rose and swung on Pharaoh, returning his punches blow for blow, howling, screaming, scratching at his face, drawing blood and leaving shards of dangling skin.

On cue, the ladies of the house joined her. Charging from beneath overturned chairs and tables, they hiked up their skirts and swarmed on the four men.

They fought for bitter seconds. The surprised men protected their faces and groins as the wall of women descended, scratching, kicking, punching, and biting, until a heavy blast rang out, freezing them where they stood. Quiet fell over the room, and eternity clanged past.

"Oh my God!" May covered her mouth and pointed at Dimples, who was taking tiny steps forward, her lips open in a silent scream.

"Call a fuckin' ambulance!" Leila wailed.

Sammy stomped his feet and waved his gun in the air. "Goddamn it, Papa! You said we wasn't gonna hurt no women!"

Blood bubbled from Dimples's lips, and she fell into Leila's outstretched arms, dragging her friend down to the ground with her. The front door banged violently as an invading wind blew the scent of death over the room, and as the gunmen regrouped, the ladies bolted, once again scattering for cover, leaping over lifeless bodies and sliding in a river of blood.

Pharaoh grabbed Big Gussie and shoved May toward his son. "Here. Git behind these bitches! The money! We gots to git downstairs and git Slim Willie!"

Stepping over Roscoe's body, Pharaoh aimed at the lock and fired. Motioning, he ordered Redman, Sammy, and Jug to follow him, then headed down into the darkness.

▒▒▒▒▒▒

Downstairs, Slim looked up just as the lock blew. The door banged open, and moments later he saw a shaky pair of multicolored high-heeled shoes at the top of the stairs. Early and Kess had drawn their guns but checked themselves at the pleas of May and Big Gussie.

"Don't shoot! Lawdhamercy, Slim, they got us out front! Don't shoot!"

Slim stood, and Frank and Ronnie jumped in front of him. "Naw." He pushed past them and pointed toward the bar. "Get down, boy," he commanded, as Bishop stood with an icy root beer in his hand.

"We coming down!" Pharaoh yelled. The women were forced down the stairs as he and his men followed, guns cocked.

Bishop stared. Pharaoh Smalls and his son, Sammy. Redman Walker and his drinking partner, Jug Taylor. Even over the cloud of gunpowder he could smell the fear rolling off the men. Desperate, killing fear.

"My man, Slim Willie!" Pharaoh cried. "You ain't had to get up out your special chair just for me! I know you said my money wasn't no good 'round here no more." He trained his weapon at Slim Willie's head and grinned. "But of course yours is always good with me!"

Slim Willie grinned right back.

"All we want is the money, Slim," parroted Jug. His gun hand trembled, and his voice squeaked out in a high-pitched whine. "Jes' give us what we come for an' we turn right around an' leave."

Slim Willie laughed then. A short, deadly sound that scared Jug so badly his hand trembled and he nearly dropped his gun. Bishop watched as his father moved so fast he looked like a bolt of white lightning. Slim grabbed Jug's gun hand and forced it back, the sound of snapping bones filling the air. Jug's scream was cut short as Slim slid his stiletto straight through the man's heart and then retracted it with finesse.

Redman Walker hit the stairs and flew up them two at a time.

Pharaoh moved. He brought his arm up and put a hole first in Frank, then in Lazy. Then he leveled his gun again. Not at Slim Willie but at Big Gussie.

Snatching the woman in a yoke, he warned, "Fuck around if
you want to, Slim. I'll blow this bitch's head off! We gone upstairs
and crack that safe, motherfucker. Now move, upstairs!"

Slim stared for a long moment at Big Gussie, then raised his
arms and turned toward the stairs, and Bishop knew Pharaoh was
a dead man. You didn't threaten Slim's women and expect to live.
He watched quietly as Pharaoh grabbed Big Gussie in a choke
hold and followed Slim Willie upstairs.

Sammy's eyes were wet when he looked at Bishop. He blinked
rapidly but kept his gun pointed as he climbed the stairs backward, one by one, until he too disappeared from sight.

For long moments the basement was tamped down in silence, and
then Casper moved. Bolting up the stairs, he ran toward the door.
Bishop was right behind him, and at the top of the steps he flung
himself through the doorway and stumbled over something soft
and heavy. He looked down and saw the new girl, Reenie, her
platinum wig cascading around her tender face, a partial boot
print dusting her forehead.

"No," Bishop whispered. "God, no . . ."

"Don't look." Casper pulled Bishop into his arms. "Everything's okay," he whispered. "Everything is gonna be fine."

The house looked like a battlefield. Bishop clamped one hand
over his eyes and held tight to Casper with the other. The odor of
blood and gunpowder stung his nose as the Isley Brothers fought
the powers that be from the speakers. The white man guided
Bishop through the parlor like it was a minefield, whispering instructions along the way. "Step up and over, Bishop. Don't look
down. Okay, move to your right. More. That's it. Big step, now.
There you go. Straight ahead."

They came upon Dimples, bloody and lying on her side. "Oh,
shit," Casper moaned. "Don't look, Chicken Boy. Jesus fucking
Christ, just keep your eyes closed and don't look."

Moments later they reached Slim Willie's office, and at the sound of his father's voice, Bishop shook Casper off and opened his eyes.

"Pharaoh," Slim Willie was saying, "one a us gone hafta bleed in here tonight, mothafuckah."

Slim sat before his safe. Pharaoh and Sammy aimed pistols at his head. On his desk were stacks of playing cards and liquor receipts. Slim's nose twitched and he rose to his feet. Without taking his eyes off Pharaoh, he commanded, "Turn 'round, Bishop. Casper, gone an' take the boy back outside."

"Sit the fuck down, Slim." Pharaoh swung his gun around to Bishop. "Sit back down and spin that dial, or I'm put a hole in his scrawny yellow ass before you can blink."

*Mistake,* thought Bishop.

Slim Willie smiled. A horrible smile that showed every one of his teeth. His hand quick-caught Pharaoh at the throat and tightened around his neck like a noose. The room filled with the sound of snapping bones, and blood spilled from the corners of Pharaoh's mouth. His pistol dangled from his limp hand.

Sammy screamed, "Turn him loose, Slim! Turn him loose!" His eyes darted toward Bishop, but his gun stayed aimed at Slim Willie. For a moment the boys held each other's gaze, and Bishop saw a glimpse of the scared, bucktoothed Sammy he'd known in the third grade. He was still scared, and a dark stain had spread across the front of his pants.

Slim Willie let Pharaoh go and reached for Sammy.

The boy's gun coughed, and Slim staggered, a blotch of red slowly staining his white suit. Wind rushed past, sending Tally Ho's scattering from the desk and onto the floor, and then Bishop's ears were filled with his own screams.

With one hand pressed to his chest, Slim Willie lifted young Sammy into the air by the neck and squeezed for long moments until the boy's eyes rolled back and he fell lifeless to the floor.

Casper moaned and vomited, and Bishop caught his father as

he staggered forward. In the parlor, the album ended and the scratchy sounds of the spent 33 could be heard skipping through the speakers.

"Daddy." Bishop lowered Slim Willie to the floor and cradled him in his arms. "Daddy, no. Please."

Slim Willie reached for his son's hand. He struggled to speak. "Be . . . be . . ."

"Don't talk," Bishop begged.

Slim Willie gripped Bishop's neck. His lips were on his ear.

"Daddy . . ." Bishop moaned as his father's wet hand slid down his arm. And as Slim Willie fought the gray blanket that rushed down to cover him, the wind crept through the room, picked up the words that rode on his breath, and blew them directly into his son's ear.

"B-b-be . . . be . . . a man."

Bishop lowered his head to his father's chest and cried until he felt hands upon him. He looked up and saw Big Gussie.

"Dimples?" he asked.

She shook her head, then allowed him to press his face into her body and wail. Big Gussie rubbed his shoulders briefly, then pushed him away, her skirt dappled with blood like an artist's smock.

"Stand up, Bishop," she commanded. "And stop all that goddamn cryin'. It's on you now. Get your shit off! That motherfucker over there is still breathin'. Go finish it!"

"No, Bishop," Casper whispered. "No."

Tears fell from his eyes as Bishop rocked and moaned and cried out, "Oh . . . Slim . . . Dimples . . . no . . ."

Big Gussie smacked his face twice. Hard. "Dry it up, goddamn it, and don't you *dare* cry! Boy, you is now a *man*! You's the *son* of a man!"

Bishop lifted his head and clarity filled his eyes. He pulled himself to a stand and the wind carried him over to the man wheezing on the floor. Sirens wailed in the distance, and the odor of spilled blood hung in the air.

"Chicken Boy," Casper begged. "Don't do it. I can't be here . . . the law . . . I can't . . ."

Bishop reached down and plucked the gun from Pharaoh's yielding hand. He turned to Casper. "Go, motherfucker," he whispered, his voice icy. "Then go."

"Sorry. So sorr . . ." Casper muttered. He reached out and clutched Bishop to his chest, then fled, his footsteps thunderous on the hardwood floors.

Bishop stood over the dying Pharaoh, who closed his eyes on the boy, refusing to beg.

"Be a man," the wind commanded, and dry-eyed, Bishop obeyed.

He pulled the trigger twice, and then twice more.

Outside the house police lights flashed and sirens screamed, and as he fell to his knees and pushed his face into his father's bloody chest, William Bishop Bartholomew Johnson was filled with a certainty that could not be disputed.

He was truly a man, and he was truly alone.

# PART ONE

# CHICKEN

# ONE

## Bull Run, Alabama

Chicken could be one mean motherfucker.

I knew this the moment I laid eyes on him. Short and tough, with sandy hair slicked all over his head, it was easy to see how he got his name, and the way Old Man Wilkes slaved him out at that Snatch Hatch . . . shucks, when a scrawny yellow nigger like him felt ugly, all hell was bound to break loose.

It was hot for September when I met him. Indian summer, Poppa Daddy called it. The kind of day that spotted bass jumped out the waters of Black Shoals Lake and teenage girls swam half-naked in Dudson Creek.

Chicken had just gotten out of jail, and I sat sweating under the awning of Millie's Fabric Store—chewing on a string of black licorice and watching Jessie-Belle Lawson's hips as she and her daddy strolled up and down the open market, squeezing peaches, sniffing melons, and piling onions and peppers on top of big hunks of roasted chicken and sausage.

Sugar Baby, my granmaw, had gone inside to buy some fabric for the Bull Run Girls Junior Drill Team, and I rocked back and forth on a wooden crate diggin' the happenings on the crowded street.

Jessie-Belle looked good, even on a dog day. A church girl gone bad, she sat next to me in senior lit, and every brother on the campus of Bull Run High had fantasized about those curves circling 'round her curves, coming off of her curves, but none more than me. Today she'd decked her banging body in a white skirt with a halter top and a pair of high heels, and as she strutted past I took off my baseball cap and covered my johnson, which had swollen up like a snake that's ready to spit.

Jessie-Belle, or Jezza-Belle as she was known in the bottoms, was on a short leash, but that had never stopped her. She and her father, a squat-necked preacher who once played defensive end for the Dallas Cowboys but now made guarding his daughter's virtue his full-time job, walked back and forth between the vendor tables, portable carts, and makeshift stands. Every so often the good Reverend Lawson would turn around and bust me eye-balling Jezza-Belle's assets, and I'd squint up into the sun and make like I was admiring the beauty of J.C. Himself. The glare on his face told me he wasn't fooled. It also told me what he'd do if I ever got close enough to his daughter to do more than just look.

I'd been in Bull Run for eleven years. Eleven years since the night my father saved my life, then walked back into a burning house to die in my mother's arms. Eleven years since my grandparents, Ike and Sugar Baby Armstrong, had flown to Oakland to fetch me, Malcolm Marcus Mosiah Armstrong, the only son of their only son.

I leaned back on the crate as the sputtering of a strained motor drifted down the street, its engine backfiring, the popping sounds getting lost in the noisy crowd of Saturday shoppers. As fine as Jezza-Belle was, and as hard as I was diggin' on her, I also kept one eye trained across the street on Fleck's Pharmacy, where Barney Judd and his boys stood outside smoking and joking, bumping into passersby, and generally cuttin' the fool.

More than thirty years had passed since the days of Jim Crow, and Bull Run was still a town divided. The only place black and white went together was on book pages and piano keys, and poor white trash like Jimmy Stone, Ralph Dobson, and Barney Judd fed on our color conflicts and kept them raging full steam.

Me, Ralph, and Barney went way back. As kids, we'd boxed together over at Dockside Gym, where I was the only brother fighting on the roster. By the time I was thirteen I had a left hook like a mallet, and my Poppa Daddy decided to tear down his old barn and build a place where I could win in the ring without having to prove myself all over again with a bunch of white boys outside in an alley.

Ralphie Dobson was a decent fighter, but Barney was a redneck with true skills. He was mean and nasty, the kind of boxer who kicked ass first and took names later, both in and out of the ring. We'd met on the canvass once and it came out a draw, but the minute I switched gyms and was no longer on his team, he quit faking the funk and got a hard-on for me that had lasted for almost five years.

Barney came from a large family of riffraff trailer trash who, outside of boxing, generation after generation had produced less than dirt. Them Judds were known to despise black folks, and shopping with Granmaw or no, Barney wasn't above jumping on a brother and scuffling in the street, so I kept my eye on him and his ragbag crew while I waited for Sugar Baby to buy her fabric and come on out the store.

The heavy rumbling drew closer, and a faded blue truck belonging to Old Man Wilkes crawled down the street kicking up dust as waves of heat rose up in front of it.

"Eggs . . ."

Lester Wilkes made his produce run once a week, and his raggedy pickup swayed as the wood-slated bed bumped along the path, his fragile cargo in the back cushioned in crates and tucked under thick layers of cloth.

"Egggsss . . . for sale . . ."

The old man eased the truck over to the curb, his fat arm hanging out the window, a Pall Mall pinched between his fingers.

"Come an' git yo' fresh egggsssss!"

There was an empty space ten paces in front of me, between a perfume vendor and a johnny pump. Wilkes eased the pickup in and shifted into park.

"Eeeeeggggggs! Fresh egggsss! Jest a buck'll git you a dozen fresh eggggsss . . ."

Wilkes opened his door and hopped to the ground. I sat up straight as he glanced around the market, then nodded, apparently satisfied with the crowd.

"Git your ass down, boy," I heard him snap as he limped to the back of the truck. He pulled a dirty cloth from his pocket and coughed, then spit into the dust and stirred the glob with the toe of his boot. Folks began straggling over to inspect his goods, and the slick little hooch-brewing man whispered from the corner of his mouth, "Hur'rup an' pull them blankets off an' let these stingy mothafuckahs git a good look."

I peered into the back of the truck. A rat-faced young brother sat with his back propped against the rotted planks. Pulling himself up, he stood on the chrome bumper and glanced around, then jumped down from the bed of the truck. He was short and looked real mad about it, his mouth set, his skin damn near the color of piss. He wore faded jeans, but them suckers sported a mean crease, and his thin arms were knotted up with muscles beneath his bleached-clean undershirt.

I'd heard all kinds of rumors about this kid and what he'd done. They said his name was Bishop Johnson and that he went for bad. I'd also heard he was coming to twelfth-grade classes at Bull Run High, but I seriously doubted it 'cause Brothaman was light in the ass and didn't look a day over fourteen.

I watched as he yanked the padded cloths off the cargo bed and stuffed them down in the spaces between the crates. He did all of this real smooth-like, moving like he was his own man on his own time, then he propped his foot up on the fender, its original shine dulled and mottled with crusted drops of chicken shit.

"Hey there, Lester Wilkes." Betty Hodge, Bull Run's first black librarian, walked up holding two dollar bills. As hot as it was, she had on a blue pants suit with fake fur around the collar, flip-flops, and a wide-brimmed hat.

"Mornin', Mizz Betty." Old Man Wilkes took off his cap and bent a little at the waist. "How's Cal holdin' up?"

Miss Betty had the nerve to fan herself. "Fair to middling, especially for a man who been struck so low. He even managed to sit up and eat a little bit this morning. Course, it ran right back out his mouth and down his shirt, the funky black dog. A stroke ain't the worst thing he coulda got, seeing how he couldn't stay his tail outta that nasty cooch joint you runnin' out there in them woods. But God don't tell you when or how he's gonna make you pay for your sins. He just assures you that your black behind *will*."

I snickered. She was talking about the Snatch Hatch. I was dying to get out to that lake and see for myself if what they said about Wilkes's jook joint was true.

"Well, God bless him." Wilkes shrugged and motioned toward his crates. "You want the usual two dozen today?"

"Yes, please," she said. "And make sure ain't none spoilt. Last week you gimme a carton with two rotten ones on the bottom."

Wilkes frowned. "That musta been my no-good nephew put them rotten eggs in there! Ain't enough I gots to feed and clothe him, since he just got outta the bad-boy house and ain't got no other kinfolk. He's lazy as hell and coo-coo too."

Miss Betty grabbed the eyeglasses hanging from a silver chain around her neck and balanced them on her nose. She stared at Brothaman, who sat with his elbow on his knee and his chin in his hand, gazing off into the crowd. "This here your nephew? The one they say kilt all them folks up in his daddy's ho house?" Miss Betty clutched her change purse to her chest and studied him closer. "He don't look like no big-time killer to me. Child look like he hungry, if anything. What your name is, honey? Tell Miss Betty what they call you."

Brothaman took all day acknowledging the old woman. Made me wonder if he was planning on opening his mouth at all.

Wilkes wondered too. "Yellah niggah, you—" He fumbled around trying to undo his belt. "You heared Mizz Betty! Hur'rup and answer when grown folks talkin' at you!"

That little nephew of Wilkes's gave him a look so hateful it froze his hand, and as big as I was, my heart did a double pump at the naked violence in his face.

"Chicken," he said, and stood up straight, pure meanness jetting from his eyes. I let out my breath, surprised to find that I'd been holding it. "I go by Chicken."

‖‖‖‖‖‖

I chewed the last of the licorice string and stretched my legs. Like the rest of the kids my age, I wore faded jeans and a T-shirt in the winter, and cutoff jeans and a T-shirt in the summer. Hot, I waved away a honeybee that had been attracted to the sticky black candy, then cleaned my hands on the sides of my shorts. The awning above me cast a bit of shade, but it was no match for the Alabama sun.

Jezza-Belle and the preacher had gone, but not before she winked at me with those sexy brown eyes and waved good-bye. Rocking back on the crate, I alternated between watching the kid who called himself Chicken and keeping an eye on the crew across the street. Them rednecks was flexin' like a mother, stealing goods from under Mr. Fleck's nose, blowing cigarette smoke in grown folks' faces, and swigging beer from naked bottles.

Meanwhile, little Chicken sweated out in that hot sun, reaching into crates and passing out cartons of fresh eggs to shoppers while getting cussed out by Old Man Wilkes from one end of the alphabet to the other. I'd heard more than enough by the time Granmaw came out the store with twenty-'leven packages in her arms.

"Hey, Granmaw." I put on my cap and stood as she pushed through the door, a blast of Millie's cool air following her. My granmaw was a tall, big-boned woman who, until diabetes got ahold of her, could swing an axe just as well as she sewed a stitch. She stood eye to eye with me, and at seventeen I had just inched over six feet.

My grandparents had started out on a cotton farm near the banks of the Mississippi, and soon after my father, Ezekiel, was born, they moved further west into Bull Run, a small factory-and-farming community outside of Pine Bluff. Granmaw, known to most as Sugar Baby, had been a master seamstress and worked for a flag-making company in Langston, and Poppa Daddy made his living raising small animals for slaughter and farming plots of tobacco on his patch of valley land.

Granmaw handed me her bags. "You ready, Mister Malcolm?" Eyeing the Chevy pickup, she frowned. "Look at that Lester Wilkes! A mess before God up in that Snatch Hatch! Wouldn't eat nary one of them eggs what come out of his old drunk hens. And who's that boy he got with him in all that heat? Don't tell me that's the killer nephew tongues been wagging about."

"Yes, ma'am." I nodded. "That's him. His name Chicken, and Miss Betty say he killed a bunch of folks in his daddy's ho—in his father's house."

Granmaw grunted and waved her hand. "Don't be so quick to judge. There's a whole slew of pots out there raisin' sand about kettles. Ain't no telling what that poor child been through to make him do whatever he done, but I know for sure what's ahead of him living with that nasty behind Lester. C'mon, Mister." She shook her head, disgusted. "Let's go to the post office, then get on back to the house."

I made a move to follow her, but then I peeped Barney Judd jogging across the street, knocking people out of his path. Ralphie and Jimmy cheered him on as he pushed through the line of customers standing by Wilkes's truck, and just as that Chicken dude reached out to put half a dozen eggs in Elder Adrian's out-stretched hands, Barney lowered his shoulder and plowed dead into him. Chicken stumbled and the eggs sailed into the air.

*Pavement's so hot them eggs is gonna fry* . . .

"Mothafuc—" Old Man Wilkes cussed as the eggs fell toward the ground, and in the second it took me to cringe and blink, there was an impossible lunge of movement. Moments later I stood shocked as Barney jogged back across the street, choking back his victory cry. Elder Adrian's hands were still outstretched, his jaw hanging loose, and the scrappy little Chicken stood there as chill as he wanted to be. Clutching two handfuls of perfectly oval eggs. And not a crack in nary a one.

# TWO

The weekend came and went, and the moment I hit school on Monday morning my eyes were peeled for Chicken. He wasn't my boy or nuthin', so I wasn't about to fish for him, but walking the halls between classes I found myself scanning the crowd wondering if I might peep him. Bull Run wasn't big as a minute, and even though we shared a high school with Langston, there were still only three senior classes in the whole district. There was no way I could have missed that tough yellow face had he been there.

By Thursday he still hadn't showed. Late that afternoon I drove Granmaw to her once-a-week hair appointment at Aileen's Beauty House in a little strip mall over on Stackhouse Way. The stench of Vigorol and hair spray made my stomach roll, and after thirty minutes of sitting there listening to little old ladies argue over whose cow begot whose calf, I was full.

"Granmaw." I stood over her as she lay back in a scoop-neck chair. White gunk covered her scalp, and her hair fell into a sink. "I'ma wait for you out in the car, okay?"

Outside, I climbed into Granmaw's black Oldsmobile Ninety-Eight we called Midnight and cranked her up. I turned the radio dial from the gospel station to a new black station out of Mobile and rolled down the windows hoping the breeze would blow some of the chemicals out my nose. I bopped to the funk of the beat as shoppers went in and out of Farmer Jack's Supermarket and the dry cleaner next door.

Near the end of the street, two black boys held the hands of a little girl as they skipped into Hong-Cho's takeout Chinese restaurant. The girl had long braids and wore a little pink dress, and both the boys were in shorts and T-shirts.

I was digging the sights and settling into the music when I saw them. Barney Judd and his boys. Coming out of the alley between Farmer Jack's and a storefront record shop that doubled as an illegal number spot. I turned off the radio and rolled down my window. White boys from Bull Run didn't give a shit about soap or water. They wore those dirty Levi's and Led Zeppelin T-shirts until they fell off.

Barney was in the lead, and even from where I sat his cockiness showed. He was walking Bogart, his full-grown rottweiler who looked just like a baby bear. The dog was just as foul as his master— the Judd boys bred all their dogs that way. I watched them head toward the ABC Package Store, Bogart's thick body pulling at his leash as he growled and snapped and strained on his muscular front legs.

I shook my head. Stupid-ass white boys. I turned the radio back on, slid deeper into the seat, and watched them push into the package store. They were wasting their time goin' up in there. Preston Williams ran the liquor joint, and his girlfriend, Black Betty, lived just under the counter, within fingertip reach. There was no way he'd sell hot juice to underage kids. White ones, at that.

Not five minutes later I saw something that made my blood go cold. Down the street, the doors to Hong-Cho's swung open just as Barney and his crew came flying out of the package store, Bo-

gart barking, Preston cursing from the doorway and waving Black
Betty in the air. They ran down the street laughing and giving
Preston the finger just as the three little kids came out of the
restaurant, loaded down with takeout Chinese food.

What they did next was low, even for white trash, and later I
would say that what they got was exactly what they had coming.

Ralphie pointed toward the kids. Barney hissed a command between his teeth, then let loose the chain.

Bogart charged.

The kids screamed, trying like hell to run and trying like hell to
stay together. The two boys finally jumped up on the hood of a
parked car with their arms reaching out for their sister. The paper
bags hit the ground and split, sweet-and-sour ribs and pork-fried
rice tumbling out of Styrofoam containers and scattering across
the pavement.

I was on the move as the little girl went down.

Jumping from the car, I sprinted across the street, but as fast as I
ran, I wasn't fast enough. Yanked up by her brothers, who were
on their knees on top of the car and hollering, the little girl scam-
pered to climb up too, screaming and slipping and almost pulling
the boys down with her.

I was less than twenty feet away when some kinda blur shot past
me and Bogart went from putting out a throaty bark to choking
on a high whimper. As the little girl kicked at him with her bare,
skinny legs, the kid who called himself Chicken ran up on the
dog—chin tucked, elbows tight—and nailed him with a short
right, a tricky left, and then the prettiest flurry I'd ever seen. The
dog yelped and staggered. Left hook, downward jab, and another
short left, this one landing between Bogart's ear and the base of
his furry jaw. *What kinda shit is this?* I wondered as the dog whined
once, then took a few sideways steps and fell to the ground.

Punch-drunk. Knocked the hell out.

∎∎∎∎∎∎∎∎

Brothaman stood over that baby bear, rocked and cocked.

The little boys jumped down from the car and grabbed their crying sister, holding on to her as they ran toward Farmer Jack's.

"What the hell you do that for?" Barney pushed past his friends and knelt on the ground. Bogart was done for. His eyes were closed, his tongue hung between his teeth, and his breathing was soft and steady.

Chicken punt-kicked a rice-dotted sparerib that barely missed Barney's head. " 'Cause I felt like it!" His hands were still up, and he looked red as hell. "Why the fuck you sic him on them little kids?"

"He wasn't gonna hurt 'em! We was just playing!"

"I wasn't."

"Yo. You knocked out my dog." Barney stood and I saw the muscles in his shoulders tense and coil. Ralphie and Jimmy Stone moved in behind him.

Chicken smiled so big I swear I coulda counted every one of his teeth. "And?" He shrugged and crouched. "There's plenty more where that came from, motherfucker. You want, I can put the same thing on you."

Barney's hands went up and his eyes got dark. "Is that right?" He sniffed. "Okay. I'll take me a slice of your skinny black ass. Yeah, I'll get me a little piece now, and take me one for later too."

I didn't even stop to think. "Damn, man," I said, stepping between them and putting my hand against Barney's shoulder. "Ain't gotta be none of that. Looked to me like the dude was just trying to protect them kids. Everybody should be cool with that."

"Naw, asshole," Barney said, slapping my hand down. "Everybody *ain't,* 'cause this little fucker ain't had no business hittin' my dog!" He pointed at me. "Yo, Malcolm! You better tell your boy how we do it around here! Get in the ring and I'll knock both your nigger asses out!"

"Nigger?"

You know how fast they say white gets on rice? Well, that's just about how quick Chicken went to Barney's ass. With his fingers digging into the white boy's throat, Brothaman said, "Say somethin' else, motherfucker. Just one more word, and I swear. I'll snap your fuckin' honky neck. Right here. Right now."

We stood frozen as Chicken squeezed and Barney wheezed. Barney couldn't breathe, let alone speak. His face looked like a fire, and two small drops of blood fell from his nose.

"Aiight then." Chicken finally turned him loose, and Barney fell back choking against Ralphie. A knife with a long slim blade was suddenly in Chicken's hand. He spit on Bogart and then turned to Barney's friends and said, "Next?"

I guess even the lowest white trash knew when to live and fight another day. Ralphie grabbed Barney, and Jimmy dragged Bogart by his chain.

"Your ass is mine," Barney whispered, holding his neck as Ralphie led him away. "Mine."

"Yeah, motherfucker," Chicken said, and for the first time since I'd seen him Brothaman looked happier than a pork chop in gravy. "You just come get it whenever you ready."

|||||||||

I caught up with Chicken as he strode across the parking lot. Wilkes's truck was parked in front of a hardware store, so he must've been shopping inside.

"Hey!"

Brothaman looked at me and shook his head, disgusted.

I fell in beside him anyway. The top of his head barely came above my shoulder. "I'm Malcolm," I said, sticking out my fist for a dap. "Malcolm Armstrong."

He ignored me and kept walking. Didn't even look my way.

"That was really something you put on Bogart back there. Barney too."

"Nothin' they ain't have coming."

"Wilkes your uncle, right?"

No answer.

"You're Bishop Johnson, right?"

"What, nigger?" He glared. "You a fuckin' cop?"

"Nah!" I raised my hands in peace. "Hell no. I ain't no cop. I'm just askin', that's all. Trying to be friendly."

"Man, roll." He walked faster. "I don't need no fuckin' friends."

"I can see that." We were at the truck, and he climbed in on the passenger side. I stood near his open window. "Them kids coulda got hurt," I said. "I was on my way over to help them, but you got there first."

He gave me a cold look. "Bull Run niggers oughtta do a better job handling they business. That way shitheads like that don't get outta hand."

I agreed. "You right, you right . . . you got a point there." I put my foot up on the pickup's running board. "So, where you from?"

"Why you wanna know?"

"Do you fight?"

"All day if I have to."

"Nah, I mean, in the ring. You had good form back there, and your flurries are probably the fastest I've ever seen."

"I used to shoot my joints up in Birdtown. Been a long time, though."

I nodded. Birdtown was about fifty miles north, near Argle, and quite a bit larger than Bull Run. I threw my hands up and went into a bob and weave. "Long time? You couldn't tell it back there."

He shrugged, looking straight ahead. "I keeps my shit tight. Never know when you'll have to knock a motherfucker out."

I was impressed. "My grandfather owns the Hands Up Boxing Club. We could use a fighter like you."

A shadow crossed his face and he actually looked at me. "When y'all train?"

"Every night except Thursdays and Sundays. Tomorrow would be good, if you can make it."

"Can't." He frowned and shook his head. "Gotta work."

I nodded. The Snatch Hatch. Friday night was jook joint night. I could dig it. "What about Saturday? In the afternoon."

"Doubt it. Work Saturday too."

Damn. I thought for a moment, then shrugged. "Aiight. Cool. We're right off Lesser if you change your mind." I reached up for a dap. He hesitated but then let me have it. "Keep your chin tucked, Brothaman."

As I walked off I could have sworn I heard him say, "And your elbows tight."

# THREE

The little boy bolted upright in his bed, his heart hammering wildly inside his chest, his breath strangely constricted. I watched him from above, a heaviness pushing at him so hard he could barely breathe. Clouds of black smoke were seeping into the room, and I sensed his panic as he tried to remember the fire-safety lessons he'd learned in school.

"Stop, drop, and roll," the kid whispered. His eyes burned and his feet got tangled in the sheets as he fought his way out of bed. "Stop, drop, and roll," he told himself as he freed his feet, dropped to the floor, and rolled straight into the darkness under his bed.

Time froze. I heard her frantic screams as the boy balled himself in a knot and took tiny sips of smoky air. The door to his room flung open as the woman screamed his name. She rushed inside searching for her baby, chased by heavy smoke, the flaming carpet licking up her bare legs.

The boy was frozen, and I could smell his fear even above the burning smoke. Tears streamed from his eyes, and terror kept him paralyzed in his hiding place. The woman tripped over his dump truck as she searched, sputtering and coughing and screaming out his name.

Baby, baby, come to Mama! Where are you? Zeke! Zeke! I can't find him, Zeke . . . oh, sweet Lord, I can't find my baby!"

The floor where the boy was hiding began to smolder. Orange tongues of fire played leapfrog, chasing one another from the carpet to the bed and nibbling the sheets before delving greedily into the mattress.

The lady made her way closer. Her hands searched in the jumbled mess of his blankets, and when they could not find him she attacked the bed in a frenzy of pain and fear. As he cowered on the floor below, something in his mother's voice compelled the boy to move. He reached out and grabbed at her ankle, then recoiled in surprise and disgust when her burned flesh flaked away in his hands.

The lady shrieked, and from my position near the ceiling I winced at her pain. She dropped to the floor, pulled him free of the burning bed, and lifted him into her arms. Unable to speak, the boy clung to her, then fought her momentarily when he realized that his mother was nearly naked. Scorched remnants of her nightclothes hung in strips from her body, and large patches of her caramel skin were blackened and puffy. "It's okay, baby," she cooed. "Mama's here, and its all right."

She turned to the window. The blue striped curtains were completely ablaze and had spread their evil to the speckled wallpaper the boy's father had tacked up the summer before. With her son in her arms and one blistered hand thrust out in front of her, the lady made her way to the door.

The hall connecting her son's bedroom to hers was ablaze. She'd fallen asleep when her husband had gone downstairs to take a shower, and had been scared out of her mind when she awakened, alone in her bed with flames attacking the room.

She turned back the way she'd come, then felt her son struggling against her and realized she held him far too tight. I trembled at the fear in her voice as she told him, "Daddy is trying to get to us, but we're going to have to help him. We have to go out the window, baby."

The boy coughed and gasped. He nodded and slid from his mother's arms. "Grab me around the waist," she commanded, and they moved as one over to the single window.

The curtains were burned completely away. The woman pressed her palms to the scorching glass, and a guttural scream tore from her throat. The boy watched as tiny bits of singed flesh stuck to the blistering panes as she pushed upward, heaving the window open with the very last of her strength.

*The night air rushed into the room, feeding the fire. Waves of toxic smoke swept over the mother and son, choking off their air supply. I cried out as the woman slumped to the floor, overcome by smoke and heat, pressing the boy's limp body to hers, burying his face in her naked breasts. As they lay there gasping and waiting to die, a shadowy figure climbed in through the window and called out their names. He was tall and naked, his back muscular, his manhood Zulu-like and grazing his thigh.*

*"I'm here, Sweet Thang." His voice was calm and steady. "Daddy-O is right here." Hovering above them, I wept as Zeke gathered his wife and son in his arms and lifted them to their feet. He led them over to the window and pushed their heads as far out as he could.*

*"Malcolm first," Sweets panted, wagging her head. "T-t-take Malcolm first."*

⁙

"Malcolm. Get up, baby."

I opened my eyes in a cold sweat. I stared at my granmaw, then sighed, wiping at my face with the end of the sheet I clutched in my fist. Ever since the fire that had killed my parents and Lil' Bobby Hutton, I'd slept in a sort of twilight stage alternating between dreamland and reality, and some mornings I woke up feeling like I'd never slept at all. Like I'd just closed my eyes and time had slipped by.

"What's wrong, Granmaw?" I sat up in my bed and pulled the sheet up to cover my chest. My bedroom had belonged to my father, Zeke, and the bed I slept in was also his. The room had a large dresser that Poppa Daddy had carved and sanded, a desk and matching chair, and a second bed piled high with gym clothes, magazines, and schoolbooks.

It was Saturday, and the aroma of fried scrapple and biscuits drifting in from the kitchen replaced the smell of smoke lingering in my nostrils. Sunshine cut a square swatch across my blanket, and the hum of a lawn mower drifted in from somewhere down the street.

"Ain't nothing wrong, Mister," Granmaw said, picking my clothes up from the floor and rearranging some of the mess on my dresser. "It's going on ten o'clock and 'bout time for you to get up, is all. I thought maybe you could get some studying done instead of spending the whole day out back in that gym with your Poppa Daddy. You gots to bring them grades of yours up if you plan to get 'cepted at a university, you know."

I groaned and slid back under the sheets. Granmaw was always on my case about my grades. I was pretty lazy about school, that much was true, but I always managed to pull out the stops by the end of the semester and walk away with a few C's and even one or two B's. I knew the way I approached shit irked Granmaw to no end, and although she never said it, the implication was obvious. There was nothing special about me. I was average on all fronts. But the mighty Ezekiel, her son and my father, had been a mover and a shaker. An athlete and a scholar. He'd won a full academic scholarship to USC, and along with my mother, Sweets, had organized a major chapter of the Black Panther party in California. Except for in the ring, it looked like everywhere Zeke Armstrong had shined I stood half-assed and shoddy by comparison. It was tough living in the shadow of a man who had lived and died as well as my father had.

"Where is Pop-Pop?" I asked from under my blanket.

I peeked out and Granmaw was smirking, one hand on her hip, the other holding out my one-million-page biology book. "Child, where you think?"

I nodded and went on ahead and sat up, because if I didn't, the next thing she'd be holding out would be a Bible. After that, she'd be swinging a broomstick. I wrapped the blanket around my waist and stood, then stretched and sat down at my desk. I flipped through my notebook and picked up a pen. "Okay. I'm up. I'll study for a minute and head out to the gym later."

"Uh-huh," Granmaw hummed, her voice low and sweet. "You durn right you will."

The house that Poppa Daddy built was a ranch-style with two bedrooms and two full baths. Fifty feet behind the house, down a stone path he and I had laid, was the Hands Up Boxing Club, a huge dairy barn that Poppa Daddy had had converted into a gym.

I grabbed two biscuits and read a couple of chapters of general biology, then skimmed the pages of my geometry book. Then I pulled on a pair of shorts and a New York Yankees T-shirt and headed down the path out back.

Renovating the barn into a gym with overhead fluorescent lighting and central air-conditioning had cost Poppa Daddy almost every dime he had, but he had been determined to do it. He'd trained my father in all-white gyms, and while he hadn't been able to provide a positive environment for his own son to fight in, it made him feel good to be able to do it for me. He'd hired an all-black crew to do everything from bulldozing the old barn to building the regulation-sized ring, and for almost five years he'd welcomed young black boys from Bull Run and Langston to his roster whether their folks could afford to pay or not.

My father had been good enough to make the county championships and then go on to a big win at state, but he'd hung up his gloves short of the regional competitions when he was accepted at USC, where he met my mother. Granmaw said Poppa Daddy had nearly died from the disappointment of seeing his only son leave the sport, but by then there were hungrier fighters begging for his attention, and after selling a piece of his farm he became a member of the Golden Gloves Association and turned to coaching boxing full-time.

I had a lot of respect for Poppa Daddy. At seventeen I had no idea what I wanted to do with my life, but at sixty-three he was still a dreamer, and had turned a passion for his hobby into a pretty decent business. But while there were one or two of his fighters who looked promising for the state finals, across town, at Fists Are Flying Gym, was Poppa Daddy's biggest problem: Barney Judd.

The air conditioner was going strong when I pulled open the

heavy glass doors and walked inside. The gym had high ceilings and smelled of leather and Pine-Sol. Moving through the training area, I spotted my granpaw by the far wall adjusting the chains on one of the five heavy bags.

"Morning, Pop-Pop."

"Malcolm!" Poppa Daddy nodded as he rethreaded the thick links through an iron notch at the top of the red bag. He waited as I hurried over to steady the weighted bottom before placing the chain on top of its pulley and locking it into place.

"You going into town this morning?" I asked, following him down to the second bag on the line.

"Yep. You comin'?"

I nodded. "Yes, sir. I guess I'll take the ride."

"You can get you some new gloves, if you want. Everlast, this time. Competition's gonna be here in a little more than six months, and if none of my fighters can stay on they feet, that Barney Judd is gonna take it all the way to Chicago."

I groaned as I braced the second bag against my thigh. My chin was pretty solid, and I was known to throw a mean punch. As a lightweight I wasn't bulked up or anything, but my height and the fact that I lived with my trainer gave me an advantage over a lot of my opponents. But as much as I shared Poppa Daddy's love of boxing, in my heart I was half-stepping and I knew I would never be great in the ring. Good, yeah. Great, never.

"I don't know, Poppa Daddy. Don't look like none of us stand a chance. Barney's mean and fast. Boobie's got a good right hand, but his hook is weak. Trey's got a busted shoulder, and Early'll never make weight."

"What we need is a rabbit," he said, moving down to the next bag. "Somebody fast who can get out there and beat Barney on all fronts. A fighter who can stick and move until Barney's ass is plain worn-out."

I nodded. "If Barney takes state, it'll be like giving him a key to Bull Run. We'll have hell to pay every time we see him. In the ring and out."

"So what about you?" Poppa Daddy's voice was steady, but I could hear the hope pushing through. "You healthy and can dance and got a solid hook. Your jab done wobbled a few knees." There was faith in his eyes as he asked, "You think you might be able to take him?"

I swallowed hard. I didn't want to be the one who killed my granpaw's dreams, but keeping clear of Barney's right cross would take a hell of a lot more speed than I had in me. "No, sir," I answered him truthfully. "I don't think I can. But I know somebody who might."

By late Saturday afternoon the gym was jam-packed. Boxers were everywhere, skipping leather ropes, pounding heavy bags, dominating speed bags with precision and finesse, and sprawled on floor mats doing stretches and calisthenics. The funk of sweating black men hung in the air as I sat on a raised platform behind the registration desk, tallying the weekly stats. Every so often the front door would swing open and I'd look up, hoping against the odds that our rabbit would hop in.

At half past five I got my wish. The doors opened and in he stepped. He had on a pair of gray sweatpants and a blue shirt that was wringing wet. An Orioles baseball cap was on his head, its bill pushed to the side.

"What's up, Brothaman!" I almost tripped over my feet as I rushed from behind the desk.

"Hey. How you?" Chicken looked around, then took off his hat and wiped his head and face with the end of his shirt.

I waited until he was done, then went in for a dap. "Better since you walked in. Glad you could make it. Come on in."

He glanced around and nodded at the framed photos of great boxers that lined our walls. In between the pictures was a corny motivational saying that Poppa Daddy had composed. "Decent setup. You say your grandfather runs all this?"

"Runs it and owns it. Used to do it part-time when my father was alive, but it's his whole life now."

He stared. "Your daddy dead?"

"Yeah," I said. "My mother too."

"Somebody killed 'em?"

I nodded. "They were Panthers who got burnt up in that fire in Oakland. The firemen and cops stood there and watched the house burn to the ground, so I guess you can say somebody did."

He gave me a funny look as we walked toward the center of the gym.

"So," I said. "I thought you had to work?"

We stopped near the boxing ring where Early was sparring with Mike Lee. A group of younger fighters had gathered to watch.

"I did. Still do."

"Oh, okay. Old Man Wilkes drive you out here?"

Chicken put his head back and laughed. "Hell, naw. If it took ten minutes to go around the world, that lowlife motherfucker wouldn't put in the time to take me across the street." He turned back to the ring and shrugged. "I ran."

I calculated the distance in my head. Over six miles. I whistled. "Damn. That's tight."

"Naw, man." He dismissed the distance with a shrug. "That's life."

I took him into the supply room and gave him a towel, a mouthpiece, and a protective cup, then measured him for regulation headgear. Back outside, I returned to my desk as Chicken stripped down to the shorts he wore underneath his sweats and hit the blue mats, putting his joints and muscles through a thorough and extensive warm-up.

I was jabbing at my calculator with a pencil when Trey Green tapped me on the shoulder. "Hey, Malcolm." He beckoned me into the training area. "You might wanna check this shit out!"

I stood and looked toward the training floor, and there was

Chicken. He was standing on one of the wooden platforms turning a speed bag into a blur of red leather. Every man in the gym had stopped to watch, and his taped hands burning up that bag was the only sound in the whole building.

It was all I could do to keep from hollering. Brothaman's hands were moving so fast it was unreal. Without taking my eyes off him, I tapped Trey's shoulder. "Go up to the house and get my Poppa Daddy," I whispered, excitement damn near choking me. "Tell him I said to come running, because walking is gonna be much too slow."

Minutes later Poppa Daddy was standing at my side. When Chicken was done murderizing the speed bag, we gave him some gloves and put him in the ring with Boobie, our top fighter. Shoulder to shoulder, me and Granpaw watched Chicken do his thing. He was amazing. A total package. Solid legs, high-speed hands, hammering left, wicked right. By the end of the match he'd earned the respect of every fighter in the house.

"Well," Poppa Daddy said as he threw two towels into the ring. Trey and Early were climbing in to help Boobie stagger out. Granpaw turned to me with a smile that seemed to take ten years off his face. "That boy over there might call hisself a chicken, but it look to me like we just found us our rabbit."

||||||||||

"Poppa Daddy's pumped," I told Chicken almost a week later. It was late in the evening and ring time had ended. He held out his hands as I cut the knot on his wraps. For five days straight he'd shown up at the gym and dominated his sparring partners, and each night Poppa Daddy had insisted he and Boobie Johnson come up to the house for one of Granmaw's famous meals. While we ate Poppa Daddy would entertain us with stories of my father's early conquests in the ring, and after dinner Chicken would catch a ride with Boobie's dad as far as Ludley Park, then he'd walk the rest of the way home.

I held the scissors between my knees and used both hands to unroll the yards of protective tape from his fists. "He thinks you got the best chance of taking Barney Judd in the state finals. Wants to bulk you up some so you can make weight, but other than that, he says you're ready."

His binds loosened, Chicken flexed his fingers. "I was born ready. Just gotta make sure my situation don't fuck it up for me."

"Like how? Fuck it up like how?"

He propped one foot up on a metal bench. "Lester Wilkes got me by the balls, man. He got papers on me."

"He's your guardian, right? Like my grandparents are to me."

Chicken shook his head. "It ain't nowhere near the same, Malcolm. Lester can't stand my fuckin' ass. He's my mother's uncle, and back in the day, my daddy dented his face for beating her. Ever since then he's hated Slim Willie and anybody who looks like him. Them courts ain't did nothin' but let me out of one jail and stick me in another."

"But he'll sign the contract for you to train and fight, right?"

Chicken frowned. "Not if it means I won't be around to scrub shitters in the Snatch Hatch." He chuckled. "Hell, I'm Lester's free labor. And if I don't like it, all he gotta do is pick up the phone and say the word. I'll be on the first thing smokin' back to Spottfield. In handcuffs."

Chicken's words hung in the balance as I tested the futility of my next question. "Damn, man, how many people did you take out?"

A look flashed in his eyes that cut me bone-deep. "Not as many as I shoulda," he said, and right then and there I saw a future promise in his face. " 'Cause one of them motherfuckers got away."

# FOUR

T wo roads ran through Bull Run: Main and Lesser. Folks on Main were usually shopping for clothes or had business at the courthouse or the medical center, but Lesser's travelers were sniffing for good times and company. Pubs, movie theaters, package stores, and a spattering of clapboard houses with wide porches sat back off the narrow, partially paved road.

The sun was going down over Jefferson County as me and Poppa Daddy drove south on Lesser in Midnight, Sugar Baby's car. The windows were down and a humid breeze clung to our faces and necks as the Oldsmobile nosed down the road, its heavy frame absorbing the bumps and pings that were common to this stretch of land. The blues tunes drifting from the radio were cut with stretches of squelch and static, so heavy were the woods on either side of the road.

We drove for about fifteen miles before Poppa Daddy signaled left and turned onto a dirt path. The roar of crickets and bullfrogs bled into the night, and I glanced into my rearview mirror and saw clouds of dust rising in our wake.

"How we supposed to find it way out here?" I muttered.

Poppa Daddy spoke around the pipe clenched between his teeth. "I reckon I can make my way."

A few minutes later he pulled off the path into a grassy clearing and I smelled water. Lights twinkled through a thick grove of trees, and the upbeat tempo of a live band drifted out to greet us.

It was Saturday and the crowd was gearing up for a long night. There were roughly forty cars parked on the grass, and Poppa Daddy eased Midnight along the perimeter of the makeshift lot. I followed him as he climbed from the car and crossed the clearing. The air was humid with the odor of algae, and my gym shoes sank into the mud as we walked down a damp embankment. In the valley, we crossed a small wooden bridge stretching over a gully that spilled into Black Shoals Lake.

The sky was pitch dark, and I could hear the lively voices carrying from the structure on the lake's causeway. I stared at the sight of the log cabin, multicolored Christmas lights strung from every corner, its floor joists disappearing into the dark waters of the lake.

The Snatch Hatch.

Poppa Daddy's stride was sure as he walked up to the entrance. Two men stood near a railing smoking reefer and drinking beer.

"Five dollars." A bull-chested man sitting just inside the doorway pointed toward a cigar box filled with bills. He looked ready to bust out of his jacket, and the dirty material had been ironed so many times it was shiny. Behind him, the hut was in full swing. The band sat ass-to-elbow on the small raised stage—a drummer, a bass guitarist, and a fat man massaging his organ keys.

Immediately my eyes were drawn to the ladies. This was a sight I'd waited for, and Lord knows I wasn't disappointed. Juicy asses everywhere. The women sported long wigs and false eyelashes and wore scoop-necked tops with titties galore bubbling up from their necklines. Paired off with their customers, they danced up a storm in the middle of the room, some the hustle, others a funky slow grind, and some were dry-humping their partners so hard I wanted to jump out there and get it on too. Hoots and whistles came from above, and I looked up, surprised to see men sitting in the rafters, their suit-clad legs and polished shoes swinging in the air.

Poppa Daddy glanced around, then shook his head. "We ain't customers. Just come to talk a spell with Lester is all."

The man pointed again. "Five dollars."

"For the kid too?"

"Five dollars. Each."

Granpaw slapped a ten-dollar bill into the box.

"Wait," the bouncer told us.

As we waited I found my foot tapping to the beat of the band. *Shotgun! Shoot 'em up, baby! Work it on out!*

A fine dark-skinned woman in a slinky red dress was working her stuff onstage. She was brickhouse-built, and the guitar player lay on his back near her feet, stroking his strings and squinting up her dress.

*We gonna . . . dig potatoes!*

*We gonna . . . pick tomatoes!*

Wilkes pushed through the crowd and limped across the room.

"Ike! Good to see you, my man!" He grinned. "What brings you out tonight? Need some company?"

"Naw." Poppa Daddy ignored Wilkes's outstretched hand. "There ain't a thing you got I need, Lester. Told you that many a times." His eyes swept over the room. "Come to talk about that boy you got livin' out here with you. Bishop. Your great-nephew, ain't that right?"

Lester nodded. "Yeah, he here. They gave him five years for what he done, but some fool up in the governor's office had mercy on him. Let him out in my custody." He frowned. "I took him in out the goodness of my heart. You know his momma wasn't nothin' but a whore."

Pop-Pop smirked. "The same kind you got rollin' around in here?"

Lester chuckled, his eyes dark. "The very same kind. Of course, these in here get paid for their troubles. Little Dimples got herself hitched with a red nigger so natural-evil he made her give it away for free."

Poppa Daddy grunted and reached into his jacket pocket. He opened an envelope and took out a single sheet of paper. "Looka here, Lester. I got a proposition for you. My grandson done took a liking to your nephew, and I can vouch for the boy's boxing skills. What you think about signing for him to train a couple, three times a week, then fight in the state finals next spring? You know I run a program where boys like him can find another path."

"Boys like him?" Wilkes nodded toward an open doorway, and I glimpsed Chicken standing over a sink, just inside the room. His sleeves were pushed above his elbows, and he dunked whiskey glasses in and out of sudsy water. "A boy like him shot and killed a man. That's the kinda path Bishop's on. He ain't fit to hang around a kid like your Malcolm. I know you and sweet Sugar Baby done your best to raise this one right."

Poppa Daddy swelled up. "Leave her out of this, Lester. Don't even let her name touch your tongue."

"C'mon, Ike. All I'm saying is you don't know jack shit about my nephew. He did eighteen months in the bad-boy house. If it wasn't for me signing them governor papers, they woulda kept his rotten ass in that shit hole until he turned twenty-one."

"I know a child don't belong in a place like this."

"A place like what?" Wilkes looked surprised. "The Snatch Hatch?" He laughed and slapped his thigh. "Isaac Armstrong, old as you is, you still don't know your ass from a hole in the ground. Where you think that little niggah come from? He slid out of a whore up in Slim Willie's Place! Come in this world rolling 'round in gin and pussy juice. Sheeit. Bishop ain't got it no worse here than he had it up in Birdtown."

Chicken moved into the doorway. He'd seen us. Suds dripped from his hands, and his eyes and mouth were hard.

"Well, what about schoolin'?" Poppa Daddy questioned. "The boy been in Bull Run comin' up on three months. Ain't the child entitled to an education?"

"I'ma sign him up first thing Mondee mornin'."

Granpaw's jaw worked, and I watched him searching for a juncture where they could connect. "Then what about his future? Just because he been one way don't mean he gots to stay that'a way. The kid is good with his hands. Fast. Maybe the fastest I've ever seen. I'm offering him a chance to get in the ring and make a name for himself. To fight!"

Wilkes's whole face went dark, and for the first time I caught a glimpse of the real man inside. Not the laughing little fellow who went around skinning and grinning and selling eggs from the back of his beat-up truck but the cold-blooded Lester Wilkes who ran a prostitution ring out in the middle of the woods where even hardened lawmen were scared to walk.

"Fight? You say you want him to fight? The boy been fighting for his asshole for eighteen months. Ask me, that's fight enough."

"But what—"

"Forget it, Ike. Now if you and your grandson come here to patronize my business, step right up. The gals are hot, and since we old friends, the first drink is on the house. But if fighting my nephew is all you got on your mind, he ain't but seventeen and the courts say I got dibs on him until he's twenty-one. That means he ain't fighting nowhere, no time." Lester grinned. "Shucks, you done paid your cover charge, might as well stay and enjoy yourself. Prices is reasonable on everythang." He winked. "And I do mean everythang."

<hr />

We were leaving the Snatch Hatch when Chicken came out of the washroom. I turned around when I heard his voice, and right away I knew Old Man Wilkes was in trouble.

"I'ma fight, motherfucker."

Lester froze. He gave his head a small shake, then his face lit up with his perpetual grin.

"Gone, Bishop. Crowd's swelling. Better get them glasses washed before we run out again."

"Ain't my crowd. Ain't my problem."

Wilkes pointed. "Watch your mouth, boy. Don't let this boxing shit go to your head. If it wasn't for me, you still be fighting for your asshole."

"You don't own me, Lester. I'll be eighteen by fight time and won't need nobody's say-so."

Wilkes's meaty hands curled into fists. "We'll see about that come next spring, if you live that goddamn long."

"I said I'ma fight, and if that means I gotta start right now with you, so be it."

"*Niggah*—" Lester lunged.

Chicken waited all day for Wilkes's fist, clumsy and slowed by age and alcohol, to reach him. He ducked easily and then gave Wilkes one of those toothy smiles. "Put your hands on me, Uncle Lester, and I'ma hafta take you outta here. Everything you own is gonna be in probate."

Lester lunged again, and Chicken sidestepped, a perfect movement executed with so much fluidity and finesse I wanted to throw my hands up and clap. He stuck out his foot as Lester sailed past, and the old man went down.

When Lester found his feet, bone-chilling danger shone in his eyes. "You done fucked up," he said.

Poppa Daddy got between them. "Cut that shit out, Lester. He's just a—"

"Gone, Ike. Before you get fucked up too."

Right before my eyes a wall of bodies swarmed behind Wilkes. Dangerous men who looked ready to kill.

A glint of metal rose in Chicken's hand, and I saw that evil-looking pearl-handled stiletto again. "Gone, Malcolm. Pop-Pop." He nodded toward the door. "I'll catch up witcha later. Got some family business to tend to, and yawl don't need no part of it."

Poppa Daddy said, "Ain't no sense—"

"Get the fuck out!" Wilkes shouted, and fear rose in my gut

and filled my chest. "You heard the boy. Ain't gonna be no fight, but like he said, this here is between family and I ain't gonna say it no more."

Poppa Daddy nudged my shoulder, and we backed toward the doorway, ours eyes locked on Lester Wilkes and his men. We were almost outside when he spoke again. "You right, Lester. This is your place, so I'll go. But mark my words, if you hurt that boy in any way, I'll be back."

Wilkes laughed, a chilling sound that would haunt me all the way into town.

"You come on back, Ike. You just do that." He pointed, his eyes deadly. "And when you do, mothafuckah, be sure to bring a pine box along with you."

||||||||||

We rode home in silence, the weight of Wilkes's threat sitting between us. Back at the house I avoided Pop-Pop's eyes, scared that he would see my rage and my fear. I went to my room, closed the door, and locked it, then stretched out on my bed fully clothed. I lay there with my eyes wide open in the darkness for nearly an hour.

My decision made, I got up and took a jacket and a pair of soft leather gloves from my closet, then eased out of my room, taking care so the hinges wouldn't squeak. The door to my grandparents' bedroom was open, so I tiptoed down the hall. I had to take a piss but didn't want to risk cutting on the bathroom light or flushing the toilet. The kitchen was dark, but I crossed it easily and unlocked the door beside the refrigerator. In the garage, I put on my gloves and lifted my bike from a hook on the wall. I had a key to Granmaw's car, but without her permission I refused to use it. I sure wasn't gonna wake her up and ask if it was okay.

At the end of our property line I stood before a pecan tree and peed against it in a hard stream. Moonlight shone upon Lesser Road as I pedaled my bike toward the outskirts of town. The night air held a chill, and I was grateful for the jacket. The traffic was almost nonexistent. My legs felt purposeful as I rode mile after mile along the boundaries of the roadway. I didn't have much of a plan, but neither did I need one. Right was right, and wrong was always wrong.

I'd been riding for several miles when twin beams crept up on me from behind. I heard Midnight purring as the headlights danced on the road. The car slowed beside me and the window went down.

I squeezed my brakes and stopped, straddling the bike between my legs. I looked him dead in his eye, defiant as all hell. "He don't belong there."

He didn't have but two words for me. "Hop in."

I climbed off my bike and pushed it into a thicket of heavy brush along the road. Noting the mile marker for later, I got in the car as Poppa Daddy stepped on the gas and continued down Lesser.

Ten minutes later we had passed Ludley Park and were nearing the dusty turnoff point when the headlights picked up the form of a small man. He was on the left side of the road, jogging toward us. I leaned forward, peering, and Poppa Daddy hit the brakes and rolled to a stop.

Brothaman wore gym sweats, and his shirtsleeves were still riding above his elbows. He stared at us, his breath making small clouds in the air. His eyes were clear and unwavering, his chin tight. "He put his hands on me," he said quietly, "and I'ma kill him."

I swallowed.

Poppa Daddy nodded. "Hop in."

# FIVE

I'd never liked being an only child, and being raised by grand-parents instead of parents had made things that much harder. Yeah, Poppa Daddy did all of that fatherly shit with me, and my own mother couldn't have loved me any more than Sugar Baby did, but still, there was a difference, and having Chicken around full-time was a straight-up addition to my world.

The first couple of days he was with us I kept checking the window, expecting Wilkes and his posse to drive by and shoot up the house. When they didn't show, I thought for sure the law was gonna come for Chicken, toss him up and drag him back to jail, but Poppa Daddy took care of that.

"Got somebody up at the courthouse owes me a favor. Next week this time the names on them custody papers is gonna be mine and Bishop's." Days later we received word from the county clerk that Granpaw had been declared the legal guardian of Bishop Johnson, and the following morning he and Sugar Baby had Chicken enrolled at Bull Run High.

Because it was a juvenile facility, all inmates at Spottfield were required to attend regular classes, and Chicken's state records combined with the official school reports that were sent down from Birdtown had landed him in the senior class right along with me. But there was a big difference between the standard classes I attended and those where he was assigned. It surprised me to no end to find that Brothaman had made it on the enrichment list and was placed in advanced-standing classes for both science and math.

Of course Chicken's rep had made it to the high school way before he did, and even if it hadn't, the anger rolling through him showed in almost everything he did. He was no half-bad nigger, that much was for sure, and while the guys in school tended to cut him a wide path and keep their stupid comments out of earshot, Chicken scored a hit with the sisters from day one, and quite a few bold white girls stuck they titties up in his face too.

Katie Dobson, Ralphie's younger sister, looked like a plucked alley cat and made no bones about the fact that she thought Chicken was hot. She brushed up against him one day in the cafeteria line, rubbing her narrow hips across his ass. Chicken jumped back like he'd been scalded with hot grease.

"What's wrong, Brothaman?" I asked, laughing. "That white girl's got a jones for you. She's ready to put that sweet stuff on you, man. Go for it!"

Chicken turned down his lips and cupped his nuts. "My baby girls are waiting up in these bad boys, and every last one of them is *black*. A white girl couldn't even suck my dick."

"Shit." I laughed and reached for a dap. "White, green, orange, I ain't turning down no head!"

Chicken left me hanging. "That's because your ass is lost and don't know it."

"Oh, like y'all didn't do white girls up in Birdtown, right?"

"Not in my house. A white man raped my grandmother, and my father hated that nasty blood flowing through his veins. Nope. Black was beautiful in Slim Willie's Place. In fact, it was damn near the finest shit in the world."

"Finally! A brother with some good sense!"

Gebra Burns stood waiting behind me on line, and I turned around to give her a dirty look. She was one of those sisters who was tall and black but somehow still invisible. I'd known Gebra since third grade, and while she was a brainiac, a future surgeon who had big titties and some nice hips, the rest of her just wasn't my type. "Yeah, you heard me." She rolled her eyes. "I said your friend has good sense. Maybe you should rub up against him and see if you can catch some."

"What?" I said, waving her off. "He's all that just because he don't dig white girls?"

She hefted her book bag up on her shoulder and smirked. Her teeth where bright white against the darkness of her skin, and for the first time I noticed that she was actually kinda cute. "No, not because he's not into them, but because he's figured out that he has a responsibility to sisters that airheads like you can't even comprehend."

Chicken laughed and reached around me to pass her a tray. "When a fine chocolate sister speaks, just listen and learn, my brother. Listen and learn."

I glanced at him and shrugged, piling food on my tray. "Why for when she's talking out the side of her neck? When are sisters gonna start feeling some responsibility towards us? When they gonna start making the brothers feel like they're about something?"

The look she gave me made me feel like I'd been caught eating boogers. She followed us over to our table and sat down like she'd been invited or something. "Sisters do feel responsible for y'all, stupid. Brothers belong to us in a way that we'll never belong to you. Besides, we push y'all out our coochies and let you nurse from our titties, so we already know you're something."

I bit into a fry. "Girl, you crazy. That mess don't even make no sense. Pass the salt."

Chicken slid a saltshaker my way and chewed off half of his

grilled-cheese sandwich. "Yeah it does, Mister Malcolm Marcus Mosiah Armstrong. It makes a whole lot of sense. Wasn't your father a Panther?"

"Yeah. So?"

"Well, then, you should know!"

I *was* lost but I wasn't about to show it. "I do know! Damn! Can I eat my lunch in peace?"

"Man." Chicken frowned, then turned a milk carton up to his mouth. He took a couple of long swallows, then pushed his tray away. "Check it out, Malcolm. Lemme break it down for you. See, when a brother fucks with a white woman, it's usually because they so fuckin' humbled by the white man that they really saying, 'Mister White Man, I'm nothing and you're something. I'm inferior to you, so in order for me to feel like any kind of any fuckin' thing, I gotta strive to be just like you. Therefore, I'ma start out by getting me some of the same thing you got, 'cause if Mister White Man likes it, then I know it must be good! And since I'm nothing, my women and my sisters and my daughters must also be nothing. And since you're something, Mister White Man, your women and your sisters and your daughters must also be something, so I gots to get me some of that *same* something you got!" He shook his head. "Brother, you better learn to love that what's in your own image."

Gebra put her hand on my arm. I wanted to shake it off, but for some reason I didn't.

"It's a self-hatred thing, Malcolm," she said, and while her eyes were steady, I couldn't find a damned thing sharp or bitter in her voice. "There's a bunch of brothers out here who suffer from it. They pretend that race is irrelevant, but that's only a cop-out to justify their insecurities. They don't understand that it's the black in them that makes them special, so they go get a white girl to try and prove their worth to themselves, and to the rest of the world."

I shrugged. "Don't preach that 'Say it loud' shit to me. I know who I am."

Chicken stood up and grabbed his tray. He stuck an apple in his pocket and winked at Gebra. "You's a smart girl. Fine too. One day when my brother here wakes up, he's gonna find himself a woman just like you."

⊞⊞⊞⊞⊞

I let all that "Black is beautiful" stuff Chicken and Gebra were talking roll right off me. I'd never been with a white girl, never even tried to, but I couldn't say I'd turn one down if I had the chance either. And anyway, Jezza–Belle Lawson was a straight-up sister, but my hopes of getting some of that seemed to be going right out the window. At least two Sundays a month Granmaw insisted I go to church. "Boy, you need to hit your knees and beg for salvation!" she'd say as she brushed out her wig and put in her teeth. She'd grease my scalp and make me put on a suit and a button-down shirt, then I'd squeeze my dogs into a pair of "ooh-goddamn" shoes, and with Poppa Daddy rockin' and wavin' from the porch, we'd be on our way.

When Chicken came to live with us, he was made to toe that same line. Every other Sunday we'd get decked out and greased down and head for the Church Without Spot or Wrinkle located smack in the middle of the bottoms. Jezza–Belle sang in the junior choir, and there wasn't a robe in the world made that could hide what she was packing. I wanted her and she knew it. I'd undress her with my eyes while she sang alto, inching that holy zipper down that sanctified satin until I got to that virginal white shirt beneath it, but that's as far as it ever went.

In December Granmaw bugged the hell out of me and Chicken until we both sent off our applications to the University of Alabama, and Sherrie Respass, our twelfth-grade guidance counselor, seemed confident that despite my half-assed efforts, we'd both get in. Chicken wanted to major in engineering, and since I hadn't the foggiest idea of what my talents were and had developed little to no interest in anything except boxing and girls, I just about tore that application up checking off boxes then crossing them out as I tried to decide on a major.

"See there, Peter Peter Pussy Eater," Chicken said, laughing and shaking his head. "That's your problem. All you got is fur burgers on your brain. You ain't got a passion for nothin' else, so you can't make no halfway decent decisions. You gotta look at where life puts you, then choose what you gonna do about it. Man up, nigger! Learn how to get your shit off. Make a decision, then stand up on it. No matter what happens or where the fuck it takes you."

"Shut up," I said, embarrassed. "Why you talking all that trash?" He'd called me out strong, but in my heart I suspected he was right. Sometimes even I could see that my shit was just plain old raggedy.

"I did decide," I said, going along with his program and selecting engineering. "I just ain't the kinda brother who digs being attached. That's why it looks like I'm all the time chasing a different girl. Besides, wanting pussy and getting it is two different things. I want it all the time, but I don't hardly get it at all." By now my application was a big inky mess, so I ended up having to circle my choice instead of checking off the box.

The months seemed to fly by with Chicken in the house. He settled in with us just fine, but he was single-minded and way too damn intense. Hell, he spent more time out back in the gym training and helping Poppa Daddy instruct the new fighters than I ever did.

Ho house or not, I could tell his folks had been good people 'cause he came alive under Granmaw and Poppa Daddy's love, but even so, he was still ornery as hell, and sometimes it looked like he just closed up inside himself and said "fuck you" to the world. He also stayed on my case. Said I needed to get my act together when it came down to school, chasing tail, keeping my room tight, every goddamn thing. He felt I was sitting on my ass when I should have been fighting on my feet.

"Why you gotta take everything so damn serious?" I asked him. We were folding shirts and pants fresh off the clothesline, and Chicken was ragging me as usual.

"Man, just look at how you handle your stuff. No thought to nothin'. You good people, Malcolm, but you skating through life like it ain't no big thing."

I glanced at his pile and then at mine. My gear was balled up and twisted, but Chicken's clothes looked like they'd just come from the Oriental cleaners. His pants were folded at the crease, and his shirts could have just come out the package.

"Gone, man. Leave me alone. This shit is gonna get wrinkled as soon as I put it on. It don't make no sense fussing over it."

"See? That's what I'm talking about! You a 'that'll do' type of man, and you come from better than that. You could have it all, Malcolm, if you just dug deep enough in your nuts to see what you made of."

I thought it was pretty jacked up of him to tell me that, even if he was right. But no matter how merciless he was, I knew part of it was because Chicken missed his folks and felt cheated by their murders. There just had to be a big part of that night that still haunted him. I'd catch him staring off into nowhere, turning red and looking all evil, and when I asked him where his head was at he'd bury his nose in a book or go off running through the woods trying to shake it off. But he didn't really need to tell me where his mind was during those times. I already knew.

In Birdtown.

Sugar Baby would fuss over him and coax him into her arms, but Pop-Pop simply let him be. "The boy done led a violent life," he'd remind us. "Whatever memories you still got of them animals who murdered Zeke and Sweets, Bishop got twice that. It ain't been but two years since he watched his daddy die. Not to mention the life he took and the time he done for it. If walkin' through them woods and reading all them books is gonna help him heal, we'll do our best to keep him in good shoes and strong glasses."

I didn't have to be a rocket scientist to dig that. Chicken had already told me what had gone down in Birdtown. How some old customers had done a push-in at his house and killed a bunch of folks. How one of the gunmen managed to get away. How he shot the man who killed his father, then held his dead mother in his arms. He never said much about his time in jail, other than to wonder why he got out so early. When I asked him what jail was like, he told me it was just the darker side of a man's soul.

"Mal," he said. "I know cats who are leaving Spottfield and going straight to the penitentiary, but a couple of them brothers done learned to be free in their minds. The rest?" He laughed. "The state might free their asses, but their minds, Mal. Their minds will never follow."

We had a lot of good times too. Chicken was right. I was the kind of cat who stayed horny, and for any kid, especially a boxer, that can be dangerous. I turned eighteen in January, and the night of my birthday Poppa Daddy called me and Chicken out on the back porch.

It was wicked outside; frost covered the naked tree branches, and the narrow stream running behind our property was a solid block of ice. Poppa Daddy was dressed in a plaid hunting jacket I'd given him for Father's Day and wore a fur-lined leather hat with the flaps pulled down over his ears.

"Here." He passed me a paper bag. Inside was a half-filled plastic jug, the brown paper twisted around its neck. It wasn't hard to tell where the other half had gone. Puffs of smoke came from Pop-Pop's mouth as he blew into his bare hands. His eyes were bloodshot and he reeked of corn brew. "Time you boys to learnt what good brewed hooch is all about." He nodded toward the jug. "Did this for your daddy Zeke too."

I raised one eyebrow. Little did Poppa Daddy know, but I had a thing for cold duck. I could drink him under the table any night and still piss compass-straight the next morning.

"Gone, son," he urged me on. "It's all right. You's a man now."

I lifted the jug to my lips and took a long swig, then hissed and choked as tears streamed from my eyes. Cold duck didn't have shit on this!

"Sip it, dammit!" he hollered. "This some classic shit! Put hair on your goddamn chest! Gone, Bishop." He waved at me to pass the jug. "You's a Armstrong now too, son. Go easy now."

We passed the jug between us, me smacking my lips between each sip and Chicken swallowing the liquid heat and coughing it up until it ran from his mouth and nose.

"Aiight, now." Pop-Pop slurred and stepped off the back porch, his boots crunching in the frozen grass. He unzipped his pants and turned toward Granmaw's vegetable plot. I tried not to laugh as he pissed in what had been her cabbage and tomatoes. "I think," he yelled over his shoulder, "it's about time you boys learnt a lil' sumpthin' 'bout the honeys and the bees . . ."

Poppa Daddy's tongue was liquored stiff as he gave me and Chicken an ass-backward speech about girls and sex that had us falling on the ground, rolling on the cold porch and holding our sides.

He squinted up at us, then zipped his pants and pointed. "Laugh if you want to. You ain't gotta jump on the first . . . *Whorella* or, or, or . . . *Sluttisha* who comes your way! Gone out there and seed you a garden! Ole Ike Armstrong gonna make for damn skippy you stick around and help it grow! And remember," he concluded, "that stuff them gals got between they legs is some kinda good, but watch out now! It'll wobble your knees! Don't go jumpin' off in them waters without your headgear!"

If Poppa Daddy thought his talk would slow us down when it came to girls, it didn't work on me. Sex was good in my neighborhood, and it wasn't long after my birthday that me and Chicken passed a bottle with Fast Annie Wright and Sukkie Baines, her city-slick cousin who had a thing for bright-skinned boys with curly hair. Annie was sexy and thick in that meaty sort of way. Sukkie was heavy-breasted and so hairy folks called her Chew'bacca.

Cramped into the backseat of Sugar Baby's car and smelling like a case of Wild Turkey, I fumbled with Annie's girdle and hook-end bra until my hands found warmth and wetness. I kissed her throat and nibbled on her breasts, then entered her deeply with my fingers as she undid my pants and freed my johnson, guiding me toward her spread legs.

"Wait," I told her, pulling a rubber from my back pocket.

Annie panted and sucked on my bottom lip. "We don't need that. I'm on the pill."

Bull*shit*, I thought, ripping the package open with my teeth. I might be half drunk, but I wasn't full stupid. Poppa Daddy had schooled me better than that. Taught me to be responsible for my *own* birth control. I stared into Annie's eyes. She sure looked sexy under that half moonlight, and while I liked her all right and thought she was smart and cute, I slid that latex cap over my johnson and made sure he was sealed in extra tight. Shit. They didn't call her Fast Annie for nothing.

I pulled her onto my lap, and with one of her feet propped on my shoulder and the other trying to push out the back window, I went to town, squeezing her ass and hitting her wet spot with long, deep strokes. Annie was hot and we went at it hard and fast. She whispered all kinds of nasty shit in my ear. "Yeah, baby. Fuck this hot pussy. Tear this shit up. Oooh, yeah, daddy! Feel how wet it is? Splash in it, motherfucker. Fill this funk-box up. Goddamn, that dick is big!"

Annie turned me on so bad I started talking to her too. "Yeah, baby. Talk that dirty shit to Daddy! C'mon, ride it. Get down on every inch." I cupped her ass cheeks and slammed her down hard, over and over again. She yelped and tightened her stuff around my shaft. "Is it big enough for you, baby?" I panted. "Can you take it all? Get that nut, baby. Get that nut!"

She came first, kicking and moaning, and moments later, I joined her.

I closed my eyes, kissing her forehead and rubbing my cheeks

against the coarseness of her hair, and it wasn't until we had settled down to catch our breath that I remembered Chicken and
Sukkie. I opened my eyes. Brothaman wasn't even close to getting
any. Slouched in the front seat and struggling with his wine,
Chicken was slobbering into the girl's hairy titties calling her Gussie,
Leila, Boogalou—everything but Sukkie—as he dug around in his
pockets trying to make her accept his few crumpled dollar bills as
payment for her troubles.

IIIIIIIIII

I suspected Chicken couldn't get with a woman unless he was
paying for it, but as much as I loved women and every little thing
about them, Poppa Daddy's warnings did keep some balance in
my life. Most afternoons and evenings you could find me and
Chicken out back at the gym, and when we weren't training, or
teaching the younger boxers, Chicken kept the gym's books and I
tallied the fighter stats.

If we were going to have a shot at winning at state and then
moving on to the nationals in Chicago, Chicken had to qualify
as a lightweight, and thanks to Sugar Baby's country cooking and
a kick-ass weight-training regimen, Brothaman had thickened
and put on weight, his sinewy body becoming buff and well
developed.

And Poppa Daddy was more than happy with his progress.
When Chicken climbed into the ring, Granpaw just glowed all
over, and I had to admit that there had never been a time when
the gym had been more alive, the fighters pumped with more op-
timism and team spirit. But in spite of all that, there was a grain of
fear casting shade on our shine. Granmaw's diabetes was getting
worse, and the long-term effects had caused her feet to swell up
till they almost popped and her vision started to blur.

I heard her up at night, slippers scratching the floor from her
bedroom to the bathroom. Saw the deep sores on her feet and
legs, the dry rashes on her skin. Soon, injecting herself became too

painful, and Pop-Pop shook like a dog every time she had to stick herself in her stomach, thighs, or upper arms. To my surprise it was Chicken who stepped in with hands that were gentle and sure as he inserted the syringe into her insulin vial and then held our Sugar Baby in his arms and guided the needle smoothly into her flesh.

Twice she'd nearly gone into a diabetic coma, her blood sugar dropping so low that we couldn't understand a mumbling word coming out of her mouth. She'd passed out too, and after that we made sure that she was never left alone, usually relying on our neighbor Grace Kittrell to sit with her whenever all three of us were out.

I'd smelled death at an early age. The fire that killed Zeke and Sweets might have burned their bodies, but it scorched my soul, and it was just a few years later when my Nana Charming, Sugar Baby's mother, took me on a train ride to Louisiana.

Nana Charming had received a telegram late one night saying her older sister, Ma'Dear, had passed on. Her eyes had been dry as she packed a suitcase, insisting that I go with her so I could meet "them Sweetwater Sanders" she always talked about. Poppa Daddy had raised hell when she pulled me out of bed in the dark of night. He insisted we wait until daybreak to travel, but as old as she was, Nana Charming was more than a whip. She told Poppa Daddy she was duty-bound to see that her sister got in the ground before another nightfall, then stared him down until he moved out her way and sat quietly in his chair by the door.

Ma'Dear's funeral had been held right inside her grandson Top Jar's house, and as I stared into the mud-brown face of the woman who was my great-aunt, my heart truly hurt. Top Jar's daughter, my cousin Euleatha, had tried her best to climb in the casket with the old lady, and as Nana Charming wrestled Eulie down to the floor and rocked and shushed her, tears filled my eyes because I could feel the pain radiating from my cousin's soul. I'd never seen the bodies of my parents, and I couldn't even imagine what it would feel like to look at my granmaw laid out in a box, but now as I watched her shuffling from room to room, losing the light in her eyes a little more each day, I remembered Euleatha's grief over losing her Ma'Dear, and didn't even want to imagine how I would survive if something like that was to happen to my Sugar Baby.

# SIX

April 20 found Bull Run in the middle of a soaking storm. Rain whipped up tree limbs and sent creeks of water cascading down the road in front of our house. The stone path leading back to the gym was all but submerged, and inside boxers milled about in an atmosphere of excited tension. Bags were packed, forms signed, and rosters checked. All that was left was the chartered bus ride to the Lufkin Arena, where the Golden Gloves state finals were fought each year.

The anticipation of the day had taken its toll on just about everybody. Deep lines creased Pop-Pop's face, and weariness shone just behind his eyes. I knew he'd been awake the better part of the night tending to Granmaw, but I also knew he could survive the excitement of this day on coffee and adrenaline alone.

I, on the other hand, felt like shit. With my head pounding, I slouched at the front desk watching the rain beat against the windows and wishing I could turn down the volume on the chatter and hum of the gym. I was wearing a sweatsuit with two lighter shirts beneath it and had alternated all morning between pulling off my top layers when a hot flash struck me and then bundling back beneath them when cold chills made my nose drip and my teeth chatter.

"Feelin' any better?" Poppa Daddy laid a heavy hand on my shoulder. Chicken had just come out of the locker room, where he and the other fighters had been massaged just to a point so that their muscles didn't get limp. I'd wanted to be back there with them but had doubted whether my legs would carry me that far.

"No." I shook my head, the slight movement making me dizzy. "Feels like I swallowed crushed glass and my head is fuzzy. The room keeps spinning."

"Damn," Chicken said. "That ain't good."

Poppa Daddy frowned and shoved his hands in his pockets. "Naw, that ain't good, son. Sound like a bug of some kind done got you." He pressed the back of his hand to my forehead. "You warm. Runnin' a fever." He glanced out the large bay window where dark storm clouds belched and rumbled. "Weather sure as hell don't help none. C'mon." He moved toward the door and beckoned me with his head. "Won't be no fightin' for you today. Let me get my jacket and we'll head up to the house and get you in bed."

"I ain't sick—"

"Yeah you are." Chicken frowned and propped one foot up on a chair. He waited until Pop-Pop disappeared into his office before he spoke. "This is fucked up, Mal, and it ain't gonna be the same without you."

Damn if I didn't all of a sudden feel much better. That was the nicest thing Chicken had ever said to me.

"Thanks, but I still wanna go."

He shrugged and threw a soft punch that landed on my arm. "Chill, Malcolm. Get better. It ain't no thang, man. Just a chicken wang on a lightbulb strang. Tellie is taping every fight, and I'll give you a blow-by-blow commentary when we get back."

"Bullshit," I said, then sneezed and wiped my nose with the

back of my hand. "I might not be able to fight, but I'm sure as shit gonna be ringside and rolling in real time."

Chicken looked at me for a long moment, then shook his head. "No you ain't. But win or lose tonight, it's been real, Brothaman. And it's been because of you."

"How you figure?"

He spread his arms. "You opened up your door, man. Your family . . . you been real."

Before I could answer, Poppa Daddy came out of his office. "Let's go, Malcolm." He covered his Kangol with a film of clear plastic.

"But I ain't sick—"

His hand went up, then he zipped his jacket and braced himself to go out in the driving rain. "You heard what I said. Now let's go. And pull that hood up on your head before you catch the Japanese new-moan-ya."

I grumbled under my breath but stood up. I was so weak my legs shook. "Aiight, then." I sneezed, then dapped Chicken with my elbow. "Keep your chin tucked, Brothaman."

My friend nodded. "Yeah, and my elbows tight."

<hr />

I was buried beneath a mound of blankets, sweating up a storm. Granmaw had made me stick out my tongue so she could smear a thick glob of Vicks VapoRub at the back of my throat, even though I'd told her the label said it wasn't for internal use.

"Turn your tail over," she told me as she yanked up my shirt and slapped a mound of it on my back. She massaged it into my muscles. "I been eatin' Vicks since before you was born, and it ain't killed me yet." She pasted a spoonful of it onto the ports of the steam vaporizer sitting on the floor by my bed, and I groaned because I knew next month this time my room would still smell like camphor balls.

I drifted in and out of sleep, chills rolling over me as I coughed, wincing at the scraping in my chest and the splintering pain in my head. My dreams were distorted, filled with smoke and fuzzy images of Zeke and Sweets, and it wasn't long before sweat coated my body and soaked my pajamas.

A voice penetrated my fog and I opened my eyes with a start. The shadows had lengthened into darkness, and outside the rain had slowed. Granmaw stood hovering above me, panic in her eyes.

"Wake up, Malcolm."

She stood clutching the edge of my dresser. The terror in her voice scared me, and I struggled to sit upright, fear churning with the bile in my stomach and rising toward my mouth.

"Malcolm," she whispered. "Poppa Daddy just called. There's been an accident, and him and Tellie is gonna need your help getting to the hospital while the boys try to get back home."

"Huh? What?" My mouth formed words as I struggled to understand.

"It's Bishop," Granmaw moaned. Her hands clawed at her dress. "That boy he was fighting . . . he near 'bout dead. That white boy is in the hospital, and his peoples . . . his peoples is fixin' to kill Bishop."

‖‖‖‖‖‖

I was in my clothes and behind the wheel of Granmaw's car in less than five minutes. Poppa Daddy had chartered a bus for the event, and since he didn't want to take the whole team up to the hospital, he'd told Granmaw to have me bring him the car.

I forgot all about my fever and runny nose as I sped down Bull Run's streets toward the arena. All I could think about was those rednecks. There was no doubt about what they'd do if given the chance. They'd do Chicken just like them white folks had done Emmett Till a long time back. They'd beat him, burn him, shoot him, and drown him, and when that was done, they'd fish him out the river and whip his black ass all over again.

I made it downtown without getting stopped by a cop even though my foot was like lead on the gas pedal. The parking area in front of the arena overflowed with cars and pickups. I drove around to the left side of the building, honked the horn, and waited like Granmaw had said.

"I ain't runnin'!" Chicken protested as Poppa Daddy and a group of about ten fighters muscled him toward the backseat. I got out the front seat and let Tellie get behind the wheel, and as soon as Boobie's father brought the bus around, the rest of the team rushed on.

"I'm ridin' the bus!" Chicken insisted. "It was a fair fuckin' fight. I beat his honky ass fair and square, and I ain't runnin'."

Poppa Daddy pleaded. "Bishop, think! These crackers don't give a damn whether you fought fair or not! Alls they see is their boy laid out and bleedin'. When white blood spills, they wanna see some black blood runnin' out there with it."

In the end Poppa Daddy almost had to threaten him. "You got that much fight in you? You so ready to die you wanna take a couple of your friends down with you?"

"What?"

He gestured to the boxers who hung on to Chicken by the arms, legs, and waist. They were owl-eyed and scared. "You think them rednecks is gonna be satisfied with just you? Don't you know if you get on that damn bus they gonna jump on every goddamn thing that even looks black and go to crackin' they skulls?"

Chicken went still and his teammates turned him loose.

"If you that much of a man," Poppa Daddy said, taking off his hat and rolling up his sleeves, "that you willin' to go up against a mob of mad white trash, I might as well gone and bust you upside your head right now and put you outta your misery."

Chicken folded himself into the backseat of the car. Minutes later the bus was headed back to Bull Run, and the car with Pop-Pop and Tellie in the front, me and Trey in the back, and Chicken mad as hell in between us was speeding toward Jefferson County Hospital.

"We can fix this," Poppa Daddy muttered over and over.

Tellie sped through a traffic light, then shook his head. "I don't know, Ike. That white boy took a couple of pretty good gut shots. I saw his breath leave his body and fly out the door, and up until the time they ran us out, he still hadn't moved."

"He was breathing, though. We can at least be thankful for that."

Tellie glanced at Granpaw, then reached over and touched his shoulder. "Let's hope he keeps on breathing. I heard the ring doctor say that boy mighta had something wrong with his heart."

Poppa Daddy covered his face with his hands, and even from where I sat I could see how they trembled. "All these boys done been checked out good. They physicals is current and they supposed to be healthy. Ain't my fighter's job to go easy in the ring. Bishop went there to win a fight, and that's just what he did. The boy done worked too hard and come too far to get hemmed up by some shit like this. He just beginning to settle into hisself and get his head right."

As we pulled into the semicircular driveway of Jefferson County Hospital, Tellie slowed down and eased toward the emergency entrance. A crowd milled about in the light rain, and an ambulance sat out front with its lights on. Poppa Daddy wanted to find Barney's family and extend his prayers and well wishes, but just as Tellie turned off the engine and Pop-Pop stepped from the car, the crowd went berserk.

"There's them niggers!"

Granpaw barely made it back into the car before they swarmed. "Go! Go! Go!" he screamed as Tellie fought to restart the engine. Murderous white faces, friends and parents of the other white fighters, pressed in around us, yanking on the door handles and leaping on top the hood.

Tellie swatted back toward Trey. "Get down, son! Get down!"

Bottles came crashing toward us, and berry-colored liquid smeared my window.

"We gonna kill that nigger!"

"Set them black motherfuckers on fire!"

Tellie slammed on the brakes and I lurched forward, banging my nose on his headrest. Bodies slid off the car and hit the wet pavement. Tellie stomped the gas so hard half his tires got left on the ground. "We gotta get to the po-lice, Ike," Tellie said, panting. He ignored a stop sign and sped through an intersection.

The Bull Run Police Department stood on a grassy knoll on the west side of town. At the station Poppa Daddy and Tellie filled out the complaint forms while Chicken sat on a bench sandwiched between me and Trey.

"Did they get hold of him?" Bill Watson was the desk sergeant, and Poppa Daddy seemed relieved to see a familiar face. Mr. Watson was a big hunk of beef with blue eyes and square shoulders. He and Poppa Daddy had been friends since he was a starting linebacker the same year Pop-Pop had been the first black quarterback to play for Bull Run High. Grammaw said they'd become friends only because Watson had been the only one on the team willing to share a room with a Negro during their road games. Pop-Pop said it was because they both loved football and had fair souls.

Whatever it was that had drawn them together, right now Poppa Daddy was on fire as he explained the white mob's rage to his old friend. "If they hadda got him, they woulda kilt him."

Watson nodded and sipped from a coffee mug that said I LOVE GRANDPA. I glanced up at the clock above his head; it was broken, its hands fixed at ten of two. "Yep. They got some pretty crazy folks over at Roseland. Just last week we pulled two bodies from an abandoned trailer. Somebody set the trailer on fire, but not before planting some lead in their heads."

"They said they gonna kill him, Bill." Granpaw's hands shook as he struggled to hold on to the pen and fill out the forms.

I glanced over at Chicken and couldn't find a speck of fear in his eyes. His feet were planted and his arms crossed. He looked ready for anything.

Poppa Daddy pleaded. "Everybody heard 'em. That gotta be worth y'all pullin' out some protection for this child."

"Yeah, Ike." Watson stood and placed his cup on a shelf behind his desk. He took a stack of forms from a box on the floor and set them in front of Poppa Daddy. "You'd think a death threat from a blood-hungry bunch of assholes would be enough to rustle up some protection around here"—he motioned toward the stack of papers—"but we got more complaints than we got manpower and reinforcements." His eyes were sad as he shook his head. "I wish there was something we could do, but there's not."

"They comin' for him, Bill. They liquored-up and ornery, and ain't nothin' gonna satisfy them 'cept spillin' his blood."

Mr. Watson looked helpless. "You call us if they come. I'll make sure a car gets sent out right away."

Granpaw scoffed. "The boy'll be dead before you can pull that car out your damn lot."

"I'm sorry, Armstrong. There ain't much else I can do."

Poppa Daddy leaned forward and met those sad blue eyes head-on. His eyes blazed, and he spoke through his teeth. "Then I'll protect him myself, if I have to. I'll be damned if I'ma let 'em swing him from some goddamned tree."

"I understand, Ike. Do what you have to do."

"Oh, I intend to. Pull out your wallet and slap your money on it."

# SEVEN

Just like their daddies before them, they came in the dark of night.

We waited on the front porch, Poppa Daddy smoking a cigar, and me listening to the call of tree crickets and katydids. The sky was crowded with low-hanging stars, and the night air was warm but dry.

Headlights flickered on the road crossways to our property, and Granpaw shifted his weight in his padded chair. He wore long sleeves, overalls, and a pair of dusty work boots. The brim of his cap hid his eyes as he sat in the pitch dark cradling his shotgun in his right arm.

It had taken some convincing to keep Chicken out of sight, but love had prevailed.

"Me and Malcolm is gonna set a spell on the front porch tonight," Poppa Daddy had explained as we huddled around the kitchen table. There'd been no evening meal. Sugar Baby was too sick to walk, let alone stand up at the stove, so Granpaw had set out a couple of tins of sardines and a half-eaten box of crackers he'd found in the pantry. The food had gone untouched. "And," he continued, "you, Bishop, you gonna stay inside and take care of my Sugar Baby."

"Naw, Poppa Daddy—" Chicken protested.

"Look, son." Weariness shone in Granpaw's eyes, and his age rode high on his back. "I used to have me a hardheaded boy just like you. Full of piss and pot liquor. Now, I know you been through a war and you's a fine soldier. But this time you gots to stand down. I know these here white folks. Knew they daddies and granddaddies, and the whole lot of 'em are just mean and rotten. I might be able to peace 'em down by myself, but with you there, well . . . blood is gonna have to be spilt."

Chicken shrugged. "Fuck around, lay around. They gotta bring ass to get ass. My blood gets spilled, theirs gonna too."

Pop-Pop seemed to consider this for a minute, then he spoke real quiet. "Yep. I 'spect you right. I'm sure you can take whatever you got comin'. Problem is, my Sugar Baby can't. Them boys go to stirrin' up a ruckus over you, and the stress is likely to kill her. Now, since I know how much you love my wife, I know you'll be mindful of her condition and do like I ask. Stand down, Bishop."

Chicken plain staggered under all that weight Poppa Daddy had dropped on his shoulders.

"All right, Pop-Pop. If you say so, then I guess it's best."

▮▮▮▮▮▮▮

Dirt and pebbles danced in the glow of the headlights as the pickup maneuvered down the path toward the house. The rumble of the engine stirred me, and I sat up in Sugar Baby's rocker and pulled a hand-sewn quilt around my shoulders. A gift from my old auntie Ma'Dear, it had a patchwork design in the colors of humanity, and it fell over my knees and draped across the rifle Poppa Daddy had given me on my thirteenth birthday.

Poppa Daddy looked over at me when I moved, but he didn't speak. He just kept on rocking, his rhythm neither slowing nor quickening. A trail of sweet smoke came from his cigar, and he looked peaceful and untroubled.

The pickup braked at the edge of the stone path. The Chevy was dark in color and had a busted grille and heavy front-end damage. Three white men rode in the cab, and three more were in the bed. The driver got out and slammed his door heavily behind him. Two men jumped from the back and stood beside him.

The crickets hushed and Granpaw kept rocking, the creaking of his chair hitting the porch the only sound in the night. Bug and Blue Judd, Barney's uncles, stood before us, and at their side was Caleb, Barney's younger, meaner brother. They were dressed in lumberjacks and Levi's, their dirty hair showing beneath their caps. We knew these men well. The older ones had gone to school with my father, and the younger ones had taken up raising sand where their daddies had left off. Blue stepped forward, wiping his nose with the back of his hand.

"Evening, Uncle Isaac."

"Blue." Granpaw nodded, rocking his shotgun. "How do?"

"All depends. Hear tell you got somethin' we looking for."

"I reckon you done heard wrong."

Blue swiped a matchstick across his leg, and a blue-orange flame ignited. He held it against the end of a cigarette and sucked until the tip glowed. "That lil' bastard ain't nothin' to you. Barney's my nephew. My flesh and blood, and a Judd'll die for his kinfolk."

"Bishop is my grandson," Poppa Daddy said simply, "and Armstrongs die for theirs too."

Caleb pushed toward the porch. The bulge of a pistol showed through his shirt, and I knew his uncles were packing too. "Send that nigger out, old uncle. 'Less you ready to die for him tonight." He moved to climb the stairs, and my heart jumped into my mouth.

"Get your boy, Blue." Poppa Daddy swung his shotgun around, and I let the nose of my rifle peek through the quilt. "I know he young and his head is swole, but he gone have to bleed if that boot of his hits my step."

I was scared shitless, but I knew Poppa Daddy wasn't bluffing. His orders had been simple but direct: not a soul got next to Bishop unless they came through us. Aim low, if possible, but once you pulled the trigger, make sure you left a hole in somebody.

"We ain't got no fight with you," Bug said, pulling Caleb by the shoulder. I could see the rage in Caleb. See how his muscles shook as he fought against himself. The fool in him wanted to rush up the steps and charge into the house. The boy in him wanted to live. "But that little nigger's gonna pay for what he done to Barney."

The barrel of Poppa Daddy's shotgun remained true. "It was a fair fight, Bug. You been in a bunch of 'em yourself. I've watched you win some, and seen you lose a couple too. The Judds are a fine fightin' family. Barney knew the risks."

"That new kid shoulda never been in the ring to begin with! He ain't no fighter. He ain't nothin' but a scared, cheatin' dog."

"Oh." Poppa Daddy almost chuckled. "He didn't cheat, and he ain't scared. He a whole lotta things, but scared ain't one of 'em."

Blue frowned. "Then he ain't too smart neither. It ain't but a matter of time. Don't hafta be tonight, but sooner or later we gonna get him."

"Gone home, fellas," Poppa Daddy said, gentlelike. "Tell Bo and Mother Judd I'm keeping Barney in my prayers. Let 'em know my Sugar Baby is feelin' a bit better and sends her good wishes too."

"We'll get him, Uncle," Blue repeated, and it was clear from his eyes that he spoke the truth. "Sooner or later, we gonna get him."

▮▮▮▮▮▮▮▮▮

We watched their taillights fade before rising from our chairs. "I'm glad they backed off," I said. "I thought somebody was gonna get shot."

Poppa Daddy lit another cigar, and the flames cast light on the worry nestled deep in his eyes. "It ain't over, Malcolm," he said. "In fact, it mighta just got worse."

Chicken sat in the front room in Sugar Baby's chair. His eyes were lidded and his face was like stone. Poppa Daddy didn't waste any words. "Bishop, you done fucked with their pride, son, and this ain't going away. It ain't just that you beat him. Naw, it shames 'em that a black kid like you could *hurt* Barney so bad! Now they egos got to be redeemed—"

Gravel crunched outside, and Poppa Daddy spun around toward the front door. I'd heard it too. The sound of tires on the road, a running engine moving steadily down our drive.

"They're back," I said, fighting to keep the panic out of my voice.

Poppa Daddy gave Chicken a stilling glance, then grabbed his shotgun and flung open the front door. Headlights shined onto the porch and caught him in a glaring silhouette. I squeezed in the doorway and pressed my shoulder to his, my rifle aimed low.

"Ike?" someone called as the car door swung open. The driver killed the lights, and I blinked in the sudden darkness. "It's me, Ike. Bill Watson."

I felt Poppa Daddy's breath let go, his whole body slumping in relief. Beside him, I pulled back my weapon, the barrel slick with sweat.

Holding the door open, Poppa Daddy let Mr. Watson climb the porch and come inside. Dressed in his police blues, he took off his cap and nodded at Chicken, who was still sitting in Granmaw's chair. "You just missed 'em, Bill. Bo's two older boys and one of his grandsons."

"I know. I passed them speeding down Lesser. I figured they was coming from your place, and I wanted to make sure your boy was okay."

Poppa Daddy pulled out a straight-back chair for Mr. Watson, then plopped down on a narrow bench where Sugar Baby usually kept potted houseplants. I slid in next to him and balanced on the edge of the seat. "He okay, for now," Poppa Daddy said. "That bullheaded Caleb liked to got shot, but I kept peace and convinced them to gone home. But they comin' back, that's for damn sure."

"That's what I come to talk to you about." Watson took a deep breath and spoke quickly. "You might not like it, Ike, but the boy's got to go. Not for long, just until things blow over. Give Barney a chance to get out the hospital and heal, and those Judds are plumb likely to forget about this and find something else to go to war on. Then you can bring the boy back and keep on living."

"Where he gonna go, Bill? Bishop is a orphan. He ain't got no peoples 'cept my family and Lester Wilkes."

Watson frowned at the mention of Wilkes's name. "I know that. That's why I'm here. I got an idea that might just work out—that is, if Bishop is willing to start living a little different."

I glanced at Chicken. I didn't want to hear talk of him leaving us, and what I saw in Brothaman's face was brief but clear. He didn't want to go neither.

Poppa Daddy sat up straight. "What's on your mind, Bill?"

"The Peace Corps," Bill Watson answered. "Let him travel awhile with the Peace Corps."

"Ain't that overseas? In a whole 'nother country? Bishop gotta start school up at State in a few months. I thought you mighta had something a bit closer'n that in mind!"

Watson held out his hands. "Hear me out, Ike. Just hear me out." He scooted his chair closer to Poppa Daddy and explained. "Yes, he'd have to go overseas, but he wouldn't have to stay long. My wife's brother works in the Peace Corps office up in Mobile. About a year ago my nephew got in some trouble and had to lay low for a while. They sent him to El Salvador and then brought him back six months later. The same thing could happen for your boy. My brother-in-law owes me one. Lemme talk to him and see can he get Bishop in. The boy can just disappear for a while until things cool off, then he can show up for school just like you planned."

Granpaw shook his head and folded his hands in his lap. He

shrugged, slinging the idea off his back. "I don't know, Bill. Don't make no sense for him to go way 'cross no waters. Bishop is a Armstrong now, and he got a right to be here. He ain't done nothin' 'cept whup on Barney's ass."

Watson's voice rose. "What's that got to do with the price of beans in Chicago, Ike? Since when shit got to make sense for it to go down in Bull Run? Now, them Judds got high tempers and quick guns. Yeah, I'd lock 'em right up if they shot him, but I bet a dollar to a doughnut your boy would still be dead. And what about Malcolm and Sugar? You got a grandson and a sick wife too. Now, you want to keep your little family safe and this kid alive? Get him out of Bull Run. Hell, get him out of Alabama."

Silence stole over us as we tried to digest the advice. Poppa Daddy sat shaking his head; he just couldn't choke it down.

"Bishop's on probation. He can't leave the state."

"I ran him through the system, Ike. There ain't a charge on him. Everything in his file just upped and disappeared."

Granpaw looked surprised, but his mind was set. "I 'preciate the help, Bill, but I ain't sendin' my boy nowhere. I just can't—"

"I'll go."

We stared at Chicken. He sat relaxed in his chair, but every inch of him looked alert.

"I wanna go. I mean, he's right. I need someplace to lay low for a little bit, then I'll come right on back."

"You ain't gotta agree to nothin', Bishop," Poppa Daddy said. "You can stay right here. Them Judds bleed just like everybody else. Long as I got a roof over my head, you got one over yours. I'll set out on that porch every night for the rest of my life, if that's what it takes."

Chicken's face was closed like somebody had bricked it up, but his voice came out low and tender. "I know, Pop-Pop. And I appreciate all yawl done for me and still willing to do. But I think it's best all around if I leave. Just let me go."

It took him awhile, but because Poppa Daddy respected Chicken like a natural man, he finally nodded, defeated.

Mr. Watson rose to his feet. "Okay then. I'll put a call in to Mobile at first light and let you know something as soon as I can." He turned to Chicken. "You're doing the right thing, Bishop. It takes more guts to leave than to hang around and take a chance on having these innocent folks get hurt. My brother-in-law will take good care of you. I'll see to that."

Poppa Daddy got up to see Mr. Watson out, and without even looking my way, Chicken walked through the kitchen and into the room we shared, leaving me all alone.

I sat there and closed my eyes. I felt sick. Like somebody had just kicked me in the throat. With Chicken gone, where would that leave me? I leaned back on the bench and crossed my arms. My whole body was chilled. I wasn't good about dealing with losses. I'd been pretty young when my folks were killed, but I still remembered how it felt to stand outside of that burning house and realize that a big part of my world was being snatched away and there was nothing I could do about it. I had that same feeling now. Brothaman was damn near gone, and there wasn't a thing I could do to change it.

I put my head back and tried not to cry.

# EIGHT

Bill Watson had fixed it so Chicken could leave right away. The Peace Corps had an opening for him in Guatemala, and even though he didn't have a college degree and was still under twenty-one, Watson's brother-in-law had clout with the big boys and had gotten him a waiver to travel and work with them without requiring a contract.

Granmaw had cried all night begging Poppa Daddy not to send him, but once we made her see what-all was likely to happen to him if he stayed, she gave in and asked us to bring in her sewing machine from the back porch. She sat on the side of her bed and set about making Chicken some of those pants that unzipped at the thigh and turned into shorts.

Poppa Daddy wanted to go out and buy Chicken all kinds of tents and mosquito netting he'd seen on those nature shows on PBS, but Watson stopped him. "He don't need to take but one suitcase, Ike. Peace Corps is gonna provide everything he needs. You just get him up to Mobile two days from now, and he'll be set."

Mr. Watson had written out a list of instructions. Chicken was to take the bus to Mobile, where he'd get processed and take a bunch of shots to protect him against whatever diseases he was likely to come across. After that, he'd fly into New York City and catch another flight overseas.

I watched Chicken pack with a weight on my heart that I could have never predicted. He had walked out of the Snatch Hatch with only the clothes on his back, so he didn't have much to take, only the few pieces he'd allowed Poppa Daddy to buy him when he first came to us. He reached under his bed, and I saw him draw that pearl-handled stiletto from a box and slide it into his left boxing shoe. It was the same knife I'd seen him pull on Barney all those months ago, and while the blade looked menacing and deadly, the design on the handle was an impressive mosaic of colored pearls.

"You taking that with you?" I asked as he stuffed the boxing shoes into his bag. He had to know they wouldn't let him on nobody's plane with a weapon like that.

He shook his head. "Not all the way."

I knew it was wrong, but I avoided Chicken those last couple of days. I was mad as hell, and every time he looked at me I scowled and turned away. Yeah, I knew none of this was his fault, but I wanted to kick my own ass and his too. Ever since the fire I'd lived my life by keeping people out of my space. I knew full well what could happen if I let somebody get too close, but it took this scrawny runt of a man, a cold-blooded killer who I now loved like a brother, to throw me off. Somehow, I'd messed around and made a real friend, and the hole he was leaving in my life was gonna take a long time to heal.

⁑

We drove him to the bus station at about nine that night.

"I ain't sneaking out," Chicken said. He threw his suitcase in the trunk, then slid in the front seat next to Pop-Pop. "I'm leaving, but I ain't sneaking nowhere."

Poppa Daddy nodded. He'd had me get both shotguns and lay them across the floor in the back of the car. I sat back there with them, comforted by the coolness of the metal and the full load of buckshot in each chamber.

Bull Run's bus station was located on the south end of Main, and I stared at the back of Chicken's head, trying to dig him into my memory. Poppa Daddy tried to make small talk as we rode, but he gave up when all he could get was one-word answers out of us.

The bus station was dark when we got there, except for a dim light shining behind the counter. We climbed from the car, and the only other people waiting were an old white man and his wife. She was bent over, clutching her stomach, and looked gray in the face. Her hair hung in dirty strands. Sugar Baby had made Chicken scrub down from top to bottom for the trip, but it looked like white folks was allowed to travel in any old condition.

Chicken would have to change buses, and this meant he would get into Mobile in the middle of the night. There wouldn't be anybody from the Peace Corps office there to get him, so he'd have to sit tight for hours until they came in to work and could send somebody to pick him up. Poppa Daddy had wanted him to take a later bus, one that left Bull Run at 2 A.M. and would get to Mobile a little after nine, but Chicken had said no. He didn't want Poppa Daddy rolling out of bed at that hour and driving him into town. Said he preferred to wait in Mobile, where he'd be just fine.

Poppa Daddy shooed us back into the car and cranked it up. He kept the engine running as he looked back and forth between his rearview and side mirrors like those Judd boys mighta been waiting outside in the bushes. "We'll just set in the car until we see the bus, Bishop," he said, and checked to make sure the doors were locked, peeking through his mirrors left and right.

We waited in silence for almost thirty minutes before the bright beams of the Greyhound lit up Main. Poppa Daddy and Chicken both jumped out and rushed around to unlock the trunk, but I took my time.

Since there wasn't a crowd, the bus driver didn't even bother pulling into the loading zone. Instead, he stopped right beside our car and the doors hissed open.

Chicken grabbed his bag and turned to face us. His face was red, his chin set.

"God bless you, son," Poppa Daddy said. His voice was low, but I could still hear the quiver. He gripped Chicken's hand, then hugged him to his chest.

And then it was my turn. I reached out for a dap, and he let me have one. "Keep your chin tucked, Brothaman," I said, and waited for the usual response.

It never came. Instead, Chicken reached for me. He held me to him, and my nose was at the top of his head as I felt the strength in his arms.

He pulled back and blinked.

"Y'all picked me up off the streets."

He coughed and I could tell it wasn't nothing but love stuck all up in his throat.

"I ain't got the words." He shook his head, looking from me to Poppa Daddy. "I just ain't got the words."

"Me neither," I said, swallowing, pushing down what was in my throat as well.

The bus driver honked and Chicken turned away.

Poppa Daddy called, "We right here if you ever need us. Write, ya hear?"

Chicken never looked back. He just raised his hand and waved. The doors closed behind him, and the bus pulled out onto Main. I glanced at Poppa Daddy and knew without a doubt that we'd seen the last of Bishop Johnson.

"Well." I sighed as we climbed into the car, the moonlight colliding with the tears on both our faces. "I guess that's it for the Chicken."

# NINE

The house was different with Chicken gone. Everything was off-center, unbalanced and unsure. The whole summer stretched out in front of me like a big hunk of forever, and for the first time I was actually looking forward to getting out of Bull Run and heading up to college. Two days after Chicken left I was sitting on the porch when the screen door swung open and banged shut. Poppa Daddy jingled his car keys.

"I'm running up to Argle to get some stuffin' for the heavy bags. Wanna ride?"

"Yeah," I said, shrugging. "I guess."

I glanced out the window as Poppa Daddy drove, the green hills and endless grass lulling me along. I'd been sick for two days. Pining for Chicken, Granmaw said. Couldn't take nothing on my stomach and didn't hardly want anything to drink neither.

Chicken had promised to call as soon as he got to Mobile, but no call ever came. I'd heard Granmaw crying in her bedroom earlier in the day, and when I went in to find out what was bothering her, she pointed to her feet. I knew the pain was more in her heart than in her feet, but I warmed up some peppermint oil and poured it in my hands anyway.

As I rubbed the thick liquid into her swollen feet she hummed and thanked God for the blessings in her life, starting with Poppa Daddy, moving on to my daddy, Zeke, and finishing up with me and Chicken. I capped up the bottle of oil and took a real good look at the old lady laying there covered with a quilt and rocking her Bible. There was a reason men like Poppa Daddy and my father fell in love with women like her and Sweets. A reason the Armstrong men protected and took care of their own, and while I knew Chicken was solid, I wondered if I would ever be man enough to do the same thing.

We had to drive through Birdtown to get to Argle, and although we stayed on the main drag, I caught myself hoping for a peek at Slim Willie's Place. Just riding through the town hurt, 'cause it reminded me that Chicken was gone. Even though a lot of bad shit had happened to him in Birdtown, I knew the town held some good memories for him too.

We made it to Argle, and Poppa Daddy pulled into Gold's Gym Supply Warehouse. He cut off the engine and turned to me.

"You comin'?"

I shook my head. I didn't have the strength to move.

He rolled the windows down and got out, and as he walked into the warehouse in his cuffed work pants and checkered shirt, he looked older than he ever had before.

I sat in the car and watched people go in and out of Gold's. A young white lady in a gray station wagon pulled in beside me and took two little kids out the back. She wore a bright yellow shirt and gray shorts, and her brown hair was up in a ponytail. The girl and the boy had blond hair and were about the same size. They looked about kindergarten age, and it was all that woman could do to keep them off of each other as she dragged them toward the store, fighting their asses off.

She stopped at a vending machine near the entrance and put in some money. One soda pop fell out, and I wondered just how the hell she thought she was gonna get those two rascals to share it. She let the girl sip first, and then the boy, and just watching them made me thirsty too. I waited until she took the kids inside, then dug around in the car's ashtray and found two quarters.

Up close I peeped the price and cursed under my breath. I went back to the car and took out another dime, then clunked the money into the machine and pressed hard on the Coke button. Nothing happened. I pressed down for 7-Up and the button lit up: *please make another selection.* I slammed my fist down the line, root beer, Sunkist, Welch's Grape, nothing. Finally, I punched the last button, Diet Coke, and the mechanisms turned and belched it right out. My kind of luck. Diet Coke. Some shit I didn't even drink.

I popped the tab and let it flow anyway, because it was hot and I was thirsty. It didn't taste too bad neither. In fact, I couldn't tell any difference from regular at all. I downed the pop in about three swigs, threw the can on the ground, and crushed it under my size-twelve Adidases. I was reaching down to pick it up, planning to chuck it into the trash can that was chained to a pole, when I saw it.

Dread gripped me as I walked over to the newspaper racks where stacks of papers from Argle and its surrounding areas were on sale. I lifted a large stone that held down the *Birdtown Gazette.* The headline read:

LOCAL MAN FOUND KNIFED TO DEATH
SUSPECT SOUGHT

I glanced toward the store, then picked up the paper and began reading.

BIRDTOWN—A 40-year-old man was found dead early yesterday from an apparent knifing at the Delancey Hotel, a rooming house for indigents and the displaced. The manager reportedly called 911 after going to the room of Redman Walker in an attempt to collect the weekly rent.

According to officials, the manager found the door open, and when Walker failed to respond to his calls, he went inside, where he found the victim dead on the bathroom floor. A pearl-handled stiletto was buried in his chest.

I dropped the newspaper and ran into the store. I sprinted past the checkout register and up and down the aisles until I spotted the checkered pattern of Poppa Daddy's shirt. He was talking to a red-headed salesman and holding a bundle of ring rope in his hands.

He had just turned toward me when I grabbed his arm and asked, "Did that bus stop in Birdtown?"

"What?"

"The bus!" I said, tightening my grip on his arm. "Did Chicken's bus stop in Birdtown?"

Granpaw stared at me like I was some kind of fool. He shook my hand from his arm, then straightened his shirt. "Well, yeah. I reckon it did, genius. You gots to go through Birdtown to get to Argle, ain't you?"

It seemed like a concrete weight swung from the ceiling and hit me full in the gut. Chicken had done it. I knew this as surely as I knew my own name. He'd gotten his shit off. I pictured that pretty pearl handle on his stiletto, chest deep and covered with blood, and I knew he'd had his hand on it as clear as day.

Bishop Johnson was nobody's joke. He was *not* to be fucked with, and that dead man in the newspaper proved it. My friend Chicken was one *mean* motherfucker, and somehow I'd known it the very first time I laid eyes on him.

# TEN

By the time September rolled around, I was more than happy to leave Bull Run. College still scared me shitless, but staying at home with Granmaw's sickness and the sadness in Pop-Pop's eyes scared me even more. We'd finally heard from Chicken. Two weeks ago he'd sent a postcard from Guatemala that had a bucktoothed little girl standing in front of a banana tree on the front. On the back he'd written in tiny slanted script,

*Hey Everybody,*

*Sorry for not writing sooner. I'm here safe and everything is fine. I trust everybody there is doing okay and Granmaw is feeling better. Things are cool. We're building a school and I think we can really make a difference and help these people out. In my free time I'm teaching a few young boys how to box. One of them reminds me of you, Malcolm, and I'm showing him everything Poppa Daddy showed us. Until later,*

*Chicken*

Granmaw read the postcard about a hundred times, then stuck it faceup along the frame holding a picture of Jesus nailed to the cross. Poppa Daddy said, "Well. We done all we could. Bishop gonna make something outta himself no matter where he is. He's just that kinda man. He's a helluva man."

*Then what kind of man am I?* I wondered as I put my last bit of stuff in a suitcase. I was leaving home in three days, and there was no way I could have answered that question.

⦙⦙⦙⦙⦙⦙⦙

My freshman year flew by. College was all that and then some. More sexy educated black women than one man could handle, and I would have been right happy about life if it wasn't for Granmaw. Her health was getting pretty bad, and I'd been called home twice during that first year, once in early November and then again right before my nineteenth birthday. But during my sophomore year things went from bad to worse, and for the first time in my life I saw my Poppa Daddy cry, and not just wetness on the face either. Real crying. Boo-hoo crying.

When Chicken heard Granmaw was sick, he flew home from his new assignment in Bangladesh, and his presence was right on time. We were all happy to see him, and whatever it was he had been doing over the years seemed like it made him even more reflective than he was before he left, almost like he had been studying this thing we call life and trying to get it right. He was standing next to me when Poppa Daddy broke down crying that day and through his pain taught us both a lesson on just how special the love of a good woman could be.

We were in the family room at Jefferson County Hospital, waiting for the test results to come in that would determine whether or not the doctors could save Granmaw's right leg. Her foot was a mess. She'd been doing bad for so long that her medications had stopped working, and the sore on her toe had turned into a nasty ulcer that stayed wet and open until it infected the bottom of her foot, rotting away at her flesh.

My line had recently gone over, and I was dressed in my frat colors—red and white—and looking pretty good, judging by the reaction I was getting from the candy stripers who worked on the ward. Chicken stood by the window with his hands in his pockets, and Poppa Daddy was sitting on a plastic bench drinking a cup of muddy coffee and staring down at his shoes.

As soon as the door swung open I could smell the bad news coming in. I'd heard all that bullshit about how doctors are supposed to keep a straight face and act professionally distant, but this one here looked like death sucking down a six-pack, and the expression on his mug said it all before he even opened his mouth.

"I'm sorry, Mr. Armstrong." He took a deep breath, and I watched a flush creep up his cheeks until his face was almost the same color as his hair. He was a young dude, under thirty, and I guessed the big dogs had sent him in to do their dirty work. "The test results are in, and the infection in your wife's foot is just too far gone for us to save it. We think amputation is the only possible course of action if we're going to save her life."

Poppa Daddy never said a word. His face just sorta caved in, and he made this high-pitched little hitching sound as his shoulders shook. It took me a minute to realize what was going on, to understand that my Pop-Pop was crying out loud, and when the knowledge hit me my legs gave out and I slid down the wall until I was sitting on the floor with my feet out in front of me. Chicken and Poppa Daddy both came over and got down on the floor beside me, and with our arms and legs tangled, we held on to each other, Chicken's eyes bone-dry as me and Pop-Pop cried ourselves out.

Later, after we got our acts together, the three of us went into Granmaw's room, where a nurse was setting out a pan of soapy water and towels to bathe her.

"I think I can handle this." Granpaw waved her away and picked up the washcloth. "Armstrong men take care of they own," he said, smiling down at Sugar Baby. "We stand by 'em through thick and thin, come what may."

Granmaw smiled back. "They gonna take my leg, ain't they, Ike?"

He nodded but never lost his smile.

And Granmaw didn't lose hers either. "Okay then! We done talked about this, so you know what you gotta do." She motioned toward a narrow wall locker where the patients kept their personal stuff. "Gone and get it. It's in the zipper pocket of my blue bag. It's been a long time, baby, so come on over here and do it good, you hear? Do it just like you used to fifty years ago!"

I glanced at Chicken. I didn't know if we should hang around for this or not. Seemed like things was about to get personal, and I didn't even want to think it, let alone see it. I stood up. "Um, Granmaw, me and Chicken gonna go downstairs and get something to eat—"

"No, Malcolm." Her voice was full of Sugar Baby sass. "Y'all stay right here. This used to be our Friday-night thing, and your Poppa Daddy got better and better at it each week that went by. When I got real sick the doctors told us we had to cut it out, but I don't guess it can hurt none at this point, so I'ma lay back and enjoy every bit of it, 'specially since it look like this'll be the last time."

We had no choice but to stay put. Poppa Daddy got her purse from the locker and brought it over to the bed. Then he fumbled around inside until he found what he was looking for. I almost laughed as he twisted the top off a bottle of Red-Hot Sally nail polish and scooted his chair toward the bottom of the bed.

We watched as he pulled the sheet back from Granmaw's bad foot and painted tiny red strokes on her baby toe. The smell of lacquer cut the air, and Granmaw looked happy as all get-out. And why not? Poppa Daddy's hands were full of love as he dipped the small brush in and out of the bottle until he'd polished all except her wet, infected big toe, then he took her left foot in his hand and polished those toes as well.

I looked over at Chicken and knocked a tear off my face.

"That's how it's done when you love somebody, Mal," Chicken whispered, nodding toward the picture Poppa Daddy was creating with his love. "That's how it's done."

I kept that picture in my mind throughout Sugar Baby's surgery and during the few days Chicken and I stayed home while she recovered. We watched as Poppa Daddy bathed her, fed her soup from a spoon, changed the wrappings on her stump, and carried her back and forth to the toilet. We both tried to help, but Pop-Pop wasn't having it. I talked about it with Chicken, and finally I could see why folks talked up my father the way they did. They said he'd had a love for Sweets that was deeper than his love of self. Than his love of life. The same kind of love Chicken said Slim Willie had had for Dimples. And of course they did. Taking care of somebody when they're sick is one thing, but men like our fathers took shit to a whole new level.

Polishing toenails!

Something so simple but so sacred, and done with so much devotion. Poppa Daddy was a cool dog who made loving his woman look easy, and suddenly I knew Chicken had been right, and all that ass chasing I'd done didn't amount to a pile of shit. Here I'd been trying to get with a different girl every day of the week, when in the big scheme of things, when it all played out, what was important and lasting was the love of a good woman. A solid relationship. I was an Armstrong too. I had that same good blood running through my veins, and for the first time in my life I wanted something really bad. Like Chicken, I wanted a sister who would have my back all the way down to the wire and who, when shit got funky, as it always did, would grant me the privilege of painting her toes.

〰〰〰

Even after the surgery, things never got much better for Granmaw. She hung in there for another year and a half, and by the time it was all over she'd lost both legs and much of her spunk. I was just about to finish my third year at State when I got the call I'd been dreading.

"Sugar Baby's gone," Poppa Daddy said. His voice was grainy coming through the telephone, and my whole world went dark. Somehow I managed to get myself on a bus heading south that same afternoon, where I sat alone in the back row crying quietly into my hands.

I struggled through the days after her death, sticking close to Pop-Pop and trying to be strong for his sake. Taking care of Granmaw and the pain of her death had left him weak and whipped. His back was bent, his hair totally white. Neighbors and friends from the bottoms kept a flow of food moving through the house; more jelly cakes, fried chicken, and potato salad than you could shake a stick at. But even with all the people around, the house still felt empty. Felt incomplete. I'd sent a telegram to Chicken before leaving State, and by the time I got home he'd already answered, promising to be home in time for Granmaw's funeral. Just a month or so earlier, he'd been transferred out of Bangladesh to Kenya, where he was heading up some type of irrigation project.

Besides dealing with my grief, I was also struggling through a bad case of the guilts. Chicken had been forced to go, but I never should have left Granmaw and Poppa Daddy alone. After all they'd done for me after my folks died, the least I could have done was gone to school closer to home. I should have picked a junior college, one where I could drive back and forth every day, and that way I'da been around to pick up my share of the slack. To run to the store or drive Granmaw to her doctor appointments, to help Poppa Daddy out at the gym, to take a turn getting up with Granmaw at night, all of those things that would have eased life a little bit for them over the past three years and shown them how much I loved them and how grateful I was to have them.

As I rode in the back of the limousine clutching Poppa Daddy's hand I felt a sense of responsibility for him that was far bigger than any desire I might have had for college, or fraternities, or even for girls.

"You okay, Pop-Pop?"

He nodded and held tight to my hand. Just looking at him scared me. His eyes were almost closed, and the corners of his mouth were pulled way down. I'd always thought Poppa Daddy looked pretty good for his age, muscular and trim, but what time hadn't heaped on his shoulders, death certainly had. Today my Pop-Pop was only a shell of what he used to be. A brokenhearted piece of a man.

The limousine pulled into a reserved space in front of the church, and two brothers serving as ushers helped me get Poppa Daddy out the car. Buster Robinson came over, and we held Poppa Daddy between us, bracing him by the arms and guiding him toward the entrance to the church.

Inside, the organ hummed, and the floral sweetness was almost overpowering. Everywhere I looked there were lavender and white blossoms dotting arrangements of orchids and passionflowers. Buttercups and irises dominated a slew of wreaths hanging from three-legged easels.

We led Pop-Pop down the aisle toward the seats in the front reserved for the family, and as soon as I saw the white casket, pain rose from my feet and almost choked me. Poppa Daddy saw it at the same time and went to trembling, making me hold on to him even tighter. I tried to steer him toward the front pew, but he pulled away, toward Granmaw's body, and once there, he knelt on the small stool near the head of her casket.

"Look like she sleepin'," he said, and reached for the hand he'd been holding every day for more than fifty years. I nodded and forced myself to look into her face. Granmaw looked worn-out but grateful. She wore her Sunday wig and a peach-colored dress.

"You know, Malcolm," Poppa Daddy said, smoothing the material of the dress along her arm. "Me and Sugar Baby bought this dress not three months ago. She made me promise to have her fingernails painted the same color when the time came."

I looked down at her hands and saw that someone had kept that promise. As much as I loved my grandmother, worshipped her even, I was scared shitless of the dead and wouldn't have touched a cold body to save my life. And even though I kept telling myself I was stupid and it was all in my mind, as I stood there next to Pop-Pop, I almost could have sworn I saw Granmaw's chest move, like she was sipping air or taking a breath every now and then.

But Poppa Daddy acted like she was alive and warm. He touched her hair, squeezed her hands, and whispered his love into her ear, and it wasn't until he stood and leaned over to kiss her lips that he lost it.

It was all I could do to hold on to him as he collapsed down into her coffin, crying and shaking until he made me cry too. I was trying to get my arms around his chest to pull him up when I saw that I had help.

It was Chicken. He'd made it home and was on the other side of Poppa Daddy, helping me support the old man as he swayed and grieved. We managed to get him over to the pew and lower him onto the bench, and with my grandfather slumped between us, we lowered our heads and held him in our arms. We stayed this way for a while. Me, Pop-Pop, and Chicken in a triangle; Chicken and I rocking Poppa Daddy as well as each other, because each of us knew that the other two were really all we had left.

Minutes later a heavy hand fell on my shoulder and I looked up to see Reverend Washington standing in front of me. There was sadness in his eyes as he spoke. "Sorry, Malcolm, but we're ready to begin the home-going service," he said. "Sister Lou is gonna start us off with a spiritual, and after the eulogy Brother Joseph will go ahead and read the obituary."

The reverend looked at my grandfather, then held both of his hands. "Sugar was tired, Ike. Plain tired. And be assured, the good Lord don't make no mistakes."

I shuddered then, as Sister Lou's strong voice cut throughout the church, bouncing off the ceiling beams and rolling in waves over the pew where we sat. Chicken's eyes were bone-dry, but Poppa Daddy and I were both crying so hard I barely heard the eulogy, and the only part I caught from the obituary was the very end. ". . . Earlene 'Sugar Baby' Armstrong was preceded in death by her son, Ezekiel, and his wife, Serena, and is survived by her husband, Isaac, and two grandsons, Malcolm and Bishop . . ."

An hour later we were standing ankle-deep in the moist earth of an open grave, and the Church Without Spot or Wrinkle Choir was belting out verses of "Keep Your Eye on the Sparrow" and "Precious Lord."

The bodies of my parents were also in this grave, burned beyond recognition, and Poppa Daddy had felt that putting Granmaw in here with them instead of in a plot the two of them could later share was like leaving her in my father's care. I almost agreed.

Chicken had never got to go to his folks' funerals. He'd been locked up when they were put in the ground. I didn't remember a whole lot about my parents' funeral, but lately the legacy of their love was vivid and clear and I almost smiled. But then a moan like a freight train rolled from Poppa Daddy's lips. He lurched between us and sent Chicken stumbling.

"Sleep on, Sugar!" he cried. "Go 'head and take your rest! Poppa loved you dearly . . . but God loved you best!"

I watched as Chicken staggered and almost lost his footing in the soft, loose earth. His eyes were dry but haunted, and he looked sick with grief as our beloved Pop-Pop hit his knees and reached into that yawning black hole to cast the first fistful of dirt down on his precious Sugar Baby.

⸻

The house was busting at the seams.

"Brothaman, Brothaman." I dapped Chicken out as we squeezed past a group of church sisters in black dresses and went into the kitchen. I reached to grab a cup from the cabinet, but Sister Dent checked me.

"Whatchoo want, baby? Somethin' to drink?" Grownie Dent had a banging body and was a slamming sight for an older woman. Big breasts, a trim waistline, and an ass that could make you dizzy. She could pass for early thirties, but actually she was more like mid-fifties. Her husband had been a private contractor who died in a roofing accident a few years back, and I remember her being tore down at his funeral.

"Yes, ma'am," I answered automatically, accepting the pop she offered. I felt like the only stud at a happy-ho convention the way she was eyeing me, skinning and grinning and blinding me with all that gold in her mouth. I'd grown even taller during the three years I'd been gone, and had buffed up in the shoulders and chest too, so I knew I had it going on, but damn. Sister Dent was old enough to have some shame. Couldn't she see I was grieving?

Chicken laughed as we made our way into the living room. He'd shot up quite a few inches over the years too. "You was stutterin' like a duck up in there, niggah. That thang too much for you to handle?"

"Man, go on with that." I shrugged it off. "That old woman knew me since I was a baby."

He laughed again. "Old woman, my ass. You long past a baby, but I reckon she'll stick one of them titties in your mouth and rock you all night long."

There wasn't a seat to be had. Granmaw's rocker was the only empty chair, but nobody had the nerve to sit in it. Chicken and I squeezed in between a few other dudes and stood against the wall drinking root beer and digging the crowd. There was so much I wanted to ask him. About the places he'd been, things he'd done, people he'd met, but mostly I wanted to know about that dead dude up in Birdtown. I'd known Brothaman was a killer when I met him, and I also knew he could hold a grudge, but shooting a man who had just killed your father was a hell of a lot different than holding on to that fire for two long years, then hunting that ass down and stabbing him up just like that.

I didn't have the balls to come right out and call him on it, but looking into his face I could see how he could do it. Take a man out like that. You just didn't trespass against Chicken Johnson and expect him not to get his shit off, but now there was something different about him too. I mean, yeah, he'd grown and his body looked hard and thick from the backbreaking work he was doing, but his eyes had something in them that hadn't been there when he left Bull Run. They were still cautious and wary, but there seemed to be some kind of peace lurking behind them too.

He elbowed me and nodded toward Poppa Daddy. "How's Pop-Pop holdin' up?"

I shook my head. "Not good. He lost his best friend, so he's taking it pretty hard."

"Yeah," he said. "Everybody loved Sugar Baby, and ain't none of our lives gonna be the same without her."

He was right about that. Already I could feel her absence. Sense the lack of her in the atmosphere. But as much as I would miss my granmaw and as bad as I felt for myself, it was nothing compared to how bad I felt for Poppa Daddy. Chicken and I watched him sitting in his rocker trying to keep himself up. Anybody could see that beneath his polite smile his eyes were shell-shocked and sad as hell, and that it was all he could do to bear up and pray these girdle-wearing women who smelled like forty different bottles of perfume would take their wide hips and aluminum pans and head home and leave us be. Every now and then I saw him reach out and pat the arm of Granmaw's chair, then snatch his hand back like he was surprised to find she wasn't there.

"No problem coming into town, right?" I asked.

Chicken shrugged. "Didn't have none, and didn't expect none either."

I nodded. "Things been a little better. Barney's in jail. They got him on a short-eyes charge. His little brother Caleb took a bullet in the head. Fucked with the wrong nigger up in Argle and got put down."

Chicken shrugged again. "Shit happens. So when are you going back?"

I stuck my hands in my pockets and stretched. "Maybe never," I said, and motioned toward my grandfather. "Pop-Pop needs me now. School can wait."

Chicken swigged from his can, then shook his head. "That ain't what they wanted for you, Mal. Sugar Baby would flip over in her grave listenin' to you say school ain't important."

"I didn't say it wasn't important." I kept my voice even. "I said it could wait."

"Aiight, then." He frowned and crushed his empty can between his hands. "Hell can wait too, but that ain't the point. Poppa Daddy has plenty of help around here. Old ladies lined up from here to Mobile to take care of him. I heard 'em in there working out a feeding schedule, bustin' each other up to be first in line to fry his okra and mash his 'tatoes. Believe it or not, Bro', your grandfather is still a pretty good catch. Besides"—Chicken's gaze swept around the room, but I knew his words were meant to include the whole town—"what you gonna do around here? Get a factory job? Work on somebody's farm? That 'keepin' books out back' shit done played out. Poppa Daddy got himself a young buck to hold the gym down now."

I shrugged. "I don't really know, man. I just know it's time for me to finally do something useful."

I busted the look that crossed his face.

"Come again?"

"You heard me. I need to do something that's gonna make a difference in some kind of way." I tried to explain. "Look. You know I come from make-it-happen black folks, and education didn't have a damned thing to do with it. Poppa Daddy built this house with his own hands. Him and Sugar Baby worked this land side by side. Shit, both of my parents were revolutionaries who were out there in the trenches, rolling feet first in the action. Zeke was a bad nigger and Sweets wasn't no slouch. They went to college, but they didn't hide behind no desk or no textbook. Matter fact, they lived for the struggle and they died for it too. That's the kind of stuff I need to try and live up to."

Chicken didn't say a word, but I glanced up and saw Pop-Pop staring at us. There was worry in his eyes, and I calmed down and lowered my voice. "I don't know, Chicken. Maybe I'll just go to New York or Detroit and get down with some organizations that are about social change or something like that. Who knows? I just know I can't just roll back up to State and pretend like that's all my life should be about. I just can't do that."

"Well, if this ain't some of the damndest shit I've ever heard comin' out of your mouth," Chicken said. He had this bewildered look on his face that almost pissed me off. "But if you serious about making changes that are gonna have a real impact, there are plenty of other areas in the world that could stand some help. I mean, yeah, we got babies starving right here in Alabama, no doubt about it, but as far as the effect from shit like colonialism and greedy white folks, you ain't seen oppression and poverty until you been to Africa."

"Africa?"

"You damn right. Africa."

"I don't know about going to no Africa, man." I shook my head. "I was thinking more like the East Coast. I don't think Pop-Pop could take it if I went and crossed some water."

Chicken laughed. "Man, you playing Poppa Daddy straight to the left. You musta forgot his name. Isaac Armstrong don't need nobody takin' care of him! Men like him stand on they own two feet. Even with Granmaw gone, Poppa Daddy is still gonna man-up and handle his bidness."

I disagreed.

"Aiight, then. But give it some thought before you make up your mind. You wanna live up to your name? See if you got what it takes to do it in a special way. As dirt poor as black folks are in America, we living like kings compared to people in Africa."

Chicken's voice changed, almost like he was trying to be gentle with me. "Look, Malcolm. Just think about it. But if you change your mind and find that you got it in you, there's an engineering job on my team that has your name on it. We'll be moving north of Kairami in a couple of weeks, and even though you're not done with college you still got a whole lot to offer."

I blew him off. "I ain't trying to join nobody's Peace Corps."

"Nobody says you have to." He shrugged. "Do like I did. Get yourself a passport. Go down to the clinic and let them hit you in the ass with a couple of needles and shit, then buy yourself a plane ticket. The Peace Corps ain't gotta sponsor you in order for you to get paid. The money ain't much, but it'll keep you in *Playboys* and Vaseline. You could still be your own man, a free agent. That way you can roll out anytime you get ready."

I listened, but he really wasn't saying anything I could hear. The house started emptying out, the crowd thinning, and suddenly I was assed out. Dog-tired. Chicken shrugged again, then headed back toward the kitchen with his crushed soda can.

"You look raggedy, Malcolm," he said over his shoulder. "And so am I. That jet lag is a bitch. I'ma get another piece of cake, then gone and stretch out for a while." He turned away from me, but then turned right back. His eyes were clear. "You know what? Sometimes when you been blessed with a lot, like it or not, it can cost you a lot. Handle that."

# ELEVEN

"Malcolm. Get up, boy."

My eyes had been open from the moment he approached my door, and I stared into the darkness. Pop-Pop stood over me, and although Chicken was snoring to beat the band, calling in a pen-load of hogs, I could barely make out his silhouette in the bed across the room.

"What's wrong, Pop-Pop? You can't sleep?"

He sat down beside me on the bed he'd built for my father and saved for me. He stared at me for a minute and then just started talking. "We came west in 'thirty-six, the year after your daddy was born. Sugar and me figured we would probably only have one child. Seemed fittin', I guess. My mama didn't have but one, and Sugar Baby was all Miss Charming had too.

"Your granmaw was a fine little something. Proud too. One of them Louisiana Sweetwater Sanders. Folks said her mama and her aunties Ma'Dear and Mary Mack was into workin' roots, and from the way my nose jumped open the minute I saw her, there just mighta been some truth to it. Me and Sugar got married and gave each other our love, and when Zeke was born we siphoned off some of that flow and aimed it right at him."

I sat up straight in the darkness, my mouth dry. It had been Granmaw who tried to keep my parents alive for me. Granmaw who talked about my father like he'd just run out to the store and would be coming right back. Poppa Daddy hardly ever spoke about my father, and when he did, it was mostly in passing. Granmaw had told me that it wasn't because Poppa Daddy hadn't loved his only son, but because he loved him too much, and the pain of losing him had just cut him so deep.

Granpaw continued, "I loved that long-headed boy of mine, I did. Course Sugar loved him too, but early on we agreed that we wasn't gonna let our love cripple him. Wouldn't let it cut him off at the nuts. Little black boys got a way of growin' up to be big black men, if they lucky, and more than anything else we wanted Ezekiel to be a solid man. A whole black man."

"I know, Pop-Pop. Everybody knows how good he was." I reached for his hand. It had been a hard day for him. Maybe the hardest in his life, and the pain in his voice was killing me.

He snatched his hand back and held it high in the air. "Don't interrupt me, Malcolm. My Sugar Baby taught you better'n that, so honor her." He put his hand back in his lap and continued. "You right, though. Zeke was a helluva man. More man than me, and that's why I'm settin' here with you tonight. Now, us coulda kept him right here in the valley. Remember, he was our only one, and I know folks who'da been glad to give my boy a job. And folks knew Zeke too. They loved him. He coulda landed himself one a them fancy assignments settin' behind some big ole desk in town, if he wanted to. The possibilities was here for him. Right here in Bull Run. But you see, Malcolm, he woulda been livin' for me and Sugar instead of for himself, and we couldn't have that. Me and Sugar knew in order for our boy to be any kinda man, he had to find his own path and follow it. He coulda never thrived parked in the shade of our crossroads. He had to make his own life experiences and cultivate his own pastures, and when your daddy got

accepted at that big school way out in California, we was happy to
see him go. He married up with Sweets, and together they chose
they own path. Now, Zeke's road was short, that much is true, but
it was all his and he walked it like a man. A man can't hardly be a
man if he settin' in somebody else's crossroads. You might not know
it, Malcolm, but you'd dishonor me to park yourself in mine."

My eyes had adjusted to the darkness enough for me to see that
Poppa Daddy's mouth was set in a hard line. His voice held a chill
that I'd never heard before.

"Next week this time," he said, "I want you gone. Whether it's
back up north to State, or out east to Broadway, or even out West
on somebody's butt-nekked beach. Follow your own path, son.
Find your own crossroads."

Poppa Daddy looked at me for a long moment, then he leaned
over and put his arms around me. I felt him press his lips to my
forehead, then he rubbed the top of my head like he used to
when I was a kid. My heart was somewhere up in my throat as I
watched him stand and walk out of my room.

I stretched out in the bed, and for the longest time I just lay
there staring up at the ceiling. I reached over and flipped the
switch on my reading lamp, my eyes searching the framed five-by-
seven wedding photo. My mother looked young and pretty. She
wore a plain white smock shirt and cornrows in her hair. Zeke
stood tall behind her, a dark brown man with big shoulders,
sporting a gold and black dashiki. He was a good-looking dude,
with even features. A black applejack sat sideways on his short
natural. *When you been blessed with a lot, sometimes, like it or not, it
can cost you a lot.* Chicken just might have had a point, because
even after the fire and everything I'd lost in my life, I was still
smart enough to know that I still had a whole lot left.

Glancing at Chicken, who was on his back raising the roof, I
got out the bed and checked myself out in a mirror that had been
mounted so high, Brothaman couldn't even see into it. The man
staring back at me was no stranger. He was an Armstrong sho'nuff,
without a doubt. From my broad chest and high forehead to my

near-perfect teeth, our bloodline was strong, and almost all of my physical features came straight from Pop-Pop and my father. I sometimes had to dig deep to find the gifts of my mother, but I knew they were there.

Turning away from the mirror, I cut off my lamp and walked down the short hall leading to the bedroom my grandparents had shared. The moon was shining high from their window, just enough so I could see Poppa Daddy's long form, still and facing the wall.

I walked over to the bed, and as I approached, Poppa Daddy reached back and lifted the sheets, holding them open. I slipped under the covers and moved into an old familiar spot, roughly in the middle of Poppa Daddy and where Sugar would have lain had she still been here. With my feet hanging just over the end of the mattress, I settled down into a place that had always given me comfort, then put my arm around my grandfather and slept.

Chicken left two days after the funeral, but his words hung around, messing with my head. I tried to sort it all out on the bus ride back to State. I'd just about made it through my junior year, and although I was ready to break out, I wasn't stupid enough to drop out of school during the last few weeks.

When Granmaw first got sick I'd found out that her and Pop-Pop were straight-up smart for bottom folks. Their life insurance policies were worth way more than what it took to lead their simple lives, and with the portion Sugar had left to me I could afford to take off my senior year and buy myself some time until I figured out what I wanted to do with my life.

Back at school, I just couldn't slide into a groove. Everything I'd been fired up about before seemed stupid and juvenile now. Most of my friends were athletes or boneheads who were looking for a good time and bucking for super-seniorhood, and for the first time since I stepped on campus, the freaky parties and crazy drinking in my dorm were becoming a turnoff.

I muddled around for two days before finally catching the university shuttle bus down to the west end of campus. I got off in front of Moore Hall, a three-story red brick building that was home to a whole bunch of fine sisters.

The female dorms had security, so I signed in with a thick brother who sat at a desk about two times too small for him. He was reading when I walked in, and when he put his book down to pass me his sign-in sheet, I saw it was a copy of *Invisible Man,* by a cat named Ralph Ellison. I walked down the black-and-white tiled floors and took the stairs up to the second floor. The last room on the right was number 214, and I'd been chilling in it for almost a year.

I blew into my hand to check out my breath, then knocked twice. The door opened partway, and I smelled her Ashanti before I saw her face. She looked fine as hell, with one hand on her hip and a slight smile on her lips.

"S-Sheila," I stuttered. The girl had me bent. Straight sprung. I grinned like a sucker, and my tongue got so tied up it stumbled over her name like it was a boulder. She had on a see-through blouse and short jean skirt. She laughed out loud, and I swear it sounded like magic. She stepped back to let me in.

Sheila was a little bitty thang, no taller than five-three, but Lord knows there was some good stuff crammed into that tiny chocolate package. I stepped past her, staring into those sexy almond eyes of hers, and stood in her room, which was jam-packed. For some reason the rooms in the girls' dorms were even smaller than those in mine, and still held two beds, two desks, a window, and two dressers.

And the books.

Damn if some folks didn't actually come to college to get their study on. Sheila and her roommate, Cynthia, were pre-med students, and there were stacks of books ranging in subjects from basic anatomy to crime and punishment in French literature stacked almost ceiling-high near both of their desks.

I reached out and pulled her to me, drawing deep breaths from her hair and releasing some stress when I exhaled. She felt so good against me. Her arms around my waist made me feel solid and grounded.

"You okay?" she asked, pulling back and looking into my eyes. Sheila knew me. Maybe better than I knew myself. I'd met her almost a year ago at a fraternity fund-raiser, and after hanging out a few times over pizza and beer, we'd become friends. Sheila had clawed her way out of the projects of Philadelphia, and she made it clear from the jump that her first priority in life was to become a doctor.

"I'm okay." I nodded. "Hanging." I pushed some books aside and sat down on her bed. I patted my thigh and she slid onto my lap. She was soft and smelled good, and as bad as I felt inside, heat ignited in my groin.

Sheila was a tough sister; fine as hell and smart too, she could be honest until it hurt. She'd told me about some Cherry Hill plastic surgeon she'd worked for while she was in high school. How this white dude was married, but she was young and dumb and he'd taken her for a ride and gotten her high on his promises. How on her graduation day he'd handed her a check that covered her first two years of college tuition and an abortion at the women's clinic of her choice.

Whatever scars she walked away with from that experience, I was almost sure she still carried them. Sheila was a year ahead of me and had already been accepted into medical school at Washington U. I didn't care what she told me about her past, because I had one of my own, and I sure wasn't trying to hear that mess she talked about no man ever getting close to her heart. I'd quit most of that pussy chasing with a quickness when I met her. I almost became a one-woman man, something that tickled the shit out of my frat brothers who knew my track record with the honeys.

In fact, I'd fallen in love with Sheila Danburn, and I didn't feel like a sucker behind it at all. A few months earlier I'd been on my knees begging up into her eyes. "Will you marry me?" I'd asked her one night as she stepped out of the shower, her nipples thick, her stomach toned. I stuck out my tongue and licked the tiny drops of water on her neck, grinning when a large drop rolled out of that valley between her full breasts and slid down into her navel.

She didn't answer right away. She just stood there naked, with a towel in her hand and her long braids brushing her shoulders. I knew the deal when she sighed. That long, dry sound you dragged up from the deep part of your gut.

"You know I can't marry you, Malcolm," she said. "And don't take it personally either. I'm not marrying anybody." She'd walked past me without even looking at the microscopic diamond I was offering her.

Sheila dried herself off real quick, then wrapped herself in a thick ugly robe. She tied the belt around her waist and sat on the bed tucking her feet beneath it, almost like she didn't want my eyes on her body. "My life is already mapped out," she explained. "Maybe in ten or fifteen years when I've accomplished the things I've set out to do . . . maybe then I can think about being in a committed relationship, and maybe even having a family."

I was crushed. My ego and my heart both took a beating. I mean, I was considered a prime catch. Tall, sporty, a brother with skills on the court and who was cool with the ladies to boot. Sheila should have jumped straight on my tip, honored as hell to become Mrs. Armstrong. I actually cried behind that shit. Her little rejection hooked a brother right in the gut. But the more time passed and the more I thought about it, I had to admit that it was probably for the best. Don't get me wrong. I loved the hell outta her, still do, and a piece of my heart is gonna always have her name on it, but there was something missing from our relationship that I don't know if I could have lived without forever.

That something that Chicken had seen in Gebra Burns. That something we both understood Pop-Pop had had with Granmaw. That same kind of jones that Zeke had had for Sweets, and Slim

Willie had had for Dimples. I knew it would be stupid to push for more than Sheila had to give, and besides, I didn't want to fight for it. When my real queen came I wanted things to flow naturally. That way, I'd know she was the right one for me. So I accepted Sheila's decision. I respected her honesty and told myself to dig her hard while I had her, 'cause it wouldn't last forever.

And it worked. We had a good thing that even my impulsiveness wasn't able to kill, and now I sat holding her and appreciating the concern in her eyes for exactly what it was. Friendship.

I kissed her again. "How you been? Still stressing?"

She nodded. "Yep. As usual. Studying and going to lectures. More studying." She smiled, and the flash of her dimples touched my heart. "Is your grandfather doing okay?"

"He's making it."

Sheila nodded. "I'm leaving in a few weeks, Malcolm," she reminded me. Her hand was busy making circles on my chest, heating me up. "I wish we had more time, baby, but we don't." She flashed me a smile. "I'm hyped about Washington, though. I'm taking myself to a whole new realm, and it looks like everything I've been working for is finally going to fall into place."

"Damn, girl," I told her. "Let me have some of that backbone and vision you got, baby." I was laughing but there wasn't shit funny. "Here I am fighting to decide what to do when I wake up tomorrow."

"Well." She straddled my lap and put her arms around my neck. Books slid to the floor and her skirt rose up over her hips. "Cynthia went downtown to pay a bill. It should take her at least an hour. How about I help you decide what to do with yourself right now?"

Her tongue shot into my mouth and I cupped her round hips in my hands. I lifted her up until she was hovering over me and let her pull her skirt all the way up around her waist. Rubbing her softness against my swollen crotch, my lips found her nipples, hard as pebbles as they strained to break through the red silk of her blouse.

Sheila moaned and held her hands above her head so I could

slip off her top. I stood up with her in my arms, my hands grip-
ping her thick ass. Her legs were locked around my waist. Her
arms and back were firm and trim as she pushed her round breasts
out for me to kiss. I knew what she wanted. I rubbed those midnight nipples across my face and then ate them up one at a time.
She bit her lip and moved her hips in slow circles. Using one
hand, I reached into my pocket for a condom, then loosened my
belt and pushed my jeans and boxers down until they fell around
my feet. Sheila reached between us and pulled the crotch of her
panties to one side, and I pushed two fingers deeply down into
her cream, and massaged her clit with my thumb.

"Oh, yeah, baby." Sheila panted, moving up and down on my
hand. "Juice that thang . . ." I did her like this until I couldn't take
it anymore. I pulled out my dripping fingers and tasted them,
then slid on that rubber and filled her back up, but this time with
the stiff head of my johnson. Sheila sucked in her breath, then
shuddered. I balanced her ass cheeks in my palms and using my
biceps took my time lowering her down my entire length. I sexed
her long and hard, my muscles bulging, my balls screaming, lifting
her up and down, her stuff like wet satin against my stick.

Growling, Sheila raked her teeth against my neck and I felt my
orgasm rising. I stroked her faster and faster, slamming her down
against me so hard her breasts shook and my knees trembled.
Sheila screamed and arched her back, her pussy pulsating until I
let myself go too, my explosion tearing from me and filling the
condom as sweat soaked my face and dripped from our bodies.

"I'm gonna miss you, Sheila," I said, wheezing, kissing her neck
and pumping into her as my penis went limp. I felt her sex muscles squeezing, milking my last few drops and drawing them
deeply inside of the latex glove. "Goddamn, baby," I moaned, "I
miss you already."

||||||||||

Somehow I managed to make it through the last few weeks of
school. My heart wasn't in a damn thing I did, and my final grades

bore witness to this, even though I managed to pass all six of my courses by the skin of my teeth. Two days before school let out, I went down to the Peter Pan bus station and purchased a one-way ticket to JFK Airport in New York. My plan was to look up some of Zeke's old friends who lived in the Crown Heights section of Brooklyn, where shit was hot between blacks, Koreans, and some of New York's Finest. From there I figured I'd let the wind take me where it would. Folks were always looking for an extra pair of hands and a halfway decent mind to help strategize. Thanks to Granmaw, money wasn't a problem, and other than my Pop-Pop, there were no roots anchoring me to any one particular place.

The day I left, Mobile was rainy and gray. Poppa Daddy had said there was no need in coming back to Bull Run just to say good-bye. He said I had just been there, and besides, he could say good-bye over the phone just as good as he could in person. I split most of my stuff up between my room dawgs and my frat brothers. Stereo, color TV, video games, and frat paraphernalia, you name it, I chucked it. I stuffed the bare necessities into two military duffel bags I bought from an army-navy store; a couple of credit cards, a little bit of cash, some traveler's checks, a CD player, and other small shit went into a small black knapsack along with a few pictures of my parents that I'd found in Granmaw's bureau.

The bus station was in the middle of town, and it looked like every State student from campus was leaving town for the summer. The lines snaked away from the loading points, the people waiting looking bored and restless. I read the signs until I found the gate for New York City, then got on line behind a woman wearing tight jeans and a tiny shirt.

It was almost thirty minutes before I made it to the front, and after handing the driver my ticket I chucked my bags into the storage compartment beneath the bus and found a seat way in the back row.

Minutes later Mobile was fading from my view, but instead of being excited I still felt empty. Here I was going to the Big Apple to do my own thing, and I couldn't even kick up any enthusiasm for it. And it got worse. The further we got from Alabama, the raggedier my plan looked, and the more I doubted myself. By the time the bus pulled into West Virginia some seven hours later, I hadn't slept a wink, but I had made up my mind.

The bus driver, a heavy black man who was probably about forty, gave me a funny look as I waited to get off. "This ain't New Yawk, boy. New Yawk City is a place with big ole buildin's and skyscrapers and whatnot."

I nodded. "I'm straight, homes. Thanks anyway."

I jumped off and got my bags from under the bus, then went inside the terminal and found the yellow pages. I put a quick call in to a local travel agency and waited on hold while they checked on a flight, then I went outside to a taxi waiting at the curb.

"I need to send a telegram," I told the driver, a white dude with earrings in both ears.

"How about Western Union?"

"That'll work."

Minutes later I found myself standing at a counter while a teenage clerk transcribed my message.

BROTHAMAN, IT'S TIME TO RUMBLE. WILL BE ON THE NEXT FLIGHT TO KAIRAMI. ARRIVING AT JOMO KENYATTA AIRPORT TOMORROW 12:39 AM. GOT MY CHIN TUCKED. END

I took another taxi to pick up my ticket at the travel agency, which was way across town in what looked like the white-boy bottoms. They'd booked me on a flight from Charleston, West Virginia, to Washington, D.C., then onward to Kenya. I paid for my ticket, then caught a third taxi to the Hilton Hotel right there at Yeager Airport.

Once I was checked in to my hotel room, I went straight to the telephone and put in a collect call to Poppa Daddy.

"Pop-Pop?" I was cautious, trying to judge his mood before letting him peep my hand.

His voice came through strong and clear. "Hey, Malcolm! You okay? When you leavin', boy?"

I frowned, confused as hell. "Leaving? What you mean leaving? I left Mobile a long time ago. I'm calling you from a hotel in West Virginia."

I could hear him sucking his teeth. "Hot damn, Malcolm, I know where you callin' from. I accepted the charges, didn't I? I mean when you leavin' for *Africa*! That is where you goin', ain't it?"

I laughed, happy as hell that he sounded happy as hell. "How you know? You took a mind-reading class or something?"

"You Zeke's, ain't you? Armstrong *is* your last name, so what choice you have? Of course I knew what you was gonna do. You'da knowed it too if you'd just sat still long enough to listen to the sense you was born with. You didn't have to run all over west hell and go truckin' through West Virginia just to find your way to East Africa! You coulda done like Bishop and caught a flight outta New York!"

I just shook my head, my grin trying to split my face in two. If there had been any doubts lingering in my mind, Poppa Daddy's approval had rinsed them gone. This was probably the very first time in my life I'd ever felt totally purposeful and certain.

Damn if the leaves on my family tree weren't begging me to come home, and in my heart I knew that somewhere on the continent of Africa my friend Chicken and an entire tribe of Armstrong men were waiting just for me. I hung up from Granpaw and lay back on the bed, listening to my heart thump like the beat of bush drums. Sounds rushed through my ears like the roar of heavy waves slapping against the hulls of ancient slave ships. I thought of Sugar Baby, and the motherland called out to me, my roots straining like crazy, begging me to plant them in ancestral soil. And when I pictured Zeke, the legend I'd never gotten a chance to know, the dark blood of my forefathers hollered up at me from the grave, challenging me to return to the cradle of civilization. Summoning me back home.

# PART TWO

# ABENI

# Earth

Kairami, Kenya

The sub-Saharan sun ignited a pyre that licked at Abeni's skin. A terrified scream swirled in the pit of her stomach and threatened to burst from her lips, but somehow the small child managed to contain it. Nearby, the pounding of the drums rose to a frenzy as the villagers chanted with glee and danced the *marambora,* stomping their feet and kicking up soft clouds of powdered earth beneath their lightning-fast heels.

"Lean back," instructed Hazika, Abeni's *motairi.* The older woman wrapped her thick legs around six-year-old Abeni, immobilizing her limbs and securing her naked body in a fixed position. Although she had been warned of the inevitability of this day, fear stole into Abeni's heart, obliterating her mother's instructions.

"You must not cry," Ziwani had warned her only child. "You are the daughter of Banjoko Omorru, the leader of the Kinaksu people, and you must show strength and bravery when the time for your *yreau* is near."

Ziwani had endured her own initiation at the age of five and was well versed in the ceremonial requirements. A fortnight earlier she'd begun feeding Abeni a special diet of *njha* and *ngomi ya egemba*, a Kinaksu bean that prevented blood loss at the time of initiation and promoted immediate healing of the wound.

At sunrise Ziwani, Hazika, and the other women had surrounded the young girls and bathed them in a nearby creek, then each child had been massaged and her naked body bedecked with sparkling jewels lent by friends and relatives. Abeni wore a gift from Hazika, a single strand of *magrthea da mwonjae* looped around her waist. Members of a ceremonial council had then performed a *karothema ciene*, blessing the children and marking symbols upon their cheeks, noses, throats, and navels with a white chalk found on Mount Kenya.

Three days earlier Abeni had joined several other village girls at the homestead of a tribal elder and his wife who hosted the children for the purpose of the *yreau*. There had been tears in Ziwani's eyes as she left her luxurious apartment in the center of town and led a somber Abeni into the bush, and her footsteps had faltered. Tradition demanded this, yet reluctance settled around her and clawed at her heart. Abeni's babyhood had flown past with a swiftness, and although Ziwani had persuaded the king to delay the child's initiation for one year, the day had pounced upon them nevertheless.

She stared into the face of her daughter, her heart wrenching at the fear reflected there. She had labored hard for this child, and Abeni's birth had been near miracle. Fearing herself barren, Ziwani had resorted to the old ways. She'd swallowed the murky *hoaushi* tea prepared by the *mottiri* and chewed the root of the *acudria*, grimacing as its bitter milk filled her mouth and turned her breath sour. She'd offered up prayers and sacrifices to Sazemi, the goddess of harvest. And soon, after she had lain with Banjoko, there had been an absence of her menses and then a fullness to her breasts. Her belly began to rise.

But Ziwani had fretted in the moments after her daughter's birth. Male offspring were treasured, and Banjoko must have an heir, yet her womb, delivered of its miracle, was depleted and taxed. After one look at the newborn, the midwives bid Ziwani serenity and dismissed her concerns. Have you ever witnessed such a lusty cry? This one will make a fine daughter, they declared. See how uncommonly handsome she is? With skin like blackberries and long, well-shaped limbs, Banjoko will be most pleased with himself.

Their leader's face was unreadable when they led him into the birthing room. Ziwani bit down upon her lip as her husband studied the naked, squalling child. His eyes roamed her thick crown of hair, crawled along her dimpled, ebony skin, down her gangly legs, then back up to meet the piercing, knowing look in the infant's eyes. "Ziwani Omorru." His voice quaked. "My seed has been blessed handsomely in your womb. We asked for her and she is ours. She is Abeni."

And now, as the *marambora* rose to a crescendo, Ziwani fought her misgivings and entrusted her daughter to Hazika's able hands. A horn sounded rhythmically, and just as she had been instructed, Abeni inserted her thumbs between her first and second fingers and closed her fist, a silent indication that she was prepared to withstand the operation firmly and without fear. Her tiny limbs strained visibly against Hazika, and her eyes rolled upward and stared fixedly on the cloudless blue sky as if searching for answers to questions yet unasked.

The dancing and jumping ceased. Ceremonial leaves were sprinkled at Abeni's feet. Her legs were spread wide and a hot breeze caressed her bare sex. Abeni shuddered. Her small toes curled and uncurled, searching for salvation in the dusty earth. Her trembling shoulders disappeared under Hazika's firm grasp. An elderly woman from the ceremonial council appeared bearing a bucket in which a steel axe soaked in *mae maithanwa,* an icy liquid that had been preserved overnight. The woman stood wrapped from neck to ankles in black cloth, like a giant nightmare before the frightened children.

Abeni's face was like stone. They had been warned. They must not show fear or utter an audible sign of emotion. During the operation they were forbidden even to blink, for to do so would be considered *karaoge* and would cause one to become the object of ridicule amongst her companions. Like the others, Abeni kept her eyes fixed upon the serene blue sky, anticipating the unknown moment.

As the elder splashed frigid water against her gaping genitals, Abeni's body stiffened. Hazika had promised the water would make her organs numb. Would shock her nerves into forgetting all sensation. With her breath coming in short whispers, Abeni waited, trembling.

Suddenly a *maruethia* dashed from the crowd. Tall, with a body as fat as it was muscular, her face was painted in horrific streaks of black and white, and her rhythmic movement caused the rattles tied to her legs to hiss and clang. In a flash she whipped a *rwenji* from her pocket and with lightning speed swept down the line, operating on the girls with deft strokes.

Abeni heard stifled whispers as the *maruethia* moved from girl to girl in rapid succession. Suddenly it was her turn. Although her groin still throbbed dully from the frigid water, Abeni braced herself as the witch-woman approached. For the first time she questioned this special ritual. She'd been told it was one of absolute necessity. Her mother and her mother's mother before her had endured it, as had every respectable Kinaksu woman before them. It was an important African tradition, and her father would be most proud of her, she was assured.

She would not move a muscle, she promised herself. Would not squirm or cry out or bring dishonor to her family. But as the *maruethia* knelt at her feet and leaned forward to sever the flesh from her young body, Abeni could not help but grimace and press backward into Hazika's softness. With a single stroke, the *maruethia* sliced off the tip of Abeni's clitoris, and the tiny budding organ fell free, tumbling down, returning to the dusky earth.

In swift motions, the *maruethia* shaved off the fleshy outer lips of Abeni's vulva and kicked a clump of soil atop the mangled strips of flesh.

Abeni recoiled as pain exploded in her private areas, the scorching rays of the sun stoking the inferno between her thighs to an unbearable heat. Clenching her fists, she squeezed her eyes shut as blood streamed from her wounds and formed a dark pool in the loose soil, turning the parched earth to mud.

Mercifully, a cool milky liquid containing tissue-numbing herbs was splashed on her genitals from a wooden bucket. It pooled beneath her buttocks and brought her agony down a notch. Beads of sweat rolled into Abeni's eyes as the crowd began to chant in harmony, *"Ceana citto ire koiema ee-hooa, neab marerire-ee-ho!"* "Look at how brave our children are! Did anyone cry? No one cried! Hurray!"

As Ziwani and Hazika held the weakened child by the arms and led her toward the hut where the girls would be stitched with catgut and thorns and helped to recover, Abeni, in her youthful ignorance, could not help but question the basis of such torture.

Even at her age she felt violated. Confused.

Because the agony thumping between her legs had come not only with her parents' approval but with the joy of an entire village. And as they lowered her to the earth and positioned her upon a bed of sweet-smelling leaves, Abeni felt the soft lips of her mother brush her forehead and her soothing hands caress her cheeks. She wanted to call out for Ziwani, to seek refuge in the arms that had once been a haven of safety and love, but foreign, incoherent whispers fell from her lips as a deep weakness claimed her, surging through her muscles and leaving her limp. Mercifully, darkness approached to claim her, and as she closed her eyes and sped toward the shadowy curtain of sweet oblivion, Abeni Teboso Omorru was filled with a certainty that could not be disputed: a vital part of her would forever rot beneath a dusty mound of African earth. Cut. Mutilated.

And with her mother's permission.

# TWELVE

I was dead before I was born.

In a country where the funk pot between the thighs of a woman is given less merit than that of, say, a dog or a pig, even the daughter of a king is not exempt from certain brutalities.

I was different from most Kinaksu women, and it wasn't hard to see why. Sure, my tribal sisters were relegated to a life of hardship and subjugation in the bush, while I languished in a high-rise apartment in the midst of the finest shops and restaurants the province of Kairami had to offer. And as you might guess, educating the female Kinaksu consisted of detailed instructions for bean planting and soil tillage, while I, Banjoko's only heir, had been given all the refinement that Paris, London, and even Frankfurt had to offer. Yet there were times when our lives converged. When it came to that small matter that semi-existed deeply inside the delta of our groins, there was really no difference between that of a bush dweller and that of a city dweller. Pussy was pussy. You could cut them all with the same knife. And although the hand that wielded the blade was usually female, no one could deny that the muscle behind its thrust was that of a man.

Unmarried at twenty-four, I was considered an anomaly in my country for more reasons than one. My shameful acts had sent me fleeing abroad for many years, and I might have stayed gone forever had it not been for that unfortunate indiscretion with the spouse of the director-general of France. But my father was a very powerful man. A nasty scandal, a well-publicized deportation, and Banjoko's permanent cancellation of my passport saw to it that when I returned I was virtually trapped in Kenya, although I must admit I lived quite well for a prisoner.

Two years after my return I graduated from the Kenya Polytechnic in Nairobi, where I'd studied engineering. My father hired me to manage a set of offices in downtown Kairami, and I rented an expensive but accommodating apartment within walking distance of my job. Kairami was a modest-sized town, and my father was very well known. I was an attractive woman, and even now, years after the affliction that seized me during my childhood, the locals still stared and called me unclean names behind my back; men boldly propositioned me, wondering if what was cradled between my thighs was still available to be had for the asking.

Growing up, I'd lived with my parents in a spacious, elaborately furnished apartment filled with collectibles, paintings, and antiques. My parents were full-blooded Kinaksu, a large farming tribe whose annual yield, due to poor drainage fields, was never adequate to sustain them. Banjoko was their leader, though this was due to lineage rather than to direct rule. Although he embraced the old ways with great passion, he seldom ventured into the bush, as his father and uncles had acquired great wealth by investing in Kenya's complex trade system and as their eldest male heir he controlled the Kinaksu fortune. My father's office was in the center of Kairami in a modernly constructed building that served as a hub of Kenyan enterprise. The Omorru men were renowned for their cunning business practices and deft skills of negotiation, and they could be notoriously brutal and ruthless when crossed.

When I was young my mother would often frown and complain loudly at the sight of bowls of wasted food, or elaborate meals prepared by our cook that went largely unconsumed, lamenting the fate of her brethren whose backs were bent over dried tobacco crops.

"Dust!" she would cry, fishing through the trash can in horror. "Our people are eating dust as we throw beef to the dogs!"

To please her, Banjoko bequeathed a yearly supplement to each tribal family, and thus our people were able to survive in the bush despite its irrigation impediments, though still not without enduring some hardship.

Before my cutting I had been a voracious child, affectionate and bright, my mother's heart and my father's jewel. Soon after I was led into the bush to be initiated, I became poker-faced and cautious, prone to staring spells and attacks of spitting out unintelligible sounds that burst unbidden from my lips.

After my period of healing at the tribal homestead, Najeri, my mother's brother, came to live with us. He was a *jamsiki,* and too weak-willed for manly work, he would have been butchered and killed if left in the bush. Twice already he had been attacked and driven into the wilderness without food or protection. And I was viewed in a similar fashion. Ostracized because of my bouts of gibberish and habit of staring into the sky until my eyes blurred, Mother was reluctant to leave either of us alone and managed to convince Banjoko that it would be in my best interest to have the company and protection of a man who had no use or desire for women.

Thus, Najeri was commissioned to look after me while my mother shopped, and he made it clear what he thought of me, the lone jewel in Banjoko's crown. "Your coo-coo smells like sour milk." He sniffed around the bathroom when I peed. "It's a funk pot, you know. Stinks worse than a dead pig." This he said as he paraded around the apartment dressed in mother's lace panties and shaking a feather duster at Banjoko's ornate carvings.

But he had a point. It took forever for urine, and later menstrual blood, to seep from the pencil-sized hole that stood as the gatekeeper to my vagina. Small dribbles were the best I could manage, and Najeri was right: it did smell bad. With so much fluid backed up and retained in the tight cove that shielded my honor, it was impossible to stay completely dry, or completely clean.

But if Mother thought I was safe with her brother simply because he was a *jamsiki,* she was wrong. I was eleven when I first saw the nakedness of my uncle. It was dry season, and although our apartment was well ventilated and cooled, when we were alone Najeri loved to prance around naked wearing only a pair of Mother's glittering silver heels with tinsel sprouting from the tops and tiny stars glued to the toes. His feet clacked loudly on the wood floors as his manhood slapped his thighs, swinging from one side to the other. *Clack-clack, pap-pap. Clack-clack, pap-pap.*

Najeri's penis was long and looked like a tube of fat-meat. He had never been initiated, and there was a lengthy piece of drooping skin at its tip covering a knoblike bulge. He rotated his narrow hips so that it would swing-slap from side to side, clearly amused by the antics of his precious organ, although Banjoko would have had it removed at the root had he known it had been paraded before my eleven-year-old eyes.

I mostly ignored Najeri, preferring instead to busy myself with those things that troubled me from the confines of my own head. I'd get so absorbed with the scenes in my mind that strange sounds would burst from my lips, scaring my parents so badly that they once took me to see a *hanagzu,* paying him a small fortune to blow burning smoke into my nostrils to rinse out whatever demons were dwelling in the recesses of my skull.

One afternoon the doorbell buzzed, and I opened the door to find a boy who ran deliveries from a local restaurant. He had a tiny, deformed arm and wore filthy green shorts. He was not much older than me, yet he worked a man's job, carrying heavy crates of groceries and cooked foods with that little arm of his. Today both his hands were empty, his crate nowhere to be seen. I simply stared at him, saying nothing, and he stared back at me in return.

"Move!" Najeri pushed me aside and stood before the boy unashamed in his nakedness. I retreated into my bedroom where I sat by the window staring into the clouds without blinking. I could sit this way for hours unless touched, then at the slightest bit of human contact I'd explode in a frenzied battle of self-destruction—mouth wide in a *kacadu* bird scream, teeth gnashing, fingernails puncturing my own skin, legs twisted and locked so tightly my bones wanted to snap, my fists beating horribly as I tore clumps of my own hair from the roots. Today I stared at the sky until my eyes burned and blurred, then I rose and wandered aimlessly throughout the apartment, my fingers dragging along the cool stucco walls.

I was nearing the sitting room when I heard them. Sounds unlike any I'd ever heard before. I crept closer to the doorway and peered inside, then stood watching the scene without the slightest feeling of either revulsion or attraction. My uncle sat reclined in Banjoko's chair with his legs spread wide. On the floor before him was the young boy. His head moved up and down, and Najeri's penis was in his mouth. My uncle looked up and saw me watching, and without a word he pushed the boy away and stood. His penis looked thick and hard, and it rose above his navel.

With his eyes locked on mine, Najeri turned the young boy around and forced him to bend. He yanked down his dirty shorts and aimed his penis toward the boy's bottom. I watched as he pushed in and out, heard the wet smacking sounds and the painful whimpers that escaped the boy's throat. I smelled their scent as it flooded the air, thick and repulsive.

Suddenly I felt hungry. Walking past them, I went to the kitchen and fixed myself two slices of toast with jam and nibbled on them until I heard footsteps in the corridor and the front door open and close.

There were ten families in our high-rise building, but only two girls who were close to my age. One of them, Mazani Hamid, lived in the apartment next door, and our bedroom windows were catty-corner to each other. She was not permitted in my apartment because she had not been cut, although Najeri often allowed me to sneak next door and visit her. Mazani played the flute like an angel, and we had devised a silly secret signal by knocking on the common wall in our kitchens, and then meeting to talk at our bedroom windows. Her father was a surgeon from Egypt who was on assignment at Kenyatta National Hospital, where he reconstructed the faces of people who had been severely injured or scarred in accidents. Her mother was a schoolteacher who fed us sweet tea and sugar bread.

The Hamids knew about my *yreau,* as we were bush people and almost every tribal girl in my region had been subjected to the knife. I explained the purpose of it to Mazani the same way it had been explained to me, although even as my lips were moving I believed almost none of what I was saying.

"Can I see it, Abeni?" she asked, and because she was my friend, I obliged.

I lay down on her bed and pulled my panties down to my ankles. Then I bent my knees and exposed myself.

Mazani never flinched. She peered closely, then nodded, her examination completed.

My father disapproved of my friendship with Mazani, our tapping on the walls, her playing of a musical instrument, and the many hours we spent talking from our windows. But I loved the Hamids. They were broad-minded people who had lived in the United States while Dr. Hamid trained as a surgeon, and their attitudes were far more liberal than those of most Kenyans. The clatter in my head seemed to subside in the Hamid apartment. Words no longer leaped from my mouth without a push from my brain. The Hamids were heading to Paris on their next assignment, and they let me watch home movies of their family vacations and gave me videotapes of American music from a station they called BET.

Papa found out what I'd been watching and exchanged ugly

words with Dr. Hamid. I listened through the door as he challenged their parenting of Mazani and chastised them for failing to prepare her for adulthood. "She is wide open," he spat, and I knew his mouth was a thin line of distaste. "Never will she find a husband to take her in such condition. Your family will live in shame and dishonor."

But shame and dishonor would prove to be mine and that of the Omorru name.

When I was thirteen Najeri found another friend, Anital, a tall, bronze-skinned man who was also let into the apartment only when my parents were away. This new friend of my uncle was a hulking man whose clear eyes were gray in the centers and whose lips were red and full. There was a jagged scar running down his forehead that looked like a bolt of lightning. My mother knew of this friend, as I'd seen her reply to his greeting when visiting the restaurant where the boy with the tiny arm still worked, but for the most part she ignored his existence, for surely any friend of Najeri must also be *jamsiki* and thus did not warrant much concern.

Again, Mother was wrong.

At thirteen I was tall and well shaped. My skin was smooth and blackberry dark, my body full, my braids thick and hanging down my back.

"I'm thirsty," Anital complained one afternoon as we watched television in our parlor. My father had flown to a weeklong conference in Mali, and my mother had taken her favorite sister out to a day spa that catered to wealthy Kenyan women. Anital gestured to Najeri, who was sprawled across my father's chair dressed in a short skirt and a pink bra. His girlish legs were spread wide, and I could see that his scrotum had slipped free of his panties and lay heavy and bulging against his inner thigh. "Go down to the market and get me and Abeni some fresh juice. Be sure they squeeze it while you watch."

Najeri gave me a nasty look but got up and tugged down his skirt nevertheless. He swished his narrow hips into his bedroom to change into manly clothing, and taking some money from an envelope my mother kept inside a vase, he strode out the door and let it slam.

The door latch had scarcely clicked when Anital turned to me. "Stand up," he commanded. Not knowing what he wanted and not really caring, I stood and stared at him through impassive eyes. "Turn around," he said, and I obediently faced the wall.

For several moments there was silence, and then he spoke, his voice heavy. "You have a beautiful ass," he said. "Nice and high. Rounded. I like that. Sit back down."

I lay back across the sofa and glued my eyes to the television. I watched the figures moving across the screen and heard their voices emanating from the speakers, yet they failed to move me, failed to blot out the jumbled sounds fighting to burst from my own head.

A moment later Anital rose from his chair and came over to me. He nudged me over onto Mother's chaise longue and sat down beside me. His arm was heavy across my shoulders. "You are a beautiful girl, Abeni," he said, but I could tell he was lying. "You'll be ready for marriage soon, and I promise to ask your father if you can be my wife."

I stared at him. "I thought Najeri was your wife."

He laughed and tightened his arm on my shoulder, squeezing me close to him. "Your uncle is a fool," he said, and placed his other hand beneath the slit in my *safi*. His fingers roamed back and forth against my bare thigh, and I watched with little to no interest as they distorted the fabric of my skirt. "Najeri is confused about what a man should be, and I have been helping him learn better things about himself."

His fingers were now fumbling near my crotch, and when I spread my thighs, they fell apart with no resistance. He took his arm from my shoulder and leaned me back, then covered my breast with his hand. I felt his breathing quicken, and when he spoke again his tongue seemed swollen.

"Hurry, Abeni," he said in Swahili. He took my limp hand and placed it on top of the hard mound beneath his shorts. I watched as my hand slid off until it rested near the apex of his thigh. He didn't seem to notice. "We don't have much time."

*Time for what?* I thought. My lips tried to form the words, but they came out sounding like wolf barks smothered in a babble-bird's call. I was immobile and unresisting as his hands swarmed over my flesh. His red lips left streaks of spit on my cheek, my neck, and my breasts, as unintelligible sounds escaped my mouth.

I was becoming bored with his fumbling when suddenly a hot pain exploded between my legs and I felt something tear. I shrieked and arched my back. "You have been tightly stitched," he explained, thrusting his fingers in and out of me while kissing my face to calm me. "After this, I promise it will be easier."

Despite the pain, I was not particularly averse to his probings. Instead, I almost enjoyed the weakness I saw melding in his eyes, the power that my womanness wielded over his flesh. And in some strange way the pain seemed to swell, then dissipate. Bit by bit I became frozen down there, my private area seeming to shut down and die. And as I watched the rhythm of his hand moving in and out of me and felt the warm puddle of blood gathering beneath my hips, my vagina went completely numb and my only concern was for the soiled condition of my mother's favorite chair.

A moment later my concern expanded to include Banjoko's prized paintings as Najeri stormed screaming into the room, splattering me, Anital, and the entire wall behind us with endless amounts of pawpaw juice that had been chilled with tiny chips of ice.

⁜

I saw no reason to hide.

I was still wearing my bloody skirt and underclothes when my mother and aunt Dali returned. Najeri had scrubbed the sofa with

soap and cold water, but it was useless. The lemon-colored bro-
cade fabric boasted the evidence of my deflowering for all to see.

You should have seen my mother. It was as if I had died. Worse
even, because I remained alive to bear witness to the shame that
had been perpetrated on my family. Living proof of the stain on
their honor.

"Yeeee! Yeeee!" Mother wailed, beating her chest and throwing herself against the furniture. "Noooo, please, Abeni, nooooo!"
I watched as my aunt tried to calm her. Mother was a tall, jet-
black woman with thin hair, long legs, and a heavy bottom. She
had a tiny waist and moved like a giraffe.

"We will call Banjoko," her sister said soothingly, kicking packages out of the way as she lowered my mother into a chair. I wondered what they'd shopped for, and if any of the bags contained a
book or two for me. "Calm yourself! Banjoko will know what
to do."

At the mention of my father's name, Najeri wailed fearfully,
and my aunt narrowed her eyes toward the corner where he cowered on the floor clutching his knees to his chest.

Najeri trembled under her glare, then pointed at me and
shrieked, "She let him do it! I saw her, she enjoyed it! She enjoyed it!"

"Lie!" my mother screamed, and my aunt reached down and
slapped Najeri's mouth. He wailed even louder, and my mother
leapt from her chair and slapped him too. Several times.

Of course I hadn't enjoyed it. I had barely felt anything at all,
but I delighted in the reaction it was causing. I'd never seen my
mother or aunt raise their hand to any man, even a *jamsiki,* and
the sight of Najeri crying and covering his head to avoid their
feminine blows was highly amusing. I laughed. Loudly.

The room fell silent and I put my head back and really let go,
laughing harder than I did when playing games with Mazani from
the window or sharing jokes with her family.

"God help us," my mother said finally. "He has driven her mad."

My aunt gave Najeri a final blow, then came over and pressed my face into her breast, silencing me. She was a calm, solid woman who treated me well. Her clothing smelled like jasmine and honey tea, and I liked the way my lips felt pressed to her breasts. "She is not mad, Ziwani," she admonished her older sister as she urged me to stand. She led me toward the bathroom as she reminded my mother, "Abeni has had the same misfortune as you and I. She was born female, a fate that would cause the crazies in the strongest of men."

||||||||||

My aunt helped me undress while my mother fled to call my father. I saw her mouth press into a thin line at the sight of my bloody panties. "Here," she said, reaching for them. "I will take care of these. Are you in pain?"

I shook my head. I felt nothing, only a sense of dread for Najeri, who would surely suffer after failing in his commission to protect me. My skirt was ruined, so she balled it into a wad and threw it in the trash, then helped me slip into clean panties and a thick robe. I was far too big for cuddling, but she sat down on the toilet and pulled me onto her lap, rocking me and stroking my hair like she did when I was a small child.

"I have contacted Banjoko," my mother said, bursting into the bathroom. She stopped when she saw us, and pain flooded her eyes. I hadn't sat in her lap in years, had seldom even allowed her to touch me, although she had never stopped trying. "Banjoko will call Dr. Hamid and arrange to have Abeni examined at a nearby clinic immediately," she said, her eyes jealously following my aunt's stroking hand. "Our neighbor is a surgeon," she said with conviction. "He will know what to do."

I was taken by car to a large satellite clinic in a district west of Kairami. There my mother and aunt held me by the arms like an invalid as a nurse dressed in Western clothing led me into an examining room. Once I was undressed, I was covered by a thin sheet of tissue paper. My aunt held my hand and my mother cried quietly as we waited with the door closed.

I could feel the tension in the women who waited by my side, their fear and their pain, but I did not share it. Whatever would happen would happen, and worrying about something that had already been ruined seemed pointless.

It wasn't long before we heard a knock at the door, and Dr. Hamid entered. I sat up and gave him a broad smile, in direct contrast to my mother, who threw herself at his feet and let out a grief wail in her native bush tongue.

"Abeni." Dr. Hamid stepped past my mother and took my hand. "Have you been hurt?"

"She's been soiled!" my mother said. "Fondled by a *jamsiki* who broke into my home!"

"Then he must not be a *jamsiki,*" I deduced, insolence in my tone.

Her eyes rolled back and she would have fallen and struck her head if not for Dr. Hamid's quick hands. Catching her at the shoulders, he ushered her into a cushioned chair and gave her a cup of water from a cooler near the window. He turned to me. "Your father has requested that I examine you, Abeni, but I will not do so without your permission. I am a surgeon, true, but I am trained to repair facial damages, not gynecological injuries."

It was then that I realized he wanted to look at my vagina, and I marveled that Banjoko himself had requested it. From the time I was a small child I had been told to guard my nakedness from the eyes of men, even my father, and that my mother and aunt seemed eager for me to allow Dr. Hamid to peer between my legs struck me as odd. I opened my mouth to say yes, and a pig grunt came out instead. I swallowed hard and tried again, and this time my tongue quivered snakelike between my teeth and I made one long *ahhhhh* sound.

"Abeni!" my mother yelped. "Stop your foolishness! Answer this man!"

Dr. Hamid took my hand again. "It is your decision, Abeni,"

he said. He smelled like mashed yams and sweet butter. "It is your body, and no one can make you agree to this."

It made no difference to me whether or not Dr. Hamid examined me. But he was a nice man, and I did not want to cause trouble for him with Banjoko. I opened my mouth again, and this time my words came clearly. "Yes. You can look."

My aunt and mother remained in the room as I lay back on the table and bent my knees. My aunt held my hand, but my mother positioned herself behind Dr. Hamid. I let my legs fall open wide, much as they'd done when Anital pushed them apart to probe at me.

I felt no pain, but Dr. Hamid gasped out loud.

"She has been stitched!" he exclaimed.

"My God, she has been torn!" my mother grieved.

Dr. Hamid put on a pair of rubber gloves, and I felt his soft fingers on my flesh, gentle and tender.

"Has she been penetrated?" my mother asked over his shoulder. "Is she still pure?"

Dr. Hamid completed his examination and touched my legs, indicating that I could close them. He pulled the sheet up to my waist. "Of course she is pure. Why wouldn't she be? Her hymen has been broken, but the bleeding has already stopped and there does not seem to be any damage to her vaginal wall."

My mother nearly collapsed again, and this time my aunt caught her before she fell. "She is ruined!" she moaned, biting her lips and tearing at her hair. "You must repair her. There must be honor on her wedding night!"

Dr. Hamid shook his head. "This may not be the worst of it, you know. Abeni seems to be suffering from some sort of psychological damage that was probably caused by some early trauma. Haven't you wondered why she barks and hisses as she does? Why she fights those horrible sounds that want to burst from her mouth? I suggest you—" The telephone rang, and pulling off one glove, Dr. Hamid answered it. From his tone and conversation it was obvious who was on the other end of the line. "Yes, she is here. Yes, she has been penetrated."

I could hear Banjoko screaming. Giving orders for the reconstruction of my hymen. Dr. Hamid's voice rose and became hardened. Angry words were exchanged. I gazed at the ceiling and shut out the rage in Dr. Hamid's voice. No doubt Banjoko was saying far worse on his end. I stared at the off-white ceiling, my gaze merging with the porous tiles until my pupils burned and tears trickled down my face and into my ears.

Moments later Dr. Hamid replaced the receiver in its cradle and was once again standing by my side. "Your husband has threatened my family," he told my mother. "I do not respond well to threats, but the safety of my family is my greatest concern." He swallowed and looked down at me, yet I could not read the message in his eyes. "Abeni is a lovely young lady. The destruction of her hymen does not make her any less so. This thing about 'honor' is outdated and archaic. There is no medical reason why any young girl should have her clitoris"—my mother flinched at the word—"mangled, nor is there any reason the opening of the vagina should be sewn closed. The virtue of a woman lies in her heart. Not between her legs."

"It is *our* way," my mother said firmly. "It is a precautionary custom for our people, and many of your own countrymen understand and practice it as well."

"Yes, many do," Dr. Hamid agreed. "But they are also fools."

He gave me another strange look, then turned to leave the room. "Bring her back here at sunrise tomorrow. I could lose my license if I am found to be performing this type of surgery, but for the peace and safety of my family, I will risk it."

# THIRTEEN

I awakened from the operation loaded with painkillers. I lay in bed with my legs spread wide, my ankles secured to the side railings, my body numb. Never had I been so drowsy. I saw shadowy figures moving about the room, soft-voiced nurses who washed my face and urged me to wet my mouth with small sips of water. I realized I was hallucinating when the entire Hamid family appeared at my bedside, worry on their faces, love in their eyes.

"I have repaired you, Abeni," Dr. Hamid said, his face apparition-like, his voice seeming to cross endless miles to reach me. "You are not perfect, my dear child, but this way you will at least have a chance at living normally."

Mazani and her mother stood on either side of me, holding my hands with great sadness in their eyes. "We love you, Abeni," I heard Mazani say, although her lips did not appear to move. "If God is willing, we will see you again."

I struggled to emerge from the cloud of fatigue that enveloped me, and my hands were suddenly cold as I realized that Mazani and her mother were no longer caressing them. I succumbed to the mist and fell into a deep sleep, and when I awakened again the room was empty and my throat was dry.

My legs ached from being spread, but my head was much clearer. Raising myself onto one elbow and reaching for a cup of water on the bedside table, I saw a single piece of paper bearing Mazani's unmistakable handwriting, tiny print with the letters far too close together. I absorbed the note, and it took me several moments to understand that not only were my best friends gone but what they had sacrificed in my name was more than I could bear. My eyes blurred over the single line of print, which read simply: "Seeing you whole again was worth the world."

Whimpering, I forced myself to sit upright and flung the blankets from my body. My hands shook as I tore away the bandages taped between my legs, then carefully removed the napkin that covered my flesh. Bending at the waist, feeling pain tear through the drugs and bite into my groin, I scooted forward until my knees were bent and peered down between my thighs. My vagina was swollen and discolored, but the effects of Dr. Hamid's surgery were evident. Gone was the thick scar that had run from the top of my mound nearly down to my anus. Gone was the stitched skin that had enclosed my clitoris and concealed my vagina. Through grace and mercy, a stranger's hands had touched me, and gone was the damage done by the mutilation I'd endured at the hands of my own people.

Many years have passed since Dr. Hamid attempted to repair my circumcision, but what I remember most about that period of my life was the change. It was a time of change for everything and everyone near me. As you might guess, my father nearly died when he discovered what Dr. Hamid had done. It was the first time I saw my father cry, but it would not be the last. After composing himself, he used his considerable influence to have the entire staff at the clinic fired. The Hamids had moved out of their apartment in the dead of night, so I convinced myself that they had escaped Banjoko's wrath, but I was young then, and far too naïve. I knew nothing about the long arm of Banjoko, or how deeply it wounded him to have a daughter whose vagina flowered like an apple blossom.

Mother simply shut down. She stopped shopping and going out to social affairs, so great was her shame, so far-reaching was my dishonor. I'd been home for two days when my father ordered her to take me back into the bush for a second *yreau,* but I went into a self-beating frenzy that shocked them both, and I threatened to slit my own throat if anyone dared to touch me with a knife again.

I was far from normal, mentally or physically. As skilled a surgeon as Dr. Hamid was, he'd faced constraints of time and resources when performing my operation, not to mention the nervousness he must have experienced knowing the danger he would be in when his deed was discovered. Thus my new vagina was in no way a perfect replication of the one I'd been granted at birth, but neither was it the horrible disfigurement that it had become upon my *yreau.* For the first time since I was six, my urine spurted from my body in one long *whoosh.* No longer would my menses leak out drop by drop. I cleaned my vagina with grateful hands, soaping its intricate folds and pockets until its aroma was natural and pleasing.

A week or so after my surgery, I was still very sore but feeling well enough to accompany my mother to the market. It was a warm day, and I was looking forward to going back to school in a week's time. We were riding downstairs in the elevator when a neighbor gave us the devastating news.

"Have you heard about the Hamids?" he asked. "They were killed last week, you know. They were trying to get to the airport when their car was pushed off the road by a truck. The entire family died, even the girl who was your friend, Abeni. They said the truck chased them down in their car. Ran them over a railing as they tried to get away. They said—"

I could bear no more. Covering my ears with my hands, I sank to the floor and brayed like a donkey, my visions of Mazani playing the flute in Paris replaced with horrific images of her battered body crushed beneath tons of metal and lying in a rocky ravine. My heart swelled with grief and rage as my tongue twisted and foreign melodies tore from my throat. I flailed my arms and kicked at my mother as she reached for me, the shame of knowing etched in her eyes as she tried to soothe me.

"You did this! You knew!" I screamed in accusation even as she shook her head in denial.

"No, Abeni, no!" The neighbor held me back as I leapt to my feet and tried to attack her. "I knew nothing!" my mother shrieked, shielding her face with her arms. Even if she hadn't known, I knew she was guilty by association.

Somehow Banjoko was responsible for this. Somehow he had made this terrible thing happen to my friends as their punishment for giving me back what he and my mother had taken. In that moment I hated my own father as deeply as I'd loved the Hamids, and I decided I would hurt him just as deeply as he had hurt me. Cut his heart the way he had cut my loins. Sully his precious honor for the whole world to see.

IIIIIIIII

I tried to eat myself to death. Any morsel of anything that was edible was fair game and promptly disappeared into my mouth. Before the Hamids were killed I'd stood five feet eleven inches tall and weighed a curvy 145 pounds, and barely a year later I'd ballooned to almost 260 pounds. My skin looked pimpled and sickly; my hair had fallen out in clumps. People were beginning to talk.

"What is so wrong in your life, Abeni?" my father asked after the principal at my school reported me for stealing food from the school canteen. My father was a man who practiced discipline in all matters, and the sight of me, slovenly and obese, was like a spear in his gut. I saw the concern in his eyes, and even the love. It made me ravenous.

144 / TRACY PRICE-THOMPSON

"You must control yourself, Abeni. Control your appetites. Your attitude toward life is breaking our hearts. We love you, Abeni. Please tell us how we can help you."

They sent me to see a stream of specialists and child psychologists, and in the end I lost the weight, but only because I tired of consuming the endless amounts of food my body required to maintain such bulk. A year later and back down to my normal weight, I turned to other, more forbidden appetites and indulged in them as often as possible.

In Africa, men like their women well endowed, and my curved brown body and shining youth made me a hot commodity on the streets of Kairami. I cared nothing about my own flesh, yet I reveled in the dirt I smeared on my father's honor each time I took on a new man. I'd think of Mazani as I lay in the backseat of their cars or stood against a wall in a dark alley while they pounded between my legs, groping at my numb flesh, taking their pleasure from Banjoko's only daughter, the tarnished jewel in his regal crown.

I propositioned my math tutor, and the elderly man who sold *ackees* at the market. I had lunch with my father at his office, then slipped into a storage room to pleasure a janitor before leaving the building. I picked up grown men in hotel restaurants and followed them up to their rooms, where I let them do almost anything they wanted, for as long as they wanted. And throughout it all I felt nothing. Nothing in my new vagina. Nothing in my broken heart. Nothing in my battered soul.

Things finally came to a head one sultry afternoon in July. I'd been playing with fire for many months, and word of my sexual escapades had reached my mother's ears. "Abeni," she said, her voice quivering, her eyes pained, "a few of my friends are saying terrible things about you that cannot possibly be true. I had to convince them that they were wrong, to beg them not to send you before the morals council."

I stared at her. I didn't doubt what she had heard from a few of her friends. I'd been fucked by a few of their husbands, and one or two members of the morals council as well, and in a voice absent of emotion, I proceeded to tell her so.

You should have seen the way my mother trembled as I described the men I'd had, and the ways in which I'd had them. Much the same way I had trembled when the *maruethia* stood before me on the cutting line.

"Have you no shame?" she whispered, her eyes imploring me. "Is there no value to your body? No small part of you that loves your father and me enough to guard our honor?"

I did not answer her. Of course I felt no shame, and what was there to value in what they had taught me was worthless? As a small child I had loved my parents with all the innocence and trust in my heart, but guard their honor? I felt no such obligation. After all, who had guarded mine?

"Don't you see, Abeni," my mother said, her face a well of disbelief, "you could be stoned for what you have done! Killed! If Dr. Hamid would have repaired you as your father asked, perhaps you may not have had the unnatural desires for the things you described!"

I stared at her, then laid opened my soul through my eyes, hoping for once she would look inside deeply enough to glimpse the damage that I could not articulate. I showed her that hurtful thing that I could not name, the words that my lips would never allow me to properly formulate, and when she saw into me and understood the source of the blackness that had been rotting away at my spirit, her face broke apart in a million pieces, her mouth stretched open in a silent scream.

"It was for your protection," she whispered, and to her credit, she did not cry.

But my father did.

"Why?" he asked, tears running from his eyes. For such a powerful man, his heart had been laid bare on the floor. "Why the men, Abeni? Why allow them to defile your precious body, my child?"

We were alone in the parlor while my mother slammed drawers and closet doors down the hall in my bedroom as she crated up my belongings. As much as I hated Banjoko, I was still his daughter. A part of me understood that my parents loved me, but I had no answer for my father, my mouth just wouldn't allow it, and a week later he cried again as a car came for me. Tears dampened his face as I was driven to the Jomo Kenyatta International Airport and put on a first-class flight to London, where I'd be enrolled in the Lutheran School for Girls.

I was laughing when I left.

# FOURTEEN

Over the next four years I was dismissed from six different schools. But was it my fault that men wanted me? Young men, old men, black men, white men, I fucked my way from London to Greece to Paris to Frankfurt, and then back to Paris. I took on any mother's son, and quite a few of her daughters too. Each time I was expelled from an elite private academy my parents received a similar letter: *Your daughter was found engaging in sexually inappropriate behavior. Abeni is promiscuous, and we can no longer guarantee her safety or be held responsible for her actions.*

I made many friends during my travels. My European girlfriends were sex freaks, and the rich Americans were almost just as bad. They introduced me to the joys of drugs and wild parties, and while my previous sexual forays had been motivated by something dark and intrinsic, I soon learned that sexual pleasure was not reserved solely for men.

"You mean you've never had an orgasm?" Cara asked. She was the blond-haired daughter of the American diplomat to London, and the first person I'd met who masturbated in front of others without reservation. There were four girls in our campus apartment, and Cara and I shared a bedroom. Twice I'd come home to find her stretched out on her bed, rubbing a vibrating rubber penis over her pink nipples and inside the mouth of her furry vagina. The rapture on her face had prompted our conversation, in which despite my many bed partners, I'd revealed the true extent of my sexual ignorance.

"No," I admitted, and shrugged. Was I supposed to? I'd never experienced any sort of pleasurable sensation through sex, had never once expected to.

"You're from Africa, right?" She shuddered, her naked breasts quivering. "Safi told me about how they treat the women over there. Don't they cut off your pussies when you're born?"

Safi was from the Sudan and lived in the campus complex next door. We had become fast friends upon discovering that we were both African, and I'd learned that as a child she had endured a similar *yreau* as well. "No," I said, like a lioness defending her pride. "They don't cut them off. Safi is exaggerating."

"Then let me see it," Cara challenged, throwing on her robe. Jalisa and Analise, our apartment mates, left the doorway and crowded into our bedroom to get a peek as well.

*Why not?* I thought, and for the second time in my life I lay down and spread my legs to show off my vagina. But this time it would not be the jagged scar rendered from catgut and thorns that would be on display but rather the partially restored handiwork of my beloved Dr. Hamid.

Cara took a quick look. "Oh, shit," she moaned, covering her mouth and backing up as the other girls crowded in close. "Abeni, your clit is naked! There's no skin on it. It looks like a peeled grape."

"Jeez," said Analise, her eyes glassy and wide. She was an anorexic pill-head who was stoned all the time, and the sight of my vagina rendered her completely sober. "It's lumpy too. Like it went through a meat grinder. And you're not even Muslim."

But Jalisa Hanes, my closest friend, was the most affected. She was from New York, but her family had moved to South Carolina when she was twelve. Although she had a tongue like a whip, she was an exceptionally beautiful girl, and one of the few students who was enrolled on scholarship.

She shook her head. "Honey, Christians do it too, so religion doesn't have a damn thing to do with it. That's some crazy shit a *man* made up." She shuddered as anger raged in her eyes. "Ain't no God or no woman thought up no mess like that. That came straight out the head of some ancient playa hater who didn't want his woman to get her rocks off faster than him." She frowned at Cara, then tossed me my skirt. "Get dressed, Abeni. You ain't gotta lay up here like no damn freak at a show. God help the motherfucker who tried some shit like that with me, though. I'd put my foot so far up his ass, his nose would drip shit."

Regardless of their feelings about what had been done to me, my friends were adamant that orgasms were not just ejaculations that spewed from hard dicks, and told me that the next time I had sex, *yreau* or not, I deserved to get my bucket tipped just as much as the man who was sweating on top of me did.

The first thing they tried to teach me was to please myself through masturbation. Cara loved having orgasms and admitted to being a nymphomaniac. She boasted of hundreds of sexual partners, and lying in bed beside her, I would watch her eyelids flutter and her mouth grow slack as she used her electric penis to make herself scream. But no matter how I touched myself, or allowed myself to be touched, it just never happened. I would almost feel a flicker of sensation, perhaps in my breasts or deeply within the walls of my vagina, a tiny ember of heat that seemed at once promising and then utterly elusive.

The flicker would fade into nothingness and then fizz out and die, as though the nerves that connected my pleasure center to my brain had been dulled or severed. I was totally unable to feel anything resembling the nuclear fallout that my roommates described, and once again I felt cheated and deprived. So with their encouragement, I embarked on a sexual search to find the one man or woman who would make me feel good enough to curl my toes and pull out my hair.

How I managed to complete my basic education with the amount of partying and school hopping I did is a mystery to me, yet at eighteen I graduated from a Parisian high school where my final grades were excellent, although I remained promiscuous and unfulfilled.

After graduation I spent a full year in France, begging my parents to allow me to stay on in Paris, convincing them that I had landed a job designing dresses for a top fashion line, even though I had no experience in such matters. What I was experiencing, however, was the joy of a real relationship for the very first time, and with someone who was much older and far more worldly than I was, and who was also married to France's director-general.

She was a petite brunette, with tiny breasts and narrow hips. She drank too much and walked with a swagger, and there was no way she could be considered attractive. I'd met her at a party during my first trip to Paris, and soon after I graduated she stashed me away in a modest apartment overlooking the city. The evenings I did not spend soliciting men, I spent alone, reading or watching television. I spent my days with her, shopping, visiting museums, and having sex. She adored the muscular roundness of my ass, my long legs and small waist. And although she spent hours suckling my breasts and massaging the mounds of my backside, she was reluctant to explore my vagina, preferring instead that I become thoroughly familiar with the pink perfection that was her own.

In the darkness of our bedroom my eyes would be stretched wide as she climbed the hills of passion. I watched her sexual journey, envious and angry that such heat never rose from my loins, that my lips failed to grow slack, that my body never convulsed with that nipple-hardening explosion that seemed to grip my lover under my skilled touch. Perhaps I might have spent my life this way, on a desperate, reckless quest for satisfaction that could never be realized, had I not dreamed of Mazani.

She came to me periodically, when I was sad or my stress level was high, or simply when sleep caused my bricked-in emotions to weaken and collapse, leaving me naked and vulnerable to the pain that I still carried in my heart.

In my dreams Mazani was usually alive and happy, though trapped in her thirteen-year-old body. But this dream was different. In it, Mazani stared at me with dead, accusing eyes, telling me how unworthy I had been of the vagina she and her family had died to give me. She scolded me for taking their gift and flinging it in the face of every passing stranger.

It was late spring, and I was visiting my lover in a suite at the Parisian Ritz, where her husband was heading a major political conference. The press and paparazzi were out in full force, and she seemed to delight in wagging me beneath her husband's nose. During the diplomatic champagne luncheon she'd sat me at the head table and passed me off as a former exchange student, and afterward she had taken me down the hall to her suite, where she mounted me and made herself feel good. Sometime later, after falling asleep in her arms, I sat up in a panic, dragging my dreams of Mazani into the waking world along with me.

"Mazani," I'd moaned deeply, then clamped my hand over my lips, seeking to still the rising tide of twisted grunts and guttural barks that were filling my mouth and pushing against my teeth. It had been years since I had battled with the sounds inside my head, and my lover knew very little about the strangeness of my past.

"What did you say?" She leaned over me, her voice icy, an empty bottle of champagne in her lap. The heat of alcohol was on her breath. She had been sitting upright, watching me as I dozed, and the freckled face that moments earlier had been puckered in rapture was now pinched into an angry mask. I had never seen her this way. Had never known she could become so enraged so quickly.

Her voice was thick. "Who the fuck is she?"

Sick from my nightmare and struggling to control my tongue as it coiled and contorted inside my mouth, I staggered from the bed, taking the sheet with me and leaving her pale and naked, her chest and cheeks flushed with anger.

"You're fucking around, aren't you!" she screamed, leaping at me, pulling my braids and slapping my face. She picked up a Creighton vase and hurled it against a wall. Roses and baby's breath rained down on the carpet. "Black bitch!" she yelled. "I knew it! I knew it!" I watched helplessly as she snatched the champagne bottle by the neck and raised it in the air.

I was much bigger than she was, but she had the weapon. I tried to run, but my feet got tangled in the sheet and I fell to the floor.

She swung the bottle and I rolled left, barely avoiding the thick glass as it rushed toward my face. Naked, I pulled the sheet along with me as I scooted toward the door with her screaming and swearing and kicking as she cracked me in the head and back with the heavy green bottle.

I yelped in pain and grabbed at my head, nearly fainting when my hand came away slick with blood. I went into a rage. Jumping to my feet with my breasts heaving, I brought my bloody fist around in a strong arc and connected with her nose. A sharp crack split the air. For a brief second there was silence, and then she bent over and clutched her nose, letting out a bloodcurdling scream that seemed far too vast to come from her tiny body.

And then they were upon us.

Hotel security was everywhere. Her husband came running, followed by the reporter who had been interviewing him in the lobby, and rough hands were securing my arms, angry white faces eyeing my naked body and spewing hateful words that meant the same thing whether spoken in French, English, Dutch, or Swahili.

I left Paris twenty-four hours later with the clothes on my back and twelve stitches in my head. When I landed in Kenya my passport was confiscated by customs and I was taken by car straight to my father's apartment.

As I rode in the back of the hired limousine, I determined that despite everything I had endured in Kenya, it would be good to be among the familiarities of my own people, to hear my native tongue in my ears. I had been away for six years, and during that time I had lived through a multitude of experiences, many too vile to speak of, others too vivid to forget. But I had also grown wise enough to understand that the demons of my past did not have to manipulate the sails of my future.

Time, given in adequate doses, could become a balm that heals. Old wounds formed scabs that itched and sloughed off, leaving scars that might remain visible but held only the memory of their initial pain. I had come full circle with this forced return to Kenya, and it made me wonder if it was possible to truly escape the bonds of one's past, or even if one should try. Because despite the numerous roads I had traveled, some littered with pebbles, others smooth as glass, each of them seemed to serve as a brick in the path that had led me right back home.

# FIFTEEN

I was at home for three days when I decided to enroll at Kenya Polytechnic, which was less than an hour away from my parents' apartment. My relationship with my mother was still strained, although it was clear that she had missed me immensely while I was gone. She cooked elaborate meals those first few days, and I caught her staring at me often, a look of wonderment on her face, as though she was trying to imagine the places I had been and the things that I had done.

My father had changed. He seemed more determined and even more purposeful. He was planning to build a school for boys called the Brotherhood Haven, where male Kinaksu could be brought in from the bush and taught mathematics and sciences. Most of the young males of our tribe were his nephews or cousins, and I believed this endeavor would satisfy his longing for a son of his own.

His love for me was also ever strong, but my behavior had shamed and embarrassed him and he could not meet my eyes, though he stroked my hair and held my hand. He was an African of convention and tradition, and it was painful for him to imagine the darling of his heart, his own flesh-and-blood daughter, committing the vile, unnatural acts that had caused my deportation. No doubt my name and word of my deed had been spread all over the French papers, as the husband of my lover held a high government position and such a scandal was sure to make national headlines. And although it was my father who had ordered the revocation of my passport, he refused to speak a single word regarding the sordid incident.

But the pain of it seeped from his pores. I heard him as he silently berated himself for raising such a loose, wanton child, and if I were anyone else's daughter, he would have taken me before the morals council and recommended the harshest of punishments. But I carried his blood and the Omorru name, and for him, as the man of the family and the leader of our tribe, I was his personal failure.

Commuting to school each day, I took on a double course load and completed a five-year program in just shy of four. I had no friends and was not sexually active. Word of my trouble had spread. It was not every day that the daughter of one of the province's most powerful families behaved like a whore and returned to her father's house in disgrace.

It was as if I had a mark upon me. A brand of some sort that displayed my sins and the heights from which I had fallen. Oh! The hurtful things they said about me. The mud that clung to my name! Never a word to my face, yet just within earshot, some subtle indication that I was soiled. Sullied and unclean. A thing of filth that must be ostracized and avoided. Worse than a prostitute, I was a sexual pariah who had given of myself for free.

Although I had slept with women, I felt no physical attraction to them, yet I yearned for their companionship. I missed the closeness of living among girls my age, of sharing clothing and secrets and whispering late into the night. There was no such camaraderie to be had for me in Kairami. Even when traveling into a city the size of Nairobi I felt alone. The female students in my classes were devout Christians sprinkled with a handful of Muslims—all had been cut—and none wanted to associate with a woman as far from grace as I.

Many nights I wept as I lay in my childhood bed. I missed Cara. I missed Jalisa. But mostly, I missed Mazani. Just walking past the apartment where her family once lived sent my heart hurling toward my throat and caused my whole body to shake. A new family had moved in while I was gone, a Catholic couple with two small boys, and I averted my eyes when approaching their door. I could not even bear to gaze out the window as I once did. To look across and know that I would never see Mazani's dear face again in this life caused me the worst kind of pain. To acknowledge the weight of my responsibility gave me even greater pain, a pain that cut me so deeply I would lose my breath while sleeping and awaken gasping for air.

It had taken the sum of my experiences to make me understand the role I had played in the destruction of my life and the lives of those who loved me. There were millions of African women who had withstood their *yreau* without wreaking disaster and confusion upon their families. Circumcision was a venerated ancestral ritual, one intended to embrace a young girl as part of a peer group, as a cherished member of a community. I'd grown to understand the reasoning behind the procedure even as I suffered as a result of its methods, but why couldn't I simply bear up under it as had my mother and grandmother and her mother before her? What gave me the right to upset the equilibrium of Kinaksu tradition and cause others to suffer and die?

Had I been stronger, perhaps the scar-faced *jamsiki* would not have violated me. I should have fought him off. Chewed off his red lips. Scratched out his eyes and screamed for my father. Died before I let his vile fingers enter me. At least I would have died chaste and with honor. And perhaps Dr. Hamid would not have felt compelled to operate on my behalf, and poor Mazani would still be alive.

I yearned for a different sort of life. A life, I feared, that could no longer be had in Kenya. I would do anything to erase that look in my father's eyes. To be someone who filled his gaze with approval and pride. I wanted to become a daughter who shared a relationship with her mother. A normal person, an African woman of honor and bearing, yet, as was evidenced by my public shame, I was anything but.

During a brief moment of desperation I considered asking my mother to arrange a second *yreau*. This time it would be permanent. If being recut and stitched would lift my guilt and despair, if it would elevate me from the gutters of society and bring my dearest friends back to me, I would gladly forfeit intercourse and remain stitched for the rest of my life.

But I was a coward and my fear consumed me. There was nothing I could do that would bring the Hamids back, and just the thought of the blade, glinting and sharp, made my heart quiver and my mouth go dry. I was not brave enough to submit to a second cutting, so I kept to myself and accepted my guilt and the exclusion from my peers as a penance of sorts.

For the next four years I existed in a vacuum. I studied ceaselessly and dreamt of Mazani.

I graduated near the top of my class. I skipped the ceremony and decided instead to walk to the market and have my hair braided. Once each month I took my mass of hair down to wash it, then let the sun crinkle it dry as I walked to the center of town and paid a small sum to have it rebraided. Often the feel of those deft female fingers as they gathered my wool at the root and pulled and wrapped until it was knitted close to my skull was the only touch I received from another human being.

As I sat between knees that secreted the aroma of Woman, I'd close my eyes and take pleasure in the comb scraping my scalp, its pointed tip traveling north, south, east, and west as my hair was parted and sectioned. And although the braiders pulled my hair until my eyes lifted in the corners and my scalp blazed tender, I withstood it with joy and looked forward to the next time I could experience the warmth of another's touch.

"There is a position for you downtown," my father told me shortly after my graduation. "You will be responsible for reviewing contracts and issuing permits for the corporation."

I stared. I'd been prepared to find a job teaching, or perhaps private tutoring, but this was unthinkable. It was typical for a father to provide employment for a graduated son, but to give a daughter like me a position of such responsibility told me all the things that my father had been unable to say. I was thrilled.

"Thank you, Papa. I'll do a good job. I promise."

"I'm sure you will, Abeni," he told me with a smile that made me feel almost forgiven. "You are from good stock."

My department at Omorru and Associates dealt with a myriad of rail operations, including contractor bids for expansive railway repairs, government clearances and special tracking permits for oversized cargo, and placards and markings for hazardous materials. I supervised a staff of twelve: nine men and three women. Although I was the boss's daughter, I took no special considerations, preferring instead to learn the business from the ground up. From the beginning it was obvious what the other workers thought of me, but in the interest of keeping their jobs, they kept their opinions to themselves.

I knew there was little to be gained by attempting to explain my past behavior, so I did not bother to try. I let my work ethic and eagerness to learn speak for my character, and because I was friendly and nonthreatening, it wasn't long before my staff grew to accept my leadership. Though I couldn't say that they looked upon me warmly, I had gained their respect at least, and that was enough for me.

A month after starting my new job I found an apartment near Wilson Park and fell in love with it at once. I'd never given much thought to décor or fashion, but the moment I stepped inside the quaint two-bedroom loft on the third floor of a renovated ware-house, visions of artistry flowed through my head. Unlike my mother, who was partial to earth tones, I wanted to surround my-self with a rainbow of colors, hues and tones that would lift me with their intensity, brighten me with their brilliant glow.

For the very first time I shopped with a vengeance, buying daz-zling curtains and rugs, ceramic jugs, hand-whittled masks, and vivid cotton sheets. There was no organization to my scheme. Just color splashed everywhere, without rhyme or harmony, and it suited me just fine. Early each morning I showered and dressed, then grabbed a piece of fruit and left my apartment while the African sun was still rising over the plains. Walking leisurely through the park, I would munch on an apple or pear and bite back the lone-liness that was now a part of my daily existence. From the time I arrived home in the evenings until I greeted the doorman the fol-lowing morning, I hardly spoke a word, and I sometimes forced myself to sing along with an album or laugh out loud at some-thing on the television just to hear my own voice. It was at times like these that I longed for the communal nature of the bush and the constant flow of communication it provided. Here, there were no girlfriends for me to chat with on the telephone, and having a conversation with my mother was out of the question.

As a teenager studying abroad, every Saturday morning my roommates and I had walked to a nearby bookshop to buy ro-mance novels and confession magazines that were filled with fairy tales of love and lust. As young girls, we yearned for a savior to gallop in on a black horse and sweep us off our feet, fearless and strong, charging the armies of our nightmares and filling our worlds with joy with only a single kiss.

My savior arrived without the benefit of a horse or even a car. He walked into my office on the last Friday in July, a day that had been reserved for internal audits and file maintenance. I was sit-ting on the floor behind my desk, sorting through stacks of files, when Talani, my receptionist, called out my name. "Abeni?" She knocked twice on the open door and peered inside.

"Down here," I said, waving from my hidden position. Talani was close to my age and wore her clothing long and loose. Recently, her husband had come into the office dressed in traditional Kenyan garb, and without saying a word he'd eyed my navy suit and sheer pink blouse and growled at me in disapproval.

"You have visitors," she said.

I frowned and slid on my bottom until I faced her. I had no appointments scheduled, as my calendar had been cleared for the audit. Glancing past her shoulder I saw two men, one short and fair-skinned, the other tall and alarmingly handsome. Pulling myself up, I met them at the door. "Sorry, but we are not taking appointments today—"

"Malcolm Armstrong," the taller man said, extending his hand. "And this here is my friend Chicken. Chicken Johnson."

Americans.

The second man reached out to shake my hand, and our eyes met. He was short but muscular and solidly built, with smooth skin that was much lighter than mine. His shoulders seemed too large for his frame, and as soon as our hands touched he broke out in a big, clumsy smile that was so beautiful it made me smile in return.

"Bishop," he said, still holding my hand.

"Well, all right then." His friend laughed as Bishop and I stood shaking hands and smiling into each other's eyes.

Bishop finally let go of my hand and, still smiling, looked from me to his friend Malcolm, and then again at me. "You two could be related," he remarked. "You might not be kin, but damn if yawl don't come from the same tribe."

I looked at Malcolm and nodded. His ancestors were clearly of Kinaksu blood, even if there was no way to trace it.

Bishop was still smiling at me. My friend Jalisa had warned me about black men from America. "It's all a game with them, Abeni," she had told me. "No jobs, no cars, no manners, no respect—it's all about how much shit they can get a sistah to do for them before they kick her to the curb. Brothahs be begging. They need favors galore."

Rubbing the spot where Bishop had touched my hand, I led them into my office and motioned that they should put the mound of files on the floor and take a seat. I moved behind my desk before speaking. "It is nice to meet you, Bishop," I said. There was something about his eyes that was so beautiful it was almost painful. "And it is nice to meet you as well, Malcolm." I swallowed and found my chair, then nodded at Bishop. "What can I do for you?"

"We're with the Peace Corps?" Bishop said, as if he needed to jog my memory. "I called a few weeks ago, then faxed you a request to lay some irrigation pipes on your father's land. Malcolm is fresh from Alabama and ready to help us out—that is, if your father decides to sign off on our permits."

"Yes, I remember the request," I said, looking down at some papers on my desk. "My father has received your proposal, but he has not made his decision yet." I could feel Bishop's gaze upon me, burning into my skin, and although I was well accustomed to the eyes of men, none had ever looked at me in quite this way, with such interest and awe.

"Well, the problem is, we got two tons of corrugated steel coming in to the port of Mombasa the first thing Monday morning," he said, his voice tense. "We need to piggyback off the network that's already established on your father's land, then build an infrastructure that'll run twenty miles north toward Kisumu. If we don't have the permits in hand, we can't transport the pipes by truck."

It was true that my father had mentioned this project to me, but he had not been inclined to support it. He'd explained that the Peace Corps wanted our assistance in providing potable water to a drought-stricken bush community not far from our tribal lands. Their proposal entailed connecting their pipes into the existing irrigation system that had been financed by my father for the use of our Kinaksu kin.

"I'm sorry." I held out my hands helplessly. "I would like to assist you, but unfortunately my father is the only person who can approve this type of request."

Bishop slid toward the edge of his chair. "Then how can we reach him?"

I shrugged. It wasn't just his eyes that were compelling. I liked his face too. Although he was small, there was strength and honesty in his eyes. "He is out of town on business today but should return sometime tomorrow afternoon."

"Then can I call you tomorrow?"

I allowed my eyes to touch his, and something electric leapt in my chest.

"I mean"—he disarmed me again with the perfectness of his smile—"to find out about his decision. And if you could get in touch with your father as soon as he gets home, and if there was some kinda way you could, you know, put in a good word for us . . . we'd appreciate it."

I pretended to think about it for a long moment, then nodded. Malcolm looked relieved, but the smile on Bishop's face was a thing to behold. When they left my office ten minutes later Bishop "Chicken" Johnson had more than just my telephone number. He had my attention.

# SIXTEEN

Banjoko refused the Peace Corps request, and it took quite a bit of convincing on my part to persuade him to change his mind.

"Why do you care?" he asked after I pressed the issue to limits that were far beyond my usual interest. I'd met him at the rail station as he returned home from Kisumu in a private railcar reserved for dignitaries, and we were having lunch at a quaint Italian restaurant that had recently opened in Kairami.

"It makes perfect sense," I told him, my face impassive as I picked at my salad. My father was a businessman, and there were few things that commanded his attention faster than the prospect of increasing his wealth or position. "This is an ideal situation that requires almost no effort on our part. The Peace Corps will pay us a small sum for each conduit they tap into, and the human-interest aspect will generate positive press coverage for the firm."

"Fine," he said, signaling the waiter. There were tired lines around his eyes, and I noticed quite a bit of gray in his beard. "But you must handle anything associated with this on your own.

We are recruiting teachers and scientists from as far away as Tanzania to come to the Brotherhood Haven, and during the next few months I will be traveling extensively and conducting endless interviews."

I felt anxious as my father's driver dropped me at my apartment. I had instructed Bishop to call me at 3 P.M., and I felt silly as I anticipated the sound of his voice. Inside my apartment I held the telephone receiver to my ear to make sure it actually worked, then parted the curtains and let the sunlight flood each room. I sat at the window seat in my bedroom gazing at the weekend shoppers and tourists for nearly an hour, then stripped naked and stood beneath a cascading hot shower, letting the water titillate my muscles and ease my tension.

I had just finished massaging warm coconut oil into my skin when the telephone rang.

"Hello?" I held my breath until I heard his voice.

"Abeni?" Tentative. Gentle. Hopeful. "How you doing? This is Bishop Johnson."

I exhaled. "Hello, Bishop," I answered. "I am fine, thank you, and I have good news."

I could hear the relief in his voice when I told him their request had been granted. "Thanks a lot. You don't know how much this means to us. Can I take you out to celebrate tonight? I mean, I know this is short notice and all, but I really wanna show you how grateful I am, so can I buy you dinner?"

"Sure. I would like that." The words slipped right from my mouth! "And this way," I quickly added, "you can get your permits before Monday."

Bishop was new to Kairami and knew very little about the town, so we decided to stick to familiar territory and dine at a restaurant near my office.

"What time would you like to eat?" he asked.

"Uhm . . ." I giggled nervously and reached up to touch my hair. I reminded myself that it was only a business dinner, but I had nothing at all to wear, and suddenly my braids felt fuzzy. "What time will you and your friend be available?"

There was a short pause on the line. "Malcolm's not coming. My friend is not invited, Abeni. If you trust me, and if you don't mind, I'd like tonight to be a dinner for two. Just me and you."

I could not speak. I had no idea how to respond. Trust him? I had been with men who, for all I'd known, might have been hatchet murderers. Trust had never before been an issue. Yet already I anticipated the excitement of his companionship.

"Okay." My voice was light, but inside I panted with joy.

"You aiight? Can you handle that?"

I laughed. I liked his American accent. Very relaxed. It seemed Jalisa had been wrong in her assessment of black men from America. Bishop didn't require anything of me. He appeared to be the exact opposite of what she had described. "I think so. Just you and me will be fine."

"Um, one more thing," he said just as I was preparing to hang up. "Could you do me a favor? I don't have a car, so would you mind swinging by to pick a brother up?"

⁂

I called a company car and instructed the driver to pick Bishop up at his hotel. We had dinner at an intimate seafood restaurant, and although I am sure the food was excellent, I barely tasted it. There was something about this man that captivated me. His eyes, the brightness of his smile, the subtle contrast between his curly hair and his bronzed skin. We shared a mixed-seafood platter and sat across from each other talking and laughing. He asked if I wanted wine with my dinner, and when I told him I did not drink alcohol, he seemed happy.

Bishop looked well groomed in his white crewneck shirt and pressed jeans, and his casual attitude made it easy for me to relax. He was reserved but had a great sense of humor, even though laughing didn't seem as if it was something he did very often. It was strange, but of all the men I'd known, this was my first time actually having a date with one, and I was enjoying myself immensely.

"I was born in Birdtown, Alabama," Bishop was saying, "but I moved fifty miles south to Bull Run when I . . . when I left a place called Spottfield."

"I've heard a lot about America," I told him. "There was a girl at school with me in France who once lived in California." I laughed softly, thinking of Cara. "She had absolutely no inhibitions. In fact, she was one of the freest people I've ever met."

I watched him fork a shrimp into his mouth, his dimples flashing as he chewed. "Yeah, I've heard a lot of folks are free in L.A., but I've never been there. I lived in Alabama my whole life. My people got killed in a house robbery, and I didn't have any other real family, so I ended up living with Malcolm and his grandparents, and they helped bring me up."

There was so much pain in his voice when he mentioned his parents that I had no idea what to say, except that I was sorry.

"Thanks. It was a hard time, but I survived it."

He reached over and took a napkin from a metal holder, and the muscles in his arms and shoulders bulged beneath his shirt.

I changed the subject. "Was it fun living with Malcolm and his family?"

His mouth was full, so he nodded, then finished chewing. "Yeah, I guess you could say it was. He comes from good people. His granmaw and granpaw took me in when I was seventeen, and I stayed with them until I got hired on by the Peace Corps."

It was my turn to nod as I chewed a mouthful of grilled vegetables. His manner of speaking was awesome. Almost Jalisa-like in its rhythmic, casual cadence, but with a southern street twang.

"Now tell me a little bit about yourself," he asked as I took a sip of lemon-flavored water from a crystal glass.

I nearly choked. What was I to say? Where did I begin? Was I to tell him about my afflictions? About the numerous men I'd been with?

"I'm an only child," I began, "and when I was fourteen I was sent abroad to attend private schools. I've lived in London, Paris, Germany, and Greece, and when I returned home I enrolled at a university in Nairobi."

"Private schools in all those countries? Damn! Your father must be mad rich. What did you major in at college?"

"Engineering."

His eyes grew brighter. "What discipline?"

"Mechanical."

"I wanted to study construction engineering in college, but I ran into something and had to join up with the Peace Corps instead."

Again, his words were said as a mere statement of fact, and even though I sensed there was something more to them, I was left without a response. It was still relatively early when we left the restaurant, and I was reluctant to bring the night to an end. Thanks to the permit I had signed, he and Malcolm would be leaving town and going into the bush on Monday morning.

As we headed toward the parking area where our car and driver waited, Bishop surprised me by taking my hand.

"It's nice out. You wanna go for a walk?"

*In public?* I almost screamed. Instead I nodded, not trusting myself to speak, but when he looked in my eyes I saw a mirror there, reflecting something kindred. Although I was apprehensive about us being seen as a couple—and he was slightly shorter than me—my hand felt safe and protected in his, as if no harm could come to me as long as he was near.

I was awash in new sensations, on uncharted ground, spending casual, quality time with a man, caring enough to try to get to know him, and wanting him to know me in return. We strolled along the streets of Kairami, holding hands and chatting like old friends. Although Bishop had not attended a university, he seemed very intelligent and was well traveled and interested in Kenyan culture. I pointed out scenic portions of the town and other points of interest, amazed by the view of my home reflected in his un-challenged eyes. It was surprising to hear myself speaking of Kai-rami with pride, possessing its history as if I actually belonged to it, this town I had once fled with glee.

"How old are you, Abeni?"

We were stopped near a large fountain in the center of town. During the day, locals usually gathered here to eat bag lunches, men shared cigars under the shade of leafy trees, and peddlers showcased their wares along the fountain's marble edge. At night, however, the crowd was sparse—a few couples, an elderly man sitting alone on a bench, and one or two teenagers tossing coins into the cascading water.

"I'm twenty-four. And you?"

He looked embarrassed. "I'm almost twenty-two," he said, then added, "but I've lived a lot for my age."

And while I believed him, I was certain that he had not lived nearly as much as I.

We walked an area the size of a large square, and all too soon we arrived back at the car. I twirled my purse in small circles, and he tugged on my hand, pulling me close to him.

"I had a good time tonight, Abeni." His body was inches from mine.

"As did I."

"Can I see you again?"

An ember ignited deep in my tummy. It heated my blood and flooded my muscles, leaving me weak.

"I don't know, Bishop. We're very different."

He touched my hair, running his fingers along the length of my braids. "Sometimes being different can be a good thing. I'm not trying to push up on you, it's just that I'm feeling you and I wanna get to know you better."

He sounded so sincere that I found myself nodding in agree-ment, and then I laughed. "Feeling me? It's not every day a woman like me hears something like that, you know."

"As fine as you are, I don't see why not. So can I see you again? Can you handle that, baby?"

I must have been far lonelier than I'd thought. I felt myself responding to his voice, his scent, his warmth. "Yes," I said, and smiled. My hips felt fluid as I sauntered over to the passenger door. "I think I can handle that."

And handle it I did. In what seemed like moments, Bishop and I became swept up in each other's worlds. It was difficult for us to see each other, as I worked long hours and he was busy designing irrigation plans in the bush, but we managed to steal small pockets of time that always seemed to end too soon.

Three weeks after meeting him, I placed a call to New York City. Jalisa had been hired to run a large advertising agency and had moved back to the city of her birth. Between both of our hectic schedules, we managed to talk at least once a month. "I've met someone," I told her, giggling into the telephone as though she were right in Africa with me.

"Well, go 'head, Miss Thang. Who is he? Some stuck-up African dignitary whose face is plastered all over your country's money, or one of them sweet-backed, pipe-slinging Mandingo brothahs y'all grow by the acre over there?"

"Well," I said, laughing and threading the phone cord through my fingers, "he is in fact working with pipes, but he is not a dignitary and he is not Mandingo. He is a black American, although very fair in complexion. You know, the kind of man you told me was always looking to take advantage of their women. I don't have the experience with dating that you do, Jalisa, but I think you may have been wrong. Bishop is kind and attentive, and beautiful too. He is a little younger than I am—shorter too—but he is really interested in knowing me, and black American or not, I actually like him."

Jalisa made a disdainful sucking noise, like she was pulling seaweed from her teeth. "Don't get it twisted, Abeni. I said they were slick, not worthless. As much as the brothahs can work your last nerves, they're still the best damn thing since the Hula-Hoop. Ain't nothing like a black man. No other man on the face of the earth can hold a light up to him, coming or going. Why do you think white girls are all the time chasing behind them? Smooth game and all, when a brothah loves you, he loves you right."

And I was inclined to believe her. Being with Bishop gave my world new imagery and painted broad, electric strokes across the canvas of my heart. He was candid with me but did not wear his heart in plain sight. I learned that his parents had run a gambling house where women also traded sex for money, but Bishop explained that the women of his house had raised and cherished him and he'd loved each of them like family. He said his father was known as Slim Willie, a man who would die before he let harm come to any of his ladies.

For some reason I got the impression that Bishop was telling his story for the very first time. He told me so much about his life in Alabama and described his family in so much detail it was almost as if I knew Dimples, and Boogalou, and Reenie and Miz May, and the colorful people in the small community called Birdtown. I could see the dust settling on their roads, trace the lines etched into their faces, hear the music of their voices, and feel the love that had been showered upon him.

But I remained cautious in the telling of my own story. There was so much about me that I simply could not share. The way I had spent my time abroad and the circumstances surrounding my circumcision were utterly unspeakable. I mentioned my parents only briefly, and I never invited him to accompany me when I dined with them each week at their apartment. Instead, I spoke of Mazani. I made him laugh as I told him about the silliness of our friendship and the games we played as children. I told him of her musical talents, and how after watching BET music videos I was convinced that American women were the freest and the most naked, shameless creatures on the earth.

He could hardly believe that I'd traveled as often and as extensively as I had when I was barely in my teens. "You mean your folks let you go off traveling around the world when you were only fourteen?"

"Yes." I nodded. "It is not as uncommon as you might think. A lot of children from wealthy families attend boarding schools, even here in Kenya. I wasn't the youngest girl in my classes, and actually, I think I learned a lot by being exposed to people and cultures outside of Africa."

I told him nothing about my circumcision or the attempt at repairing it. Nearly every person who had seen or touched my vagina had responded to it with some degree of revulsion. I never wanted to see that kind of look in Bishop's eyes, and when the Peace Corps project was nearing its end three months after we'd met, a part of me was almost glad that he would be leaving.

I was no longer the terrified child who hissed at strangers and barked up at the moon. That numb girl who had stood against walls, lain beneath stairwells, spent hours on her knees, was dead. I was an emerging woman now, one who had finally gained some semblance of respectability in her father's eyes, and I told myself over and over again that Bishop was in my life only temporarily, and that getting too deeply involved with a transient man of his status would not only be foolhardy and impulsive, it would destroy the growing relationship that I had worked so diligently to rebuild with my father.

October had come and was nearly gone when Bishop visited my office for the second time. He came alone, as Malcolm was closing down the construction site and preparing to move northward with their men and equipment.

We sat in my office gazing at each other. I'd left the door open so my employees would not suspect that there was anything improper between us. And there hadn't been. We had taken care to see each other only in public places, and because our time together was limited and infrequent, we kept boundaries between us that had not yielded to intimacy. But there were feelings surging inside of me that I had never before experienced, and no matter how many hours I worked, how often I walked in the park and fought what I felt, alone in my apartment I dreamed of Bishop.

I was seated behind my desk and he sat across from me in a comfortable leather chair. There was so much I wanted to say, and I could see the volume of his thoughts in his eyes as well.

"You okay?" he asked after long, silent minutes.

I barely breathed. "Yes."

"I'm not."

My heart thudded. "What's wrong? Are you ill? Is your grandfather sick?"

"Pop-Pop is fine, but that's it, Abeni. I'm sick. Sick from missing you."

The force of my emotions astounded me. I felt hot all over, then a wrenching pain that almost cut me in half seared through my heart. "I'll miss you too, Bishop." My words were inadequate to relay the depth of my emotions, and it took every bit of self-control I possessed to stop myself from jumping from my chair and curling up in his lap. I ached to feel his arms close around me and have him rock me like the baby I wanted to be.

"But I miss you right now." He stood and reached into his front pocket. "C'mere. Let me put this on you."

I crossed the room and held my braids up as he fastened a gold necklace with a tiny heart pendant around my neck. It was inexpensive yet charming, and it seemed to carry the heat from his hands and warm my breast where it lay.

Bishop put his arms on my shoulders and turned me around until I faced him. When he spoke again, his voice was low and deep. "My mother didn't have any family, and this was something I bought her the Mother's Day before she was killed. I had asked them to bury her in it, you know, as my way of telling her goodbye, but Big Gussie said no. Said one day I'd find somebody who would wear it and feel the same way about it that Dimples did. And now it's yours, baby. I want you to have it, okay?"

I nodded and took a tiny step closer to him. I pressed my palms to his muscular chest, and his arms closed around me, protective and strong, and it was at that moment that I truly understood the scope of his emotions. What a precious gift he had given me. Even if it did mean good-bye. Suddenly I knew what had to be done.

"Are you free tonight?" I asked before I could change my mind. "Can you get away?"

"Yeah." He nodded. "But this will probably be the last little bit of time off I have. Tomorrow afternoon I'll be loading equipment for the advance party to Isiolo. Tomorrow night we roll out."

"Okay," I said, eyeing the dust on his jeans and his scuffed work boots. "I'll send a car for you at six." I wanted to warn him to dress nicely but decided not to bother. They would have to accept him in his natural state, casual and relaxed, and if they could not see past his common clothing to find the love and goodness that radiated from his heart, it would only be because they were blind.

# SEVENTEEN

It was not something I did often, but shortly after seeing Bishop to the door I canceled my afternoon appointments and left work early. On the way home I stopped by a catering service and ordered a simple dinner for two to be delivered later that evening. By noon I had tied my braids back and was in my apartment dusting and polishing with lemon-scented oils, dry-mopping the hardwood floors, tidying up the jumble of toiletries on my vanity, and pushing cartons stuffed with work files under my bed for storage.

I cleaned the black-and-white marbled tiles in my bathroom and put out fresh towels, then called downstairs and asked the houseboy to have a large bouquet of flowers delivered at 4 P.M. I took a break and fixed myself a cup of hot ginger tea.

By six o'clock I had bathed and oiled my skin and put on a small amount of makeup before slipping into my indigo dress. I turned out the lights and sat quietly in a chair by my picture window. It was a space that I found soothing and centering, and with only the flicker of the candle to disturb the aura, I concentrated on keeping old doubts and fears from piercing my psyche.

Thirty minutes later my door buzzer sounded, alerting me that Bishop was waiting downstairs. I keyed in a code on my security panel, which permitted the doorman to give him access, then turned on the lights and waited for him to come upstairs.

My stomach quivered as I opened the door. Bishop was so muscular and handsome, his skin so golden and smooth, he made me forget to breathe. His mustache and hair had been freshly shaped and trimmed, and he wore a cream-colored dress shirt and black slacks. When he saw me he smiled, and that flash of white lightning creasing his face was all the proof I needed that I had made the right decision. "You look beautiful, baby," he said. "You smell good too. So fine."

"Thank you," I said, sliding my hand into his. "You look nice too." I led him into my apartment, enjoying the look of approval on his face as he surveyed my style and décor.

"Nice place, Abeni," he said, eyeing the high ceilings. "You could fit about ten of me and Malcolm's bedrooms in your dining room alone. There's peace here, baby. I feel a lot of peace and a lot of you in these open spaces, and I like that. I like the colors too. Your place really fits you."

"Thank you!" I was almost gushing from his compliments. I'd had very few visitors. Outside of my parents, a few deliverymen, and my auntie Dali, no one else had seen the inside of these walls. I gave Bishop a short tour, showing off my sitting room, my functional kitchen, and my vast bedroom. He was immediately drawn to my picture window, the area that provided me so much tranquillity and harmony, and I took this as a positive sign.

Our dinner arrived at seven, and a white-jacketed waiter lit four candles on the dining table and served us before leaving discreetly. I'd indicated that our place settings should be across from each other, but Bishop slid his plate and glass over next to mine. When our simple meal of honey-glazed chicken breasts, grilled vegetables, and yams had been served, Bishop took my hand in his.

"I'm gonna bless the food, baby, okay? I know you said your

religion is based on your Spirit Ancestors and the guidance and influence they provide, so I'm just gonna call on Spirit and God both to help us out, aiight?"

"Okay."

He closed his eyes and bowed his head. "Father and Mother God and the Ancestors that made it possible for us to be here together tonight, we ask that you bless this food we are about to eat and allow it to nourish our bodies as well as our souls." Then, nodding toward my plate, he asked, "May I?"

I was flattered. It was such a chivalrous gesture and I appreciated it. "Yes," I answered. "Please."

Bishop pulled my plate toward him and used his own cutlery to slice my chicken into bite-sized pieces. With the blade of his knife, he peeled the tender skin from my yam, then sank his fork into the brilliant orange flesh of the potato, mashing it thoroughly. That done, he set my plate before me and passed me a small saucer containing softened butter and a bowl of crumbled brown sugar. He waited until I had seasoned the yam to my taste before beginning to eat his own.

We engaged in small talk as we ate, and while the meal was tasty, we both knew it was merely a task to occupy us until we could discover how to cross the bridge that loomed before us. It would have been a shame, I had convinced myself, to forsake this chance at happiness. I had shared myself with many men, so seduction was not the issue. My doubts lay in the deception that would be involved, in the denial of rights that sleeping with Bishop would entail.

I had asked myself if I could bear the look in his eyes when he learned of my past, because concealing it was simply not an option. I owed him full disclosure of who and what I was, and it was his right to make an informed decision as to whether or not he could make love to a woman like me. Despite my internal debate, guilt was never a factor in my anxiety. Repulsion was what I feared most. To glimpse that kind of disgust in his eyes would surely kill me, yet it was a risk I felt compelled to take.

"Full?" Bishop asked, as I pushed a slice of zucchini to the other side of my plate. He'd been living on bush rations for several days and had cleaned his plate.

I smiled and nodded. "Yes, I had a snack earlier, so I wasn't very hungry."

He helped me clear the table, and while he rinsed our plates in warm water, I retrieved the insulated carrying case and repacked the utensils and condiments that had come with the meal. I was drying my hands on a dishcloth when he came up behind me. I felt his arms circle my waist and pull me close as he bent and kissed me gently on my neck.

"Thanks for dinner, baby. It was really good."

I closed my eyes and nodded. Then I leaned back, allowing my buttocks to graze his groin, and the thick heat radiating from his manhood warmed me inside. We stood that way for a few moments, and then I said, "Come." I stepped from his embrace, took his hand, and led him back to my bedroom, then stepped into his arms once again. He raised my chin with one finger and pressed his mouth to mine. Slowly, our lips parted, his tongue dancing wet and naked against mine, nibbling and probing, sucking and licking at my mouth until I was out of breath. I tasted brown sugar on his tongue, and when his hands came up to cup my breasts, his thumbs lightly grazing my twin points, I felt the strangest of sensations and my nipples stiffened and ached beneath the fabric of my dress.

He squeezed them gently, rubbing their peaks in delicious circles, and it was as though a raw nerve blazed a conduit from my breasts to my loins, electrifying everything in its path and leaving me wet and slippery as a deep moan escaped my lips.

"Bishop," I whispered as he massaged my buttocks and pulled me into him. His erection was majestic against my groin, and his breathing deepened as we rolled our pelvises against each other. I closed my eyes and snagged my lower lip between my teeth and gave in to the foreign sensations that were suddenly raging through me.

And then reality swooped down on me.

I pulled away, straightening my clothing. Not in shame, but in dread. "Bishop, we need to talk."

Desire shone in his eyes and tented the fabric of his pants. He nodded, breathing deeply, and followed me over to the bed. My eyes were downcast as I sat, and he took a seat close to me and wrapped me in his arms. "You're right, baby. There's a lot to be said, and not a whole lot of time to say it in."

Oh, he was right. He was so very right, but I remained silent. We cuddled each other on my canary-colored bedspread, and he kissed me again and then spoke. "Look, Abeni," he began. "I haven't been an angel in my life, but I've never hurt anybody who didn't hurt me."

"No, Bishop, no." I shook my head in alarm. It was I who had the sins to confess. I who needed to explain. "You don't have to—"

"But I want to, baby. Lemme just put this out there, and however you choose to deal with it, I'll respect that and hope for the best. Like I was saying, I've been wronged, and I've done wrong. I'm the son of a man, and I made sure that the men who killed my family got put down too. I got sent to jail for it and was glad to do my time, and even though it's true I got blood on my hands, I'm nobody's criminal. I don't lie and I don't steal. I'm a killer, but you can trust me with your life. Before you, I'd only met one girl who I coulda liked. She was a smart sister who had skin like yours, dark and smooth, but I knew she had her eye on Malcolm, so I stepped off. I've had other chances to get with other women, but something always held me back. Long story short, I've never laid down with a woman who I didn't pay for. Call it some kinda fucked-up consequence from the way I was raised and the things that I saw, but it's the truth. There've been a few sisters who really dug me and made no bones about it that they were game for something real and lasting, but basically I was scared to death, and at that time the only kinda women I could perform with were the kind who did it for money. Until I met you I never thought I'd have a chance for something normal. To have a woman who I could open up to without getting all red just thinking about my life. I just didn't think a woman could live with me and my sins, at least not without judging me for them. But when I met you all of that changed. I'm ready to be straight-up about my life and up-front about everything I've done."

Bishop moved closer to me and took my hand. His lips were beautiful and his soul shone in his golden eyes. "So straight up, Abeni, I love you. I'm in love with you. I wanna be with you, I wanna be yours, and if you think you can live with my past, I want you to be mine."

It was beyond ironic. Here I'd found a man who could only buy sex, and I could only give it away for free. And this was also the first time a man had ever declared his love for me, but instead of cherishing it or even echoing it, I clutched my hands to my stomach and fought it.

"What's wrong, Abeni?" He pulled me to him, his voice full of concern. Pity was the last thing I wanted from him, so I steadied myself and I did not cry. Without preamble or prelude, I opened my mouth and let my truth fly out. "I've been circumcised."

"Come again?"

"Cut. Stitched, but then later I was repaired."

I kept my eyes on him as I bit the insides of my cheeks, waiting to be crushed by his repulsion. His gaze was ever tender. It didn't change, nor did it ever leave my face.

"Damn, baby. I'm not sure I know what that really means. I mean, I think I mighta heard something about it at a women's rights rally I went to in Bangladesh, but I'm kinda fuzzy on the details."

I had imagined it would be difficult to discus my *yreau* with any man, especially Bishop, but nestled snugly in his arms, still riding the waves of his declaration of love, the words flowed from me with frankness and ease. "I am Kinaksu, and as in many other tribes throughout Africa, Kinaksu girls are circumcised and stitched to keep them chaste and pure. When I was six I was taken to our homestead, and along with several of my cousins and friends, I was cut. They cut off part of my clitoris and the outer lips of my vagina, then stitched me closed, with the belief that my honor would be preserved for my husband when I married."

"Damn, baby. That musta been some heavy stuff for a little girl to handle. And then you got it fixed? Repaired?"

I nodded. "I was lucky. My best friend, Mazani, her father was a plastic surgeon. He repaired me as much as possible, but there were limits to how much he could do and I was left badly scarred."

I didn't have the heart to tell him that it was I who had caused Mazani's death. That I suspected my own father of orchestrating the horrific accident that wiped out her family.

"I'm sorry, baby," he said again. His eyes were sad, but still the love was there. "I don't know how to take this, or what you expect me to do, but I love you, baby, and there ain't a damn thing you can tell me that'll change that."

"But that is not all," I said miserably. "I was damaged by my cutting. Wounded so badly I did even more hurtful things just to block out my pain. I brought dishonor on my father, I shamed my family name, I . . ." I just couldn't go on.

Bishop pulled me into his arms and began kissing me again. My eyelids, my nose, my lips, my chin. I shivered as his hands roamed my body, caressing the swell of my hip, squeezing my full breasts, circling my waist.

"Stand up, Abeni." He rose and pulled me to my feet. His hands were gentle but exacting as he turned me around and lowered the zipper on my dress down to the crown of my buttocks. Sliding it past my hips, he let the dress fall to the floor in an indigo pool.

Beneath it I wore a white lace bra and matching panties, and I felt his eyes traversing the muscles of my back and burning into my skin as he admired me from behind. Under the gentle pressure of his fingers, I turned to face him and heard his breath catch as he gazed upon the hills of my breasts and the tautness of my stomach.

I leaned toward him as he unhooked the front of my bra and watched the candlelight flicker over my bare skin. Smiling into my eyes, Bishop touched me with a tenderness that I'd never known, then lay me gently on the bed.

"Please . . ." I whimpered as he licked my nipples, suckling from first one and then the other. I felt tiny bursts of fire leaping from my breasts and dampening my crotch, and I arched my back, feeding him my flesh and urging him to take more.

Hovering above me, he kissed a trail down my stomach, pausing to swirl his tongue in the hollow of my navel. I panted as his tongue crawled lower, every fiber in my being merging with the pool between my legs, causing it to boil and overflow.

Using the tips of his fingers, Bishop grasped the elastic of my panties and slid them down my hips and pushed them past my knees, and then slipped them over my ankles. I felt a rush of air between my legs, and I wanted to resist. No, I thought, struggling against him yet desperate to explore what his love had awakened in me. My vagina clenched and spasmed, and the stump of my clitoris pulsed as his lips bore down and his warm mouth descended upon it. "Bishop!" I cried out. I was exposed to him, my genital flaws in plain sight.

He never faltered. "I love you, Abeni."

He planted tender kisses on my thighs and licked behind my knees.

"I've lived like a dog," I whispered.

"But you have the soul of a queen."

He pushed my knees up and spread my legs wide.

And when his kisses touched me there, I heard trumpets blare and saw streaks of fire dance behind my lids. His tongue dipped into the river that raged between my malformed vaginal lips, and it climbed north to massage my imperfect clitoris with broad, loving strokes.

I clutched the back of his head and gyrated into his face, blossoming like a flower and offering up my nectar as my hips rose from the bed to meet him. Suddenly a spark ignited between my legs and I stiffened and cried out. Wave after wave of pleasure, unlike anything I had ever before experienced, washed over me, consuming me in a swelling surf, stiffening my back and propelling me over a cliff of delight.

And then I climaxed, a scream tearing from my throat as I pushed his mouth deeply into my center, defying the boundaries of gravity and not caring whether I lived or died when I fell to the ground.

Many minutes passed before I was able to move. My loins ached and my entire body felt wrung out, my desire satiated and my muscles lazy. The shadows had lengthened, the glow of the candles now our sole source of light.

"Come," I whispered. My fingers were on his belt and I touched his erection. It was my turn to give, and I wanted to repay him in the only way I really knew how.

But Bishop wasn't done. He touched my fingers, stilling them, and rose from the bed.

"Close your eyes, baby," he said, and although his voice was thick with love, I feared that perhaps when I reopened them he would have disappeared, gone from my life forever.

"Relax, Abeni. Close your eyes."

Lying naked before him, I allowed my eyelids to flutter and close. I sensed him moving away from me, and for a brief moment panic rose in my chest. And then I heard him. Near my vanity table, searching, it sounded like, for an object.

Moments later he was back at my side. "Keep 'em closed, baby, aiight?"

I nodded. At the bottom of the bed, the mattress shifted under his weight. I flinched as I felt his hand close on my right foot.

"Sshh . . . It's okay, baby. I'm here. Bishop is here, and from now on won't nothing ever hurt you."

He lifted my foot into his lap, and a sharp odor filled the air. He hummed a soft tune that I did not recognize, and then I felt a cool liquid being applied to my toenails. It was the most amazing moment of my life. After what I had just felt, and what I was still feeling, there was no doubt in my mind that Bishop had opened my eyes and let the future in. I could have stayed there with him forever. Enjoying the sensation of his hands on my feet. Small strokes, broad strokes, man hands that were strong yet placid, caring hands, loving hands, capable hands, faithful hands. Bishop's hands, polishing my toenails.

# EIGHTEEN

I had instructed the driver to return at nine, and leaving Bishop lying across my bed I walked naked into the kitchen and placed a short telephone call, then showered and changed into a clean dress. He seemed a little surprised when I said I wanted to go out, but he didn't protest. When the car arrived, we slid into the backseat, and Bishop looked at me with an eyebrow raised. "You gonna let me in on the secret, or what?" His smile was radiant, but it did little to calm the nervousness spreading through my stomach.

I took a deep breath. The car was navigating through Kairami traffic, and we didn't have much farther to travel. "I am taking you to my parents' apartment. I want you to meet my father."

Bishop fell silent for a moment, then nodded. "I was wondering when you were planning on taking a brothah out the closet. I've heard a lot about your father, about how he runs things to the max here in Kairami. I figured since I was only gonna be around for a hot minute, you might not want to go through all the trouble of explaining me. Or that maybe this just wasn't a relationship you were proud of."

"That's not it at all," I protested. "I have never taken a man home with me before. That's just not the way things are done here."

He settled back in his seat and put his arm around me. "Well, that's how they're gonna get done tonight."

His confidence was not enough to dispel my uneasiness. A thousand scenarios played out in my mind. I had told my parents to expect a guest, and while I told them Bishop was an American traveling with the Peace Corps, I had given them no indication that we were involved in a relationship.

Minutes later we pulled up outside of my childhood home and I instructed the driver to return in an hour. Bishop reached for my hand as we approached Zayd, the middle-aged doorman, and I felt so uncomfortable that I wanted to flee. When we were alone in the elevator, I let Bishop hold me, drawing strength from his scent.

"You're shaking, baby," he said, kissing my face. "Why?"

"I'm afraid," I admitted. "My father . . ."

Bishop grinned as the doors slid open, then took my hand once more. "Don't worry about your daddy, sweetie. Chill, baby. I got this. I've been traveling with the Peace Corps for years, and I've learned to get along with all kinds of men. By the time the night is over, me and your daddy are gonna be good friends."

⁂

My parents welcomed us into the apartment, and Bishop was gallant as he complimented my mother on the décor, and then later on the tea and flatcakes she served. I was awed by the way he carried himself in their presence. Respectful and humble but as an equal, a man in his own right, and without a hint of being intimidated by the power my father wielded.

I had been prepared to suffer through pregnant moments of uncomfortable silence, but instead the mood was jovial and warm. My mother had gone to the kitchen to fix more tea. Banjoko was dressed in a jacket and trousers and wore slippers on his feet. He and Bishop were in deep discussion regarding the Brotherhood Haven. I sat on the sofa across from the men in my life, perplexed. Neither of them could contain his excitement.

"I am a bushman by blood," my father explained. "And while I have great respect for my Kinaksu tribesmen who work the soil, Kairami is starving for highly skilled technicians."

Watching this animated exchange was simply amazing. But what was even more remarkable was the picture they presented as they sat knee to knee. Physically, the African and the African American had been cut from totally different cloths, but both were serious-minded and possessed great inner strength.

"Our goal," Banjoko was saying, "is to educate more Kinaksu youth in the areas of science and technology. Many years ago the young men of my tribe were fierce warriors. They were renowned, even beyond the Zulu or the Watusi, for their fearlessness and physical strength. Today the Kinaksu continue to display great strength and stamina, but it is used to cultivate endless fields of tea and beans, while their minds remain understimulated. Abeni tells me you have a passion for helping those in need, and what your country is doing through its Peace Corps is worthy and admirable, but if the future of the Kinaksu is to be assured, we must start plucking our young men out of the bush and planting them in the classroom. They must be taught the skills necessary to become future leaders, and to accomplish this, we must find people who can teach our youth to compete in a global market."

"I'm with you on that," Bishop agreed. "I love kids, and I have a lot of respect for teachers. Some of them have really made a big difference in my life. I worked at my grandfather's gym for a while, teaching young boys the art of boxing. You'd be surprised at how fitness and discipline in training can affect the way a kid views the rest of his life."

"You are right!" my father exclaimed, pounding Bishop on the back. "You are right! The courage and dedication that are required to learn boxing skills are the same attributes we must work to instill in the students at the Brotherhood Haven."

My mother came in, and with a nod I silently declined her offer of more tea. I was on the edge of my seat, my eyes locked on Bishop.

"Well, sir," he said, then looked at me, "if you're ever looking for somebody to step up to the plate and develop a comprehensive boxing program for your students, I'm your man."

Father and I were both confused. "But your work has been completed here. The irrigation system has been tapped and the new pipes have been primed. Your team should be moving north shortly, am I correct?"

"Yes, that's right. The team has to move on, but I don't. I'm my own man, and I'm basically doing my thing on my own time."

My breath snagged in my throat.

"But there are endless possibilities awaiting you!" Banjoko exclaimed. "The training you'll receive with the Peace Corps will prove invaluable in the future. I think you would be a great asset to the Brotherhood Haven, and because I believe a program like yours would benefit my students, I would hire you to develop one today. But what"—my father spread his arms in confusion—"what would compel you to do such a thing? Why would you be willing to remain in Kairami, simply to teach our youth to box? What could I offer you that would entice you to stay?"

Bishop met my father's gaze with confidence. "Your daughter," he said, then crossed the room and knelt at my feet. He pressed his lips to my hand and said, "I want to marry Abeni."

⁚⁚⁚⁚⁚⁚⁚⁚

I was not sure why my father agreed so readily to Bishop's proposal, but nor was I surprised. I was twenty-four and unmarried, an anomaly in Kenya, and since there appeared to be no man in Kairami, certainly none of the Kinaksu, eager to marry a woman whose honor had been so thoroughly debased, perhaps Banjoko thought this marriage might restore me to respectability.

"Abeni is our only child," he had warned Bishop, the joviality disappearing from his voice. "Her mother and I love her, and while her life has been problematic, as her name implies, we asked for her, and she is ours. You taking her as your wife will not change that, but it will entail great responsibility, and I will look to you to ensure her happiness."

My mother cried and I allowed her to hold me, surprised to find a small measure of comfort in her arms. "Is this what you want, Abeni?" I was so overjoyed I could only nod. I had never been more certain of anything in my life, and cloaked in the promise of Bishop's love, I finally felt protected and secure.

Whatever my father's motives, marriage to Bishop would prove to be a bliss that could not be rivaled. My parents arranged a large ceremony to be held weeks later at the same Kinaksu homestead where my *yreau* had been performed. And with Bishop by my side, mingling effortlessly with my Kinaksu family, even the memory of my cutting could not overshadow my joy.

He had expressed only one regret: that his grandfather could not be there to share this day with him. "But Malcolm will be here," he'd promised. "No doubt about that."

When Malcolm returned to Kairami from an assignment in Mombasa, I became even more conscious of the depth of their bond. They loved each other in subtle ways, and I was thankful that Malcolm extended his love to me as well. "This is good," he told me shortly after the ceremony as Bishop shook hands with the male Kinaksu and prepared to cut the ceremonial goat. "You're exactly what he needed, Abeni, and I know he's gonna do his best to make you happy."

Malcolm was like an overgrown puppy—happy, boundless, and filled with energy. I understood how important he was to Bishop, and already I loved him too. He opened his arms to give me a congratulatory hug, and the top of my head barely reached his chin.

"Thank you, Malcolm." I kissed his cheek and smiled.

Later that night, as we stood together in a bathtub filled with warm water, Bishop lit scented candles and bathed me by their glow. I trembled like a small bird as he dipped a soft cloth into the soap-filled water and trailed it across my body. He began at my neck, letting the bubbles cascade over my breasts and dribble down my stomach before disappearing between my thighs.

Breathing deeply, he turned me around, bracing me in his strong arms, then washed my shoulders and slid the cloth down my back, then slowly, ever so slowly, rubbed my buttocks with strokes that were so sexy and sensuous I moaned and pressed myself back against him, panting at the feel of his coarse pubic hairs scraping against my tender skin.

When we were washed, Bishop dried me with a thick Egyptian towel, then wrapped it around my torso and lifted me into his strong arms. I was a tall, muscular girl, but he held me with ease, and I closed my eyes and pressed my cheek against the hardness of his chest as he carried me into our bedroom. He lowered me to the bed with a gentleness born of love, then parted my towel and stared at my bare flesh.

"You're beautiful, baby," he whispered, and I glimpsed the naked need in his eyes. He lay down beside me, our skin tones contrasting, his manhood thick and glorious, arched and straining toward my center. I took it in both hands and marveled at its power, and in a sense it was the first penis I had ever truly touched.

We kissed and caressed each other until perspiration beaded on our skin, and when Bishop finally mounted me, sliding his thickness into me inch by blessed inch, my clitoris pulsed and my vagina clenched, and I held tight to his arms and climaxed with a force so powerful I thought I would die.

# NINETEEN

Bishop had very little in the way of personal belongings, so making room for him in my apartment did not present a problem. I had offered to look for a house outside of the city, but he wouldn't hear of it.

"I like it here, Abeni. I like the town, I like the people, and I like how I feel whenever I walk through these doors. Your essence is in the walls, baby. I can feel you here, even when I'm alone, and I like it like that." He reached for me and rubbed the small of my back. "Besides, if we ever have a baby, we can put him in the spare room."

"Or her!" I laughed, letting him kiss me.

"That's right," he agreed. "Or her."

We honeymooned at a resort near Mount Kenya, spending two wonderful weeks learning new things about each other and making endless, powerful love.

Upon our return to Kairami, we settled into our new life as a couple, and I took great pleasure in pampering Bishop and being pampered even more in return. Every day I left work by four and rushed home to bathe and oil myself with his favorite scents, then change into something sexy while I prepared new and exciting meals.

"Aw, hell. I done got you spoiled," he would tell me, laughing as he oiled the parts between my braids or pressed my dresses for work.

"Why are you so good to me?" I asked.

He thought for a moment, then said, "I didn't have long with my parents, but what time we had was good. When I got out of jail, Sugar Baby and Poppa Daddy picked up the slack without missing a beat. With them I heard all about what Armstrong men did and didn't do. What I heard most was, 'Armstrong men take care of their women.'" He shrugged. "I'm a Johnson, and that's a fact. Slim Willie's blood runs hot in my veins, but maybe I'm part Armstrong now too." His voice trailed off, and a faraway look entered his eyes. "Besides, I get to honor my mother every time I honor you."

I felt bad about his loss, and despite the trials I had faced because of my family, I knew I was fortunate to have them in my life. Bishop had Malcolm and an elderly grandfather. That was it. Later that night I did something I'd never before imagined doing. I prayed to Spirit and the Ancestors to touch my womb and my husband's loins and to send us a child who would heal Bishop's heart and fill the abyss created by his parents' passing.

And when we made love, I clasped my legs tightly around his back, loath to let him withdraw, and long after his penis became soft and flaccid and slipped from my folds, I held my legs tight, harboring the seed that was navigating through my body and rushing forth to fertilize my womb.

░░░░░░

The Ancestors were merciful and judged us worthy. Just three months after we married, a sickness fell upon me each morning when I awakened and a foul taste arose in my mouth. After several such mornings, Bishop put his arms around me as I crawled back into bed, my stomach flipping and curling.

"C'mere, girl," he said with a chuckle as I groaned in misery. "You been feeling bad almost every day this week. I haven't seen no blood this month neither."

I hid my face beneath the blanket, embarrassed by his mention of my menstrual flow. I had been taught to view my monthly bleeding as something foul and unclean, and during the years of my infibulation and the tiny hole that was my only portal, it certainly seemed to be so.

But Bishop had no such inhibitions. Unlike the African men I'd known, he found nothing disgusting about the female body performing its natural functions. He insisted on showering with me when I bled, just as he did every other day of the month, and twice during that time he'd spread a towel beneath me in bed, then taking care not to crush my tender breasts, made passionate love to me. Afterward he bathed us both.

"You know what this means, right, Satin?" He had told me my skin was so dark and smooth it was like a satin gift from God, and I liked the sound the word made slipping from his lips. I shook my head and fought another wave of nausea. He pulled up my nightgown and cupped the heaviness of my bare breasts. "They're full, Abeni." Then he slid his hand down to my flat belly. "I think we mighta went and did something wonderful, girl. I think we're gonna have us a baby."

Two weeks later a blood test followed by a pelvic exam confirmed Bishop's suspicions.

"I'd say you were about six weeks along," said Dr. Olwana, a female gynecologist who had been referred by my aunt Dali. She ordered additional tests and scheduled a follow-up appointment for me in four weeks.

Bishop was the only man waiting in the sitting area, and when I emerged from the examination his grin of expectation became magnified into a broad smile of joy.

"Six weeks along," I parroted the doctor, and right there in a room filled with women, he pulled me into his arms, lifting me off my feet as he gave me a deep tongue kiss.

"I'm so happy, baby," he whispered. "I'm gonna take damn good care of you."

We waited a few days before sharing the news with my parents, and seated at their dining room table munching on fruit and cheese one Saturday afternoon, I experienced a level of joy that was completely unrivaled.

"Banjoko, Ziwani," Bishop began, "I wanna thank you for trusting me with your beautiful daughter. I never thought in a million years that I'd find somebody as special as Satin. She means the world to me, and I've made it my business to see that she's happy for the rest of my life. Without giving out all the hot details, me and Satin are pregnant. We're gonna have a baby."

"A baby?" Dali exclaimed, setting her fork down and reaching for my hand. "This is wonderful!"

Tears sprang to my mother's eyes. She cried at the slightest bit of happiness in my life, and upon hearing she would soon be a grandmother, she rose from her chair and stood by my side. "Abeni," she croaked, beaming down at me with a look of wonder on her face. The ever-present distance between us dissipated, and I reached out and hugged my face to her stomach. Her hands were in my hair and stroking my back. "A baby . . . this is the greatest gift of all. The gift of a fruitful womb. I am so happy for you."

But it was Banjoko who was the most elated. "Congratulations!" he boomed, shaking Bishop's hand and then kissing my cheek. "My first grandchild! Dali is right, this is wonderful news! My darling, Abeni. With this child lies our hope and faith for the future. I am very proud of both of you. Now, let us celebrate!"

I was overjoyed. I had done something my father was proud of and had finally gained his respect and approval. Bishop joined my father for a toast and a drink, while I satisfied myself with a cup of freshly made carrot juice.

I was sick until my third month, and then suddenly I blossomed as pregnancy began to agree with me. My skin glowed with health, and my hair, already thick and strong, fell around my shoulders like an ebony mane. Bishop was doing well at the Brotherhood Haven. In addition to leading a course called the Focus Factor, where he taught mental discipline and the history and techniques of great fighters, he had sketched out his own design plans, then hired a construction crew to build a gym in a building adjacent to the main school facility. I paid him several visits at work and was awed by his superb physical strength and the way his body moved in the ring. One of the other young men, a science teacher from the West Indies, had also done a bit of boxing, and observing the two of them as they pointed out techniques and methods to the score of wide-eyed boys crowding the ring was truly amazing.

During my sixth month I began working half-days, and to occupy myself I started searching stores for the perfect theme for our developing nursery. I decided to forgo the traditional nursery colors and tap into my own creativity. I spent hours selecting an array of nontoxic paints. I asked for Bishop's input on an original color scheme, but he told me whatever I picked would be fine with him. On countless afternoons I mixed a myriad of paints and took endless notes until I discovered hybrid colors that were exciting and unique. After considerable thought, I settled on a strawberry-salmon and lemon-lime, and alternated the four walls with these colors.

Bishop seemed astounded by the final results. When I finally permitted him to enter the nursery he was surprised into speechlessness, and at first I wasn't sure if that was a good thing or not. The kindly wife of an Omorru and Associates employee had hand-sewn a tiny quilt and pillow sham for the crib, and by my eighth month I had received gifts of clothing, toys, and several practical items from Banjoko's wealthy friends, and a box filled with hand-carved ducks and birds from my family in the bush. All that was left to complete the portrait of our lives was our much-anticipated baby.

"Girl or boy?" I had asked Bishop during the early days of my pregnancy.

"Doesn't matter," he had said with a shrug. "Let's just concentrate on getting us a healthy baby, and I'll be happy no matter what."

I wished I could share his sentiments. It mattered greatly to me, the sex of my child. I waged an internal battle that alternated between terror and resignation because I understood the tribulations life could bring to an African girl in these parts.

It was true that I had been more fortunate than most. My father was wealthy, and more important, he had high social status, and I had been spared a life of toil and hardship in the bush. I had reveled in a luxurious apartment and received an adequate education, and had never known the pain of an empty stomach or the ache of an overbent back. Yet, I'd also lived and learned, and there were some things that transcended class and social status in Kairami. Some areas were so steeped in tradition and cultural norms that very few women escaped them unscathed, and it was this certain knowledge that haunted me in the dark hours of the night as I lay beside Bishop listening to his calm, even breathing.

In my dreams the baby was born sexless, a smooth, blank space where a penis or vagina should have been. Relief would flood through me, even as Bishop cried out in despair and the nurses shook their heads in pity, and then my smile would fade as a deformed vagina slowly morphed and materialized, hellish and three-dimensional, where moments before there had been none.

I would awaken with a scream on my lips. Icy fingers of fear would clutch my heart as my unborn child kicked and stretched inside my bulging womb. I'd snuggle close to Bishop, backing into his naked body spoon-fashion, placing his arm protectively around my waist, his strong hand cupping the crown of my swollen stomach, and then, sighing and entwining my legs with his, I would sleep.

I was in the midst of such a nightmare when I felt it. A deep, searing pain that began in my pelvis and radiated around to hammer at my lower back. A sensation like boiling water pushed against my bladder. "Bishop," I moaned, flinging off the sheets and stumbling into the bathroom. I made it to the commode just as a gush of warm fluid spewed from my vagina and my middle was squeezed in a vise grip.

"Easy, baby."

Bishop was there and I reached for him, biting my lip against the tide of pain, grateful for his hands on my face, my arms, and my back.

"I think," I moaned, leaning forward and pressing my face into his groin, "I think my water broke."

He chuckled softly. "I was hoping like hell that's what it was. I would hate to think my woman was on the toilet pissing harder than me." He lifted me to my feet, and we both saw the blood-tinged liquid running down my legs. "Okay," Bishop said, supporting my weight as he guided me across the bathroom. "In the shower for a quick rinse-off. I'll call the hospital and the driver, and then we're outta here."

I panted through the contractions as Bishop soaped me briefly, then rinsed me off. I was barely conscious of anything except the pain as we sped toward the hospital. Dr. Olwana met us there and gave me a short examination, then hustled me into the delivery room.

"You're doing fine, baby," Bishop murmured over and over, holding my hand as I bore down and rode the pressure that lanced through me. It was uncommon for Kinaksu men to be included in the birthing process, but early on Bishop and I had insisted he be involved at every level. I squeezed my eyes shut and clutched his hand as they urged me to push. After several tries I felt something round pop from my vagina, and after another push the baby's torso and legs slithered free as well.

"It's a girl!" Dr. Olwana exclaimed, and I heard Bishop's shout of glee.

I opened my eyes and gazed upon the beauty of our baby, her

face a tiny replica of the man I loved, and in that moment all my nightmares were banished and anxiety dissipated like particles in the wind.

"Thank you, baby. Thank you." Bishop was kissing me, murmuring over and over, but all I could hear was the squalling wonder that was She; and with her warrior father by my side, I prayed to the Ancestors to permit this child the sovereignty that had been granted by virtue of her birth, and as the prayer flew from my lips, Spirit whispered in my ear and gave me her name: Hundiata.

work and dressed her in a pumpkin-colored shirt and shorts that had been a gift from my aunt Hazika. "I'm taking her down to the American consulate today," he told me. "They'll snap a couple of passport pictures, then I can register her as an American citizen born abroad. That way," he added, noting my alarm, "when you get your passport back, we can fly to Alabama and I can show you how collard greens from down South are supposed to taste."

Bishop grew annoyed and quiet whenever the issue of my passport arose. He wanted to go home, wanted to visit his parents' grave and needed to see his grandfather, but he didn't want to leave me and Hunnie behind. My passport remained canceled, and on the one occasion I mustered up the courage to ask my father to have it reissued, he gave me a look that allowed me to see my life for exactly what it was, and if I had fantasized that all was forgiven and he'd forgotten my shame-filled past, the fire in his eyes made it clear that I was mistaken. Yes, I was married to a wonderful man who loved me more than he loved life, and certainly, I had a beautiful, healthy daughter and an enviable job waiting for me the moment she reached six months of age, but in spite of these things, my freedom was not absolute. There were limitations and restrictions imposed on me that I could not transcend. I could not decide to book passage and take a simple vacation outside of my country, and while marriage and a child had rendered my boundaries less oppressive, Bishop's yearning for home made me acutely aware that they still existed.

I wrestled in silence with the issue of my freedom, and a week before I was scheduled to return to work, I arranged to have lunch with my father at his golf club.

"I'd like to have my passport reinstated." I had been careful to dress modestly and to pay him deference in the weeks preceding our meeting, yet after years of living in Kairami and internalizing the ideals of a patriarchal society and its legitimization of the influence my father wielded over me, what I meant to convey as persuasive and direct actually came out sounding weak and ineffective.

He sipped his tea casually before answering. "Why must we revisit this, Abeni? It would kill your mother to lose you again. You are living a wonderful life now. Those dark days are far behind you, and Kenya is your birth home. You have a good husband who does wonderful work at the Brotherhood Haven and who treats you well, and you have given us a beautiful granddaughter to preserve our bloodline. What more do you need, my child? Why can't you be happy with things the way they are?"

"I want my freedom, Father," I told him. "Bishop has a grandfather who loves him in much the same way you love me. He has given up everything to remain here with us. And now he wants to see his grandfather. He wants Hunnie and I to accompany him to the United States."

I heard his sharp intake of breath, and the look in his eyes nearly shattered me where I sat. I could feel my muscles and bones atrophying and cracking, then crumbling to the floor like elephant dust.

"My blood," he spoke through lips so tight they barely moved, "is in the soil of Kenya. Never again will you be permitted to take a drop of it from this country. Hundiata is *Kinaksu,* and will be raised in a manner befitting my granddaughter. You nearly ruined your life with your headstrong notions and unnatural desires, but your mother and I are stronger now. Wiser. Abeni Teboso Omorru, I swear on the souls of my Ancestors, you will never leave Kenya.

"Nor will Hundiata."

Bishop was a doting and attentive father who relished the task of preparing Hunnie to greet each new day. He would awaken her at dawn to warm a bottle of breast milk, then bathe her in milk-soap water and oil her brown skin until it shone. He had established a routine that seemed to suit them both, and when my car arrived at 7 A.M., I'd leave jealously as he sang to her and tickled her face with his mustache.

For the first eighteen months of her life Hunnie spent her days with my mother and Dali. Bishop's car detoured past my mother's apartment each morning, then sped back across town to have him at work by nine.

In the afternoons Bishop left work at three and had his driver take him to retrieve Hunnie before bringing them both home to our apartment. While there were some who felt he was too involved with the daily needs of an infant, I was proud of Bishop and looked upon his devotion to our daughter as further proof of his love for me.

I watched their interactions for hours, but could never find the right words to capture and express the beauty of what was transpiring between them. Bishop and I nurtured her equally, both of our arms were her enclaves of comfort and love, and my parents became an extension of that love, showering her with attention and affection and filling her with the security that extended families in my country often provided.

When Hunnie turned three, Bishop flew home to America. Malcolm was getting married to a girl from their hometown named Gebra Burns, and he wanted Bishop there at his side. During the first week he was gone my mother called me in a panic because Hunnie refused to eat. By the third day my father was insisting she be taken to the hospital, but instinctively I knew that Hunnie was not ill. My daughter simply missed her father, and it broke my heart to hear her pitiful cries for him, especially during the long nights that he was away.

There was something different about Bishop when he returned.

"Daddy loves you," he whispered at the airport, clutching Hunnie so tightly she dropped her juice cup. "Daddy missed you so much."

"Your face is scratchy," she scolded him in her sweet baby voice, but her arms remained clasped around his neck, happy to have him back as well.

Bishop kissed me warmly, but our conversation seemed stilted. He told me that Malcolm and Gebra had flown to Hawaii for their honeymoon, and that his grandfather was aging and anxious to see Hunnie. His voice and demeanor were even, yet I sensed a change in my husband that began in his heart and stared at me from his eyes.

"We need to find Hunnie a nursery school or child-care center," he announced two days after his return. "She's not a little baby anymore, and she needs to be around other kids her age."

I was mortified. "B-but why?" I asked, trembling. This would kill my mother, who after diligently caring for Hunnie for three years would surely take it as a personal affront. "She loves my mother, and Dali too. They have a routine and she is comfortable with them, Bishop. I feel better having her with my family than I would leaving her with complete strangers."

"Oh, yeah?" he asked, grabbing his hat and striding toward the door. "Well, I sure as hell don't!" He slammed the door on his way out.

I was concerned. Of course we had argued and disagreed in the past, but until now our opinions had converged wherever Hunnie was concerned, and I could only wonder what Bishop was feeling inside. He refused to discuss the matter further and left it to me to break the news to my parents.

"Why is he taking her away from us?" my father asked, alarmed.

"He wants her to have other children to play with," I said weakly. "He says Hunnie is very intelligent and could benefit from being in a more structured setting."

"Of course she is intelligent. She is an Omorru. But Hundiata is well cared for here. Already she speaks two languages and can write her name. How does he explain her progress if she is not learning new things with us each day?"

I felt beaten under their barrage of questions and could provide them with no answers. Somehow my father's anger at Bishop had transformed into disapproval of me, and I spent the next hour opening and closing my mouth, wanting to dispute my husband's decision and thus appease my father, yet unable to summon the strength to do either.

In the end Bishop won out, but his victory was for the battle and not the war. He found a day-care center he thought was suitable, and while Hunnie cried in the beginning and complained of missing her grandmother and Aunt Dali, she eventually settled in, making many new friends and becoming the darling of her teacher's eye. Over the next two years Hunnie grew tall and strong, dark like me but each day looking more and more like Bishop. It amazed me that there were times that I was sure the eyes that greeted me with laughter and wonder each morning belonged to my husband, but there were also days when staring down at her, my father's face laughed up at me as well.

For the most part her morning routine remained the same, but instead of Bishop awakening to her cries of hunger at dawn, now Hunnie at five was old enough to climb from her bed and slide in between Bishop and me each morning. We had adapted to sleeping in modest clothing by the time she was two, and I delighted in the feel of her small body nestling between us, snuggling into the warmth created from the heat of our bodies.

Although we were not consciously trying, Bishop and I were prepared to parent a second child, but month after month my menses flowed with the regularity of the moon. Yet there was no disappointment in my failure to conceive a second time, as Hunnie was more than enough to fill our lives with joy and complete the triangle of our love.

We were living our days as most people do, believing ourselves the masters of our destinies, entrenched in a routine that was comfortable if endless, working, making love, quarreling and making more love, raising a daughter who was happy and self-determining, and unless you looked carefully, you might not have noticed the cracks forming in the veneer of our lives. It had been easy for me to forget the horror of my past, to pretend certain things had never happened, to distance myself from the acts I had committed as if those crimes belonged to some other girl.

Until Mazani came back.

In my dreams the friend of my youth stared up at me from

troubled eyes. She was submerged in water, her hair floating above her head like black seaweed, although I heard her voice clearly and sensed her message of impending doom. "I'm sorry, Abeni," she said, shaking her head. "I'm so sorry."

"What?" I would scream, and plunge my head beneath the surface of the water trying to reach her. But all I found were fish. Fish of all species and sizes, swimming in schools, and somehow I knew they were symbolic of Hunnie. When I withdrew my head from the brilliant blue of the water, Mazani would once again be visible, the warning in her eyes woeful and unmistakable. "I'm sorry, Abeni. I'm sorry."

I would awaken from these dreams shaking in terror, with the faint aroma of seawater in my nostrils. Quietly, so as not to disturb Bishop, I would ease out of bed and flee to Hunnie's room, crawling into her bed and holding her tightly as she slept, as if the strength in my womanly arms was enough to defend us both from her destiny.

Soon enough I would learn that it wasn't.

# TWENTY-ONE

We had been summoned to my parents' apartment, and because it was my father who made the call, I understood its seriousness. Bishop had worked late and was not very eager to go back out after dinner, but I told him Banjoko had requested we both be present, and as my mother had been recently diagnosed with arterial sclerosis, I was fearful that this visit might involve news of her declining health.

Dali let us into the apartment, and when I reached to greet her with a customary kiss, her face was somber and she did not meet my eyes. "I am going to my room to help Hunnie practice the new song I taught her," she said, taking Hunnie's hand and turning her around at the door. "Come, Hunnie. We will sing to each other until we know all the words."

I watched them walk away, mildly surprised, but when I glanced at Bishop there was fatigue in his face but no real concern. My parents were waiting for us in the parlor. My mother sat stiffly on her chaise longue, and my father stood by the window with his back to us. The air was charged with tension, and immediately a burning knot formed in the pit of my stomach.

"How's everybody doing?" Bishop asked, and although my mother gave him a small nod, neither she nor my father spoke. "So what's up?" Bishop directed his question at my father's back. "You wanted to see us, right? Everything okay?"

"It is time." My father turned around, and I was struck by the stoniness of his face. It was a face I had seen only during the worst periods of my life, the last time being years earlier when I asked to have my passport restored, but never had he shown this side of himself in Bishop's presence. "It is time to prepare Hundiata for life as a Kinaksu."

I looked from my father to Bishop, and even in my rising panic I noted the similar strength in their eyes. My ears were buzzing and I felt gorge rising to my throat.

Bishop asked, "Oh, yeah?"

My father spoke with none of the usual warmth he reserved for Bishop. His stance was that of a bull facing a lion, aggressive and prepared to do battle. "In Kenya, there are many customs that you may not be familiar with, Bishop. As part of our culture, and to ensure the health of our daughters, we have our children initiated with a ceremony and festivities at our tribal homeland. And the time has come for Hundiata to partake in such an initiation."

Bishop actually laughed. "Just what kind of ceremony are you talking about? I mean, Hunnie's only five. What does she know about special rituals and stuff?" He looked to me for clarification, and the horror I was feeling radiated from every orifice of my body. "What's he talking about, Satin?"

I opened my mouth, but my throat felt sealed shut, and not even the tiniest sound could I utter. I turned away from his stare, hiding the helplessness welling in my heart, but because he knew me so well Bishop read my emotions, and then suddenly he knew.

He turned on my father in rage and disbelief.

"You've gotta be out of your mind. You want to fuck up my baby girl the same way you fucked up yours?" I flinched at Bishop's language, as did my mother.

My father spoke. "There are things your American women do that have caused the moral decay of your entire nation. But here in Kenya we are concerned about our daughters. We guard their honor and protect their reputations. Hunnie cannot remain open. It would destroy her. Ruin any chances she might have for a normal life. I know many things about you, Bishop. You were raised with prostitutes and spent time in prison. And look at Abeni." He gestured toward me as if there were no greater proof of what dishonor could bring. "Do you know why she was sent abroad? Has she told you anything about her life during those years? She was a—"

"Hunnie!" Bishop yelled, summoning her from Dali's rooms. "C'mere, Sweetie Peetie. Come to Daddy!" He strode over to my father, his finger inches from Banjoko's nose. "If you even think"—Bishop's voice was low and deadly, a pitch I had never heard before—"about touching my daughter, I'll kill you."

"You do not understand," my father said, but there was no compromise in his voice. "We failed to have Abeni reclosed, and her life came to ruin. Why do you think we permitted her to marry you? After the disgusting things she'd done, no respectable African man would have her. We will not let that happen to Hundiata. She is of my flesh, of my blood, and I will stop at nothing to ensure her honor."

Bishop's face was a mask of rage. The look he gave me was one of pure disgust. "You hear that, Abeni? After everything they put you through, after the way you suffered worse than a goddamn dog, they wanna do it to Hunnie too. Tell 'em, baby. Tell 'em both to kiss your ass where the sun don't shine. You ain't gotta fear him no more, baby. He'd have to go through me to get to you, and trust me, this motherfucker would never make it. There's no way you'd agree to anything like that, right? You wouldn't let anybody cut our baby down there, right, Abeni? *Right?*"

I could not speak. For the first time in my life I identified with my mother. I understood her plight and realized just how much she had loved me—before, during, and after my *yreau*. But I could not speak. Instead, I put my head in my lap and wrapped my arms around my knees.

A wounded noise of disbelief flew from Bishop's lips. "Oh, shit," he said, and bolted from the room. He yelled for Hunnie, and I heard her ask, "Where's Mommy?" Then the door slammed and they were gone.

There was no air in the room. I raised my head and looked at my mother, searching for what, I did not know. She met my gaze unwaveringly. "It is for the best," she said, and I almost believed her.

"One week," my father warned, his eyes deadly and resolute. "You must begin feeding Hundiata *njha* and *ngomi ya egemba,* in one week."

░░░░░░░░

I have no idea how long I sat there. Holding myself. Praying. Damning my wretched life.

"Come, Abeni." Dali's arms were on me, gently urging me to stand. I looked around the room. My parents were nowhere in sight. I allowed Dali to lead me into the kitchen, where she sat me down and washed my face with a paper cloth, then made me take small sips of water.

"My baby," I whispered as a wave of pain struck me high in the chest. I pushed the water aside and pressed my face to the cool marble of the table.

"It is difficult, I know," Dali said, her voice comforting but firm. "There are things that you understand, Abeni, that Bishop will never understand. He is not of us, therefore his perceptions of our way of life may be distorted. You must make him understand that the *yreau* is necessary for a Kinaksu girl." She put her hands on my cheeks and forced me to look at her. "You must find a way to convince your husband of this if you are to ensure your daughter's purity."

I moaned, pulling away. A heaviness pressed deeply into my

chest, weighing me down and causing my head to explode with bullets of pain. There was nothing I could do that would turn out to be right. I was torn between two worlds, trapped in a nightmare from which there was no awakening. Trapped in a culture where cutting was viewed as protective and defending. It was true that I had suffered enormously after my *yreau*. But this was Kenya, and I had also suffered greatly after being repaired, and the pain of being ridiculed and shunned as an unclean pariah had been almost as devastating as the knife. Expulsion and isolation were the penalties of an intact clitoris, an open vagina. It would kill me if my own daughter were to experience the same shame and loneliness that had haunted my life, a fate that surely awaited her if I failed in her *yreau*.

"He will hate me," I whimpered, covering my face.

"Nonsense," Dali said. "Bishop has no hatred in him. We will call a car." She grasped my wrists and forced me to stand. "And I will take you home. Together we will make Bishop understand the consequences and peril Hunnie will face if there is no *yreau*."

The apartment was dark when we arrived. Running my hand along the wall, I flipped the light switch. Followed by Dali, I swallowed deeply and went inside. Bishop was sitting cross-legged on a large pillow in the living room, cloaked in shadows and rocking our sleeping daughter in his lap.

"Bishop—" I began, but he silenced me with an upheld hand. In the glow of the moonlight I could see that the hand in the air was pale and unsteady, but it was the sight of his eyes, deadly and enraged, that nearly floored me. He unfolded his legs and adjusted Hunnie's pliant form. She was such a beautiful child, and I marveled at her perfect build. All arms and legs and growing more and more each day. Bishop stood and, cradling her tenderly in his arms, walked past me without saying a word.

I would have remained there in the foyer if Dali hadn't taken my hand and led me into the parlor. I stood in the middle of the room there until Bishop reentered, and when he strode toward me and opened his arms, I exhaled into his chest, my cheeks against the hardness of his muscles, my arms holding him tightly.

"Baby," he whispered into my hair, his voice filled with anguish, "this just can't be. What they want just can't be. Why would they even ask us to do some crazy shit like that to her?"

My throat was closed and I could not speak. All I could do was hold on to him. Hold on and pray I wouldn't be swept away by the river that surged within me. We stood together, embracing each other for long moments. Bishop trembled in shock and disbelief. I shed tears born of guilt and divergence.

Joining us and placing one arm around each of our waists, Dali spoke. "Bishop, dear, can we sit? I know this is very difficult for you to understand, and actually, it is difficult even to explain, but if you are willing to hear me out, I'd like to try."

We stood in a triangle in the center of the room, and I held my breath until I saw Bishop's nod. Slight, almost imperceptible, but indicative of his willingness to listen.

Bishop and I sat on the sofa, and Dali pulled an armchair close. It felt good when Bishop reached into my lap and took my hand, rubbing it between his own.

"I understand that your belief system is Western and liberal. That is part of what makes you the wonderful person you are, and over the years your perspectives on many issues have been refreshing and enlightening. In your country, you tend to believe that your way is the best way, often the only way. Perhaps it is, but then, what if it is not? In Kenya, we value chastity in our women, and there are many people of all tribes, religions, and social classes who believe the *yreau* to be a critical first step to ensuring honor and reducing sexual desire in young girls, and this, Bishop, is what helps them through adolescence. It helps them preserve their virginity."

Bishop leaned forward. "That's some bullshit! There are plenty of virgins out there in the world whose folks wouldn't even think about doing something like that to them." He was enraged. "And who the fuck says I wanna 'reduce' my daughter's sexual desire? I want Hunnie to have the best of *everything,* and that includes sex. Everything the good Lord gave her when she was born, my baby girl is gonna have it until the day she dies, and that goes for her clitoris and whatever else yawl let these brothers over here talk you into cutting off your goddamn coochies."

"Bishop!" Dali said. "Calm down! You are talking like an American, but you are living in Kenya! Don't you understand? You cannot impose your own value system here! It is Hundiata who will suffer if this ritual is not performed, not you. To appease your narrow-minded thinking, it is your precious daughter who will be ridiculed and taunted, looked upon as something filthy and tainted. She will never have a husband. Is that what you want for her? Is it?"

I cringed. Bishop breathed audibly, expelling his anger into the air. When he finally spoke, his words were foul and clipped. "You're good people, Dali, and I love you. But don't you tell me to calm the fuck down, and don't ever tell me what I should or shouldn't want for my baby girl. Now, you're right about one thing. When it comes to circumcising little girls, I'm one narrow-minded motherfucker! And yeah, I'm an American brother thinking with an American mind. A mind that knows a woman's worth. But there ain't no law that says Hunnie's gotta stay in Kenya, and if push ever comes to shove, or if, like you put it, people start riding her the way they rode Abeni, I'll take my child down to Jomo Kenyatta and hop on the first thing smoking back to Alabama."

"It will never come to that," Dali said sadly. "In all these years in Kairami, have you not learned anything at all about Banjoko? Don't you understand that he does not consider Hundiata's *yreau* a request but a requirement? After the horrible things Abeni went through, that period of her life where Banjoko was publicly humiliated and disgraced by his only daughter, he feels a tremendous love and responsibility for Hundiata and will stop at nothing to ensure that her chastity is protected and honor is restored to the Omorru name."

I sat like stone. Like a statue without the slightest animation. Bishop glanced at me, and when I offered no assistance, he looked away and rose to his feet.

"Thanks for seeing Abeni home, Dali. Is your driver waiting downstairs?"

Dali rose to her dismissal. "Yes. He is. But I am warning you, Bishop. There will be no escaping Hunnie's *yreau*. There is usually much preparation and festivities, but it could happen at any time. Children have been known to go missing from their beds and return with a *yreau* completed. Some disappear from schools, from playgrounds, and one or two have even vanished from day-care centers. Hunnie's *yreau* is inevitable. It is just a matter of time."

I saw Bishop rock back on his feet as if the implications behind Dali's words pierced his very flesh and cut him to the bone.

"Thanks, Dali. I appreciate the heads up. But do me a favor, Auntie. Since you're the dog who brought us the bone, here's one you can take right back. You tell Banjoko that my daddy was willing to die for a houseful of whores. I'm that man's son, and Hunnie's life is in my hands. Just what does he think I *won't* do to save my baby girl?"

〰〰〰〰

Dali had gone, yet I remained affixed to the sofa. My limbs were frozen, heavily weighted, and I could not move. Bishop had locked the door and now stood watching me from the doorway. The look in his eyes was one of love and despair, fear and desperation, and it made my bones ache to see him in such pain.

"Satin," he said. "Come here, baby."

Stiffly I moved, my body bent under the weight of my own

disgrace. Bishop met me halfway and once again took me into his arms. "Abeni," he said, "I'm gonna ask you something, and I need you to tell me the truth, baby. Okay? No matter how hard it is, I need to know the truth."

I nodded, crying softly, my face pressed into his neck.

"Is Dali right? Would Hunnie's life be ruined if she stayed here without being cut?"

Memories of my own humiliation and ostracization played in my mind. Yes. I nodded. *Yes*.

He was quiet for many minutes, the pounding of our hearts and my own blood rushing through my ears the only sounds in my universe. Then, "He's gonna snatch her, right?"

I closed my eyes and nodded again. *Yes*.

I felt his body go limp, his arms fall suddenly from my waist, and when I looked up at him the tears began rolling down my face. My husband gazed at me, his eyes filled with sorrow, and when he shook his head and backed away from me, a cold rush of air soared between us, and I knew in my heart that I had lost him.

"C'mon," he said, motioning toward me. "It's late, baby, and you gotta go to work tomorrow. Lay down and get some rest, okay?"

I took the hand he offered and followed him into our bedroom. For the first time ever, the colors there seemed garish and brash, and I wanted to shut my eyes against their intensity. Bishop stopped me near the edge of the bed. Kneeling, he unlaced my shoes, removed my socks, then stood and untied the sash of my sarong. "Hold your arms up," he said gently, and as I obeyed, he slipped my shirt over my head until I stood before him in my panties and camisole.

I waited as he pulled back the spread on my side of the bed, then I climbed in when he held the blanket open expectantly. "G'night, baby," he whispered, and kissed me on my forehead. He picked up the cordless telephone receiver from my night table and dialed a series of numbers before crossing the room. My eyes were almost closed when he flicked off the lights, and I heard only one word before he stepped from the room and closed the door behind him.

My husband whispered, "Malcolm?"

# TWENTY-TWO

The next morning I awakened bleary-eyed and exhausted. I looked toward Bishop, only to find he was already awake and had been staring at me as I slept. There were deep lines in his forehead, and he looked as though he had not slept at all. As our eyes met, yesterday's pain hurled into me, and my stomach felt as though it had been struck with a bat.

"You okay?" he asked, reaching out and touching my shoulder.

I nodded as I remembered his call to Malcolm. I didn't want to imagine what they had discussed, but deep inside I knew.

"Just a second," Bishop said, and climbed from the bed. I gazed at his golden, muscular body as he pulled on a pair of gym shorts. Bare-chested, he left our room, then reentered a minute later carrying Hunnie in his arms.

"Shhh . . ." he whispered as she came awake, fretting. "Lay next to Mommy, okay?" He laid her down beside me and got in next to her, and instinctively she nestled against the warmth of my body as I cuddled her and smoothed the two sleep-tousled braids that hung down her back. Pulling my daughter close to my breast,

I reminisced about the days when she suckled her nourishment from my body, the days when we were connected spiritually and mentally, if not physically, the days when all that was required to sustain her was contained next to my heart.

Bishop reached across her and held us both. He and I lay there together for long minutes, inhaling the same air, our feet touching, our child sandwiched protectively between us.

Hunnie finally stretched and came fully awake. Peering into my eyes, she smiled sleepily, then put her slender arm around my neck and began reciting our special chant. "I love you more than you love me."

"Never, never, that can't be!"

"Oh yes, oh yes, oh yessiree, because I love you more than you love me."

As usual, she burst into laughter at the end, and because I did not want to alert her to the ache in my heart, I joined her.

"Oatmeal or cereal?" Bishop asked, tickling her sides and turning her toward him.

"French toast!" she yelled, leaping onto his chest and straddling him. She pretended to punch him as he tickled her into giddiness. "I'm going to be a boxer, right, Daddy?" Then to me, "Mommy, Daddy said he's going to teach me how to fight! One day I'm going to be the boxing champion of the world!"

"Yeah, we're gonna get you in the ring in a couple of years, baby, but right now let's go eat breakfast and let Mommy get ready for work."

I smiled as Bishop scooped her into his arms and rose from the bed. Champion of the world. What a lofty dream for a five-year-old Kenyan girl. My daughter was limitless. In her mind there was no mountain that could not be conquered, and the implication of this was not lost on me.

"I'm not going in today," I said, throwing off the covers and slipping into my robe. "How about I make some French toast for everybody?"

Hunnie shrieked her delight, but Bishop looked almost stricken. "You don't have to go through all of that trouble, baby. Hunnie can have cereal. Or if she wants something hot, I'll just fix her a bowl of oatmeal like I normally do. There ain't no need in you taking time off from work. Besides, didn't you say you were working on a new project?"

There wasn't a phony bone in Bishop's body. He was a lousy faker and never even bothered to lie. He wanted me out of the apartment for the day. Wanted me gone, and in a split second I understood why. Understood, and respected it. Had anticipated it from the moment I'd heard Mazani's dead voice warning me from a sea filled with silvery fish. Yet I would not fight him. There was no doubt that with Hunnie safe, Bishop would return for me and challenge Banjoko. And there was also no doubt that he would lose. And then who would Hunnie have? No, when Bishop left Kenya, he must never return. Never.

The inference of it all rushed over me, and I felt something springing up from my throat, pushing against my teeth. I nodded at Bishop, fighting to hold it in. Averting my eyes, I gathered my clothing and shower materials and rushed into the bathroom. I waited until the water's fiery needles stabbed at my skin, and only then did I open my mouth and expel the torturous gumbo that bubbled from my throat. With a cacophony of twisted syllables rolling off my tongue, I barked and grunted and howled and cackled and hooted and brayed, as a lifetime of pain flew past my lips and reverberated off the water-slick walls that barely contained my soul.

⁜

There would be no more walking through the park for me. Instead, I instructed my driver to drop me at my office, where I spent over an hour making calls and scheduling two urgent appointments. I left work by ten and instructed the driver to take me into the heart of Kairami, and once there I guided him to a flat building in the midst of a large commercial plaza. Inside, I met with a brown-skinned gentleman, a few years older than I and obviously of mixed Arab and African descent. He asked me to read and sign a series of forms that outlined the instructions I had given him by telephone that morning, and then he summoned two of his assistants to witness my initials and endorsements with their signatures. I slid the packet of papers into a plain brown envelope.

My next stop was several miles away at a large office building. There, within an hour, I had all of my financial assets, including the considerable sum that been accumulating in my account since my eighteenth birthday, transferred into the joint account that I shared with Bishop.

When that was completed, I asked to be taken back to my office, where I closed my door and sat down at my desk. With tears blurring my eyes, I wrote two letters.

One to my husband, the other to my daughter.

The apartment was empty when I returned that afternoon, and for a moment I felt a sharp tug of panic, followed by an immeasurable sense of loss. If I had ever doubted it before, the lifeless apartment confirmed it now. There was no life here for me, save Bishop and Hunnie. My sole reason for being born had been to unite with the two of them, and without them, I simply did not exist. I wandered through the large rooms, letting the emptiness cloak me like a shawl.

In Hunnie's room I picked up her toys, ran my fingers across her books, pressed my nose to her pillow, and held one of her tiny sandals in my palm. Retrieving the brown envelope from my purse, I peered inside to ensure all of my day's work was there. I reached behind my neck and removed the necklace that had once belonged to Bishop's mother and dropped it into the envelope, then I licked the flap and sealed it tight.

It didn't take me very long to decide where to place it. Bishop's grandfather had taken a liking to Winnie the Pooh and had sent Hunnie several items that boasted the image of the cute little bear. The backpack hanging from a hook in her wall beckoned me. When she was smaller Bishop and I would fill it with extra clothing and toys and send it with her to my parents' apartment each day. The child-care center where Bishop had her enrolled did not allow toys or personal items, but soon she would be old enough to start kindergarten and would no doubt want to carry her school texts in it. I unzipped the interior pocket of the bag and slid the envelope inside. It fit very nicely, hardly any bulk to it at all, and after zipping the bag closed, I hung it back on its hook.

I spent the next two hours doing laundry. I washed, dried, and folded several loads of clothing for Hunnie and Bishop, allowing my few items to remain in the bottom of the hamper. I hung her heavy pink sweater on a hook beside her book bag. Her new sneakers went next to her desk. I placed several pairs of folded panties on her dresser, along with a pair of clean pants and two short sets.

Each time I walked past the telephone I was tempted to pick it up. To call Jalisa and seek her help and guidance, but before my hand could touch the receiver I'd acknowledge the futility of my situation. The hopelessness of it all. I was Banjoko's daughter, a prisoner of my own father, and there was nothing I could do to right this situation save ensure that my daughter was allowed an opportunity to live free of those same binds that were killing me.

Night had fallen by the time they returned. Bishop's eyes were shaded, yet I saw the secret hiding there. We ate a simple dinner in the parlor, Hunnie sitting on the carpet taking small bites of her grilled-cheese sandwich while coloring with bright crayons, and Bishop and I sitting side by side, eating sliced beef and sharing a large glass of lemonade.

Throughout our meal he touched me constantly, a hand on my thigh, a caress of my arm, his fingers in my hair. He touched me like a blind man reading Braille, memorizing my contours, imprinting my flesh upon his fingers and thus upon his heart. At half past nine he called to Hunnie. "Time for your bath, sweetness. Come hug and kiss Mommy while I run your water. You want pink bubbles or blue bubbles tonight?"

I sat there quietly taking in their faces, contrasting colors but so much alike, both beautiful and strong. Hunnie crawled into my lap, and I leaned back on the sofa and rocked her gently.

"Hundiata," I began, then paused to kiss her on the flat spot between her eyebrows and the bridge of her nose, "there are so many people who love you. Your Poppa Daddy, your grandmother, your grandfather . . . your auntie Dali and Uncle Malcolm, all of your Kinaksu cousins . . . The world is a wondrous place where people try to live and love each other the best way they can, but sometimes things happen that we simply cannot control."

She gave me a sleepy smile, then rubbed her eyes and lay back in my arms. The sound of cascading water rose from the bathroom, and I leaned over and kissed her lips. "Mommy loves you, Hundiata, and so does Daddy." My voice cracked and I felt the tears building. Sitting up straight, I gently swung her legs to the floor and urged her to stand. "Please remember that."

That night Bishop made love to me as if it would be our very last time. It was tender and sweet, a song of love that flowed between us. He moved down my body, kissing my breasts and my stomach and leaving a trail of sorrow in his wake. He licked me, kissed me, inhaled me, then moaned as he partially penetrated me. I spread my legs, but his penis would not cooperate and remained lodged partway within my vagina. Bishop cried out then gave up, sliding his arms beneath my body, just holding me. There was no thrusting, no plunging, no movement, other than that of our pounding hearts, our flesh quaking in grief.

I felt Hunnie beside me in the dark of the night. Despite my attempts to mask my grief, she had sensed it and crawled into our bed to snuggle in the valley between our sleeping bodies. I held her in my arms, my tears on her hair, and this is how the rising sun found us.

I knew how difficult this was for him, and I had promised myself I would not interfere. Had vowed not to make it any harder than it surely was. I refused his offer of breakfast, of coffee, and dressed quickly in the bathroom. Because I had never once seen my husband cry, when it was time to leave I put on my most ordinary smile, gave him my most ordinary kiss, and with a drum beating a hole in my heart, forced myself to kneel and do the same to Hundiata. I paused for a moment, treating my lips to the softness of her skin, the sensation of her arms squeezing me, buried my nose for one last whiff of her neck. And then I closed the door and left.

The tears came as I waited for the elevator, and just as I stepped inside, I heard him call out my name. Turning my back, I pounded the door-close button and fled.

I spent the day organizing my office and making notes. I did not have lunch, nor did I accept any calls. Talani peeked in several times to check on me, but everyone else pretty much left me alone. By five o'clock my accounts were in order, and all open-ended folders contained detailed instructions for their continuance. I called for my car and arrived at my apartment shortly after five-thirty, and even before I stepped inside I knew they had gone.

My feet sped toward Hunnie's room first, and as I had suspected, her backpack was missing from its hook. As were her pink sweater, the gym shoes and underwear, and several other articles of clothing. I dragged myself woodenly into my bedroom, where I sat at my picture window, my heart in my stomach, staring up into the sky.

Maybe I was mistaken, I told myself. Perhaps they were out having ice cream and would return in a few minutes, Hunnie's face sticky, a half-eaten cone in her hand, and Bishop smelling of strawberry syrup, traces of shortcake still on his lips. But Hunnie's passport was also missing. Her birth certificate was gone.

I sat there as time sped past, watching the African sky change from a brilliant blue to a dusky violet and finally to a moonlit black. It was after eleven when I rose from the chair. In the bathroom I urinated and took off my clothing. Slipping my bathrobe from a hook behind the door, I slid my arms into it, then opened the medicine cabinet and retrieved a small medicine bottle I had hidden there two short days earlier. Some months ago Bishop had hurt his back while boxing, and our physician had prescribed a muscle relaxer and sent him for therapy. I shook the small white pills from the amber vial and counted out thirty, one for each year of my life. Holding my breath, I tossed them back one by one, then bent and guzzled cold water from the tap until the acrid taste left my mouth.

Returning to my bedroom, I took a framed photograph of the three of us from Bishop's dresser, then pulled down the covers on his side of the bed and crawled in to wait. His masculine scent permeated the sheets, giving me courage, and clutching the photo to my chest I thought of Mazani and the Hamids, and the perils Bishop and Hunnie were sure to face along their journey.

Despite my father's reach, I knew Hunnie would be safe. If anyone could assure this, Bishop could. I had heard the stories of Slim Willie, his father. That warrior man who had loved a houseful of women enough to protect them from all harm—this was the same depth of love that Bishop had for our Hundiata. And his mother. Dimples. She had fought for her life but died knowing her son would be safe. I admired her. After all, a mother's life is a very small price to pay in exchange for the well-being of her child.

And my Hunnie. Oh, the opportunities! The possibilities! I could actually see her in America, boxing with her father. The champion of the world! I visualized her walking down a crowded New York City street, moving with the confidence of ten Jalisas. Just imagine! After the type of life I had lived, *my* daughter, charting her own course, a self-assured young lady with the independence to blaze her own paths. As my hands grew cold and the light in the room faded, I saw my Hundiata setting sail as the mistress of her own vessel, nurturing and respecting the body that had been utterly perfect from the moment of her birth. It was with this image in my mind and the convicted assurance that Bishop would ensure our daughter received all that I had not been able to give her that I drifted off, joining the Ancestors and finding a peace sweeter than any I had ever known, because although I was not destined to see her journey to fruition, I thanked Spirit, the Ancestors, and even the God of my husband for allowing me even the smallest taste of Hunnie.

# PART THREE

# HUNNIE

# TWENTY·THREE

My heart was broken, and if it wasn't for my baby girl looking at me with those big old sad eyes, I probably woulda just laid down and died. We'd cut out right after Abeni left for work, and walking out of that apartment knowing that Hunnie would never be coming back was the hardest thing I had ever done. I kept telling myself that as soon as my baby was safe in Alabama with Malcolm and Poppa Daddy I would come back and find a way to get a passport for Abeni, but even knowing this didn't make it any easier for me to let my woman go to work like everything was cool, while all along I was plotting to kidnap her only child.

I had had a hard time believing Banjoko could do something so foul to his own grandchild. I knew how much he loved her, but I'd also come to understand that there was something fucked up about him and his way of thinking when it came down to women. It wasn't that he hated them. I had known plenty of men, black and white, who could care less than a fuck about a female, but that wasn't Banjoko's trip at all. He actually loved the women in his life. He thought he was doing right by them when he followed those traditions that focused more on what was between a girl's legs than what was wrong in their own male thinking.

I wasn't trying to knock their shit either. I mean, more power to the Kinaksu and whoever else believed in cutting women if that was what the girl really wanted for herself, but I'd seen the effects it had on Abeni. The nightmares, the scars, all those crazy sounds that came outta her mouth when she was sleep and couldn't help it. Even the way she responded to me in bed. No, to me it wasn't nothing but a bunch of male ego-tripping that had almost messed up my wife, and I was ready to lay down and die before I let that happen to Hunnie. Not to my baby girl.

Malcolm had left the Peace Corps two years earlier and gone back to Alabama, where he'd looked up Gebra and was running a Habitat for Humanity construction project up in Mobile. He'd finally had enough of the ass chase, and as soon as he realized the prize he'd overlooked in high school, he headed straight to Gebra. I guess she'd just been waiting around for him to come to his senses because they hooked up fast and hard and were now a couple. Gebra worked as a surgeon just south of Mobile, and when they visited Poppa Daddy on the weekends, Malcolm helped him out back in the gym just like he did when we were kids.

"What?" he'd screamed into the telephone. Malcolm had been just as surprised as me when I told him what they wanted to do to my baby.

"You heard me! No matter what I say, he's gonna snatch her up and take her, and when we get her back it'll be all over. He'll hold her down and cut her up, and there won't be a damn thing I can do about it, except hunt his black ass down and kill him."

"Okay. Calm down, Chicken. We're gonna figure this shit out, okay? Don't worry. Nothing's gonna happen to your baby, not if you can get her out of there."

I wasn't a running man, but in the back of my mind I'd thought about snatching Hunnie and hauling ass back home. Because of

Abeni, I'd fought the thought. At first I was mad as hell at her. Straight disgusted 'cause she wouldn't stand up and tell her father to his face not to put his fuckin' hands on our baby. But after listening to Dali, I kinda understood where Abeni was sitting. She knew what would happen to Hunnie whether she got cut or not. From where Abeni was standing, it was probably six of one or half a dozen of the other. Hunnie was damned if she did and damned if she didn't, and as soon as I realized that, I almost broke completely down because it meant not only would I have to save my baby by myself, I'd also have to leave my wife.

"I don't know, man. Abeni can't leave the country. Banjoko's got big-time connections here, man, and he won't let her get a passport. The only reason Hunnie got one is because of me."

"Yeah," Malcolm agreed. "I heard Banjoko's got juice everywhere in Kenya. He's a dangerous dude, and most people are scared shitless of him. When I was in Isiolo I heard something about a man he had killed for beating the shit outta his wife's brother. The nephew was straight-up gay, and everybody knew it, but when he went to Isiolo and made a pass at this married guy, dude kicked the shit outta him in public, and Banjoko had the man killed in front of his wife and kids."

I remembered something Abeni had told me about the doctor who fixed her circumcision. How him and his family had been chased down by a semi and run over like a buncha dogs in the street, courtesy of Banjoko.

"I don't have a whole lot of time," I told Malcolm. "I need to make a move like right now."

He agreed. "But we can't go at this half-assed, Chicken. It's not just you who's running. You'll have Hunnie with you too, so shit has got to be tight for her sake."

"I need you to make a few calls, Malcolm. Get in touch with the governor, Casper Wilson. Me and him go way back. All the way back to Slim Willie's Place. He's done me a bunch of solids over the years, and he's got mad pull. Talk to him and tell him my

"I know, Sweetie Peetie," I said, lotioning her from head to toe. I pulled her pajamas on, then picked her up and tucked her under the covers. "But I promise, you can call her as soon as we get to Poppa Daddy's."

I'd chosen this hotel because it was outside of the city, and even though I knew Banjoko had big investments in Nairobi, I figured if he was looking for me, there was no better place to hide than right under his nose. I'd seen it done. Crooks chilling right around the corner from the police station, so I knew it could work. We checked out of the hotel the next afternoon and took another *matatus* to a small branch of my bank. I didn't want to risk going to our regular branch because everyone there knew me, so I looked in the telephone book and found one that wasn't too far from where we were, and gave the driver the address.

Neither Abeni nor I had been big-time spenders. I didn't make much money at the Brotherhood Haven, but then again we didn't have many expenses either. Our cars and drivers were paid for by Omorru and Associates, and until last year Hunnie had stayed with Ziwani and Dali during the day, saving us the expense of child care. The biggest thing on our plate had been the rent on our apartment, and since Abeni made good money at her job and had been paying it by herself when I met her, even that hadn't been a big deal. We were simple people and just weren't big on material stuff. Even before Hunnie was born we had lived pretty frugally, and not only had I been able to send some money home to Poppa Daddy each month, we'd also built up a pretty decent savings account that we'd opened in trust for our daughter.

I didn't have any qualms about taking that money. It had been put away for Hunnie's future, and I knew Abeni would want her to have it. But when the bank teller wrote the account balance on a slip of paper, I thought for sure she had made a mistake.

"Are you sure this is right?" I asked in Swahili. "I mean, I didn't know I had this much money in there."

"There was a large deposit credited two days ago," the clerk explained. She was a pretty girl in her late teens. Her hair was pressed straight and her eyes were bright in her oval face. I wondered if she too had been cut. I hoisted Hunnie's backpack on my shoulder, then guided her between me and the counter. Then I filled out a withdrawal slip and pushed it toward the clerk.

"I'm sorry sir," she said, sliding the form back to me. "Your withdrawal exceeds the amount I am authorized to process. You must have this approved by the branch manager."

"Where is he?"

I followed her directions across the banking floor, where I met an older man dressed in an expensive-looking tailored suit. I gave him my withdrawal slip, and clutching Hunnie's hand, I waited.

I was a pretty strong guy, but the way this dude looked at me after studying my slip almost made a brother feel stunted.

"What's up?" I said in English, 'cause certain attitudes just didn't translate well.

He looked down at my wrinkled jeans and slept-in shirt, then glanced at Hunnie. I ran my hand over the two days' worth of stubble on my face and said it again. "What?"

"Do you have any identification, sir?"

I pulled out my wallet and gave him my employee ID from Brotherhood. He punched some numbers into the computer on his desk, then stared at the photo, then looked at me, then back to the photo. A moment later, he turned it over and compared my signature on the back to the one I had just signed on the deposit slip. "Did you fill out this slip here in the branch?"

"Yeah."

"Did you actually sign this in the presence of the teller?"

"Yeah," I said, nodding toward the girl. "She gave it to me and I signed it right there at her window."

He handed it to me. "Sign it again, please. I need to witness it."

"Daddy, I'm hungry," Hunnie said, pulling on my hand.

"Is there a problem?"

"Well, yes. I mean"—he looked at me and gave me a phony-ass

grin—"this is a very large amount to withdraw, especially in cash. Wouldn't you rather have a bank check for part of it? Are you paying a bill with this, or perhaps taking a vacation? Would traveler's checks work for you today?"

It was all I could do to keep my cool. Here I was trying to get my baby somewhere safe, and this little motherfucker was talking to me like I was somebody's child. I snatched it from him and signed it again, right below my first signature. "It wasn't too large of an amount when it was a deposit, was it? Give it to me just like I asked for it. Half in dollars, and half in shillings."

Hunnie was holding on to my leg, rubbing her face against my pants. "Daddy, I want something to eat. Isn't it time for lunch?"

I pulled my eyes off him and bent down to her. "Yeah, baby. It's chow time. We'll get something as soon as we're finished here, okay?" I stood back up and eyeballed the manager again. "And hurry the hell up. My baby is hungry."

# TWENTY-FOUR

I took Hunnie to a little burger place that was in the same complex as the bank, and I sat facing the door, drinking a Coke and eating a chicken sandwich as she nibbled at her burger and fries. Her meal came with a little spin-top toy, and I let her play with it while she ate.

I ran down my plan mentally as I watched her, hoping like hell things would go smoothly and me and my baby could get on a flight out without any problems. We were gonna take a *matatus* to the airport, where Malcolm had already made us a reservation to fly home. The thought of leaving Kenya made Abeni flood my mind, but I pushed her down into that hard place in my stomach where the memory of my mother lived. I would call her as soon as we touched down on American soil, and until then, even thinking about her was dangerous 'cause it made me weak.

"You ready?" I asked Hunnie, and reached over to wipe her mouth. She nodded but didn't give me her usual smile. I took her hand and we went back outside to find us a ride. We didn't have to look too hard 'cause there was a taxi waiting right outside on the curb, something you didn't see often, so I should have known better. I stuck my head in the passenger-side window and spoke in Swahili. "Airport?"

He was dressed pretty sharp for a cabdriver, and he nodded over his shoulder, directing me to hop in. The car was an older model with torn seats, and the odor of cigarettes and stale sweat hung in the air. That struck me as funny, 'cause above the funk I could smell the driver's expensive cologne. It was similar to something Abeni had bought me for my last birthday.

Jomo Kenyatta International Airport was in southern Nairobi, and the plan was for me to take a *matatus* there and catch an evening flight. Sitting in the backseat, I couldn't decide if I was being paranoid or what. Instead of keeping his eyes on the road, dude kept looking in his rearview mirror, straight at me. I took Hunnie's backpack off her and pulled her closer to me, and after a few more times of me challenging those eyes in his mirror, he finally gave up looking and drove instead.

"Right here!" I hollered out when I started seeing signs for the different airlines. I could almost smell Alabama, and I prayed like hell that in just a couple of hours me and my little girl would be heading toward home.

"Which airline?" he asked. He spoke to me in English, even though I had approached him in an African tongue.

"Don't matter," I said, taking him right back to Swahili. "Just let us out right here." I paid him and hustled Hunnie out the cab, but instead of pulling off, he just sat there watching us.

"C'mon, baby," I said, and led her toward the Air Alaska terminal. We pushed through the revolving doors, and I looked out the window and saw he was still there. Looked like he was talking into a radio.

*Shit!* Holding tight to Hunnie's hand, I spotted an escalator on our right and we jumped on it. I had no idea where the terminal for Kenya Air was, but we moved down the long corridors and through connecting walkways trying to find it.

"I'm tired, Daddy," Hunnie complained. "You're making me walk too fast."

I looked down and saw a sheet of sweat covering her nose. "I'm sorry, Hunnie. Daddy almost forgot your legs ain't as long as his. Want a pickup?" She nodded and held her arms out, and I lifted her and sighed as her little legs grabbed at my waist. Shifting her to my right hip and slinging her bag over my other shoulder, I took off again, my stride long, my steps quick.

We had come into the airport complex at Terminal A, and according to a skycap I asked, Kenya Air was in Terminal D. Holding Hunnie tight, I beat feet until we were in the right terminal, then scanned the signs until I saw the Kenya Air logo.

"Gotta put you down for a little while," I told Hunnie. Looking around, I saw a row of chairs across from the ticket counters and sat her down there. I dug down into the bottom of Hunnie's bag and pulled out the envelope stuffed with shillings. Her toothbrush fell out and almost hit the floor, but my reflexes were still sharp and I managed to catch it.

"Damn, Daddy's good." I grinned. Hunnie laughed, and it made me feel better. Malcolm had made our reservations, and all that was left was for me to pay for the tickets and get us on the plane. Zipping the bag and taking her hand, I walked Hunnie over to the ticket line and waited.

They had a good crowd going, and I figured it was because school had let out and people were taking summer vacations. I hoped me and Hunnie looked like normal travelers, and I let my eyes scan the entire room while we waited.

I counted several ticket agents, and there were a bunch of people working behind the counter lifting bags onto belts. At the end of the long row of counters was a security checkpoint, and I guessed a couple of folks' number had come up, because they got sent down there to have their bags opened and inspected. I kept glancing around in all directions, looking for signs of Banjoko or his men and wondering whether the folks who met my eyes just happened to do it or were out to kill me and steal my baby girl.

It took about twenty minutes for us to move up on line, and I just knew somebody was gonna stick a gun in my back, and I'm sure I looked crazy the way I kept turning around staring, my eyes crawling over every inch of the terminal.

I was grateful when it was our turn to approach a ticket agent, a brother so dark he almost blended in with his jacket. I'd seen Africans like him in Kenya before, although I had no idea what tribe they came from. With even, good-looking features, they had an amazing pureness of skin that made them stand out in a crowd.

"Um, I have a flight reservation to New York, JFK Airport." It was a long trip. It would take us six hours to go from Nairobi to Amsterdam. From there, after a five-hour layover, we'd be facing a seven-hour flight to JFK.

"Name?"

"Johnson. Bishop and Hundiata Johnson."

I waited while he typed our information into his computer, then tapped his fingers impatiently on the screen.

"That will be six thousand and forty-two shillings, sir. How will you be paying for that?"

"Cash."

He gave me a look but waited while I counted it out. "How many bags are you checking?"

"None."

He grilled me with his eyes again but kept his mouth closed.

"All right, let's get your seat reservations and boarding pass, and you'll be on your way."

He tapped on the keypad a few more times, then waited.

"Hmmm . . ." He stared at the screen, and whatever he saw there made him look closer, then glance up at me.

"Do you have any identification, sir?"

I dug into my back pocket. "Yeah, I do. Right here."

I gave him my passport and held my breath.

"I'm sorry, Mr. Johnson." He frowned, sliding my passport

back along with a white stub that had a series of numbers printed on it. "You'll have to go through a security screening before I can issue your tickets. If you'll step right down to the far end of the counter, one of the men in blue airline jackets can help you."

"Security for what?" I said. "We don't even have any bags to check, so what is it they need to screen?"

He shook his head. "I don't know. To be honest, I've never seen a code like this before, but there's no way the computer will let me print your ticket or boarding pass until the code is removed by security."

I was worried. There was just no telling what was up. It could have been a simple thing, but I doubted it. Something in me said that Banjoko was on my ass, and as I led Hunnie down to the security area, every single hair on the back of my neck stood up.

Hunnie and I were forced to wait in yet another line. I knew she was tired, but she was handling it like a trouper. There were only three families ahead of us when she touched my leg. "Daddy, I need to use the bathroom."

The next person in line, a Muslim woman with her head and body covered, stepped up to be screened. Two children stepped up with her, and that meant that there were only two families standing between us and the security area, where two men, one black and one white, were going through luggage and carry-on bags by hand.

"Hunnie," I asked her gently, "do you have to go bad, baby? I mean, is it really, really bad, or can you hold it?"

"I have to go, Daddy. The last time I went was this morning, and now I need to make pee-pee."

I could have kicked my own ass. She didn't have a spare leg, so of course she had to go. Hell, I had to go too, but I'd been so busy worrying about getting on the plane I hadn't even noticed it. There was a bathroom not far from the counter. I guided Hunnie by the shoulder and turned around. "Excuse me," I said to a white guy who was on line behind me. "My little girl needs to go to the bathroom. Could you hold my spot?"

"Sure," he said. His accent was clipped and British. "But you should tell them up there where you're going. Just in case I've already gone through by the time you get back."

I nodded, and holding Hunnie's hand, I stepped off the line and walked over to the security desk. Both men were busy and had their backs to me. One guy was struggling to reclose a zipper, and the other was going through the Muslim woman's carry-on bag.

I called, "Excuse me—"

"Just a minute," the white guy said over his shoulder.

I leaned on the counter, waiting nervously, and I actually jumped as a high-pitched beeping sound cut the air, and a fax machine sitting on a desk next to a computer terminal kicked on. I watched as a sheet of paper slid out the machine and into a bin, and what I saw made my blood run cold.

The black-and-white image of my face took up half of the page, and Hunnie's picture, one I'd taken of her and Abeni myself, was on the other half. Abeni had been cut out of the photo, but me and Hunnie showed up as clear as day.

"Now, what do you need, my friend?" The white guy was done with the zipper and had come to answer my call.

I made like I didn't hear him and swept Hunnie up in my arms, then ducked quickly away, hoping the only thing he would remember about me was the back of my head. I dodged through the crowds and forced myself to walk normally as I headed for the revolving doors.

I was just about to barrel my way through when I saw my taxi driver. He was standing at the curb talking to two other men. I changed directions in midstride, bumping into a heavyset African man dressed in Kenyan clothes.

"My bad," I muttered under my breath, but I sure as hell didn't stop. I ran toward the first door I saw, near a bank of elevators. I turned the knob, pulled it open, and stepped inside.

# TWENTY-FIVE

We were in a stairwell, one that led to a multilevel parking garage. Holding Hunnie close to my chest, I took the stairs two at a time.

"W-why are you running, Daddy?" Her jaw jigged, and I felt her legs tighten around my waist.

"I'm not really running," I answered, turning on a landing and bounding down the next flight. A sign ahead of me told me it was the second level, and I pushed through the door and found myself facing a lot filled with cars and vans. An arrow pointed to a sign that said AIRPORT EXIT, and I almost ran toward it, but I checked myself. That move woulda put us right out in the open.

"You gotta get down now, baby," I told Hunnie, breathing hard and letting her slide to her feet. I looked around, then grabbed her hand and pulled her along behind me as I stepped onto a narrow ledge between a row of cars and the garage wall. We'd have to walk the perimeter of the garage to get to that exit sign, but there were a couple of minivans we could duck behind, if we had to. The ledge was narrow and there wasn't much room to maneuver. I crashed my leg into a Cadillac bumper and cursed, then turned sideways. A black sedan drove past, and I crouched down and pressed my shoulder to the wall. Behind me, Hunnie pulled on my hand.

"C'mon, Hunnie," I said when the car was gone, standing again and almost dragging her behind me. At her size, she didn't seem to have much of a problem maneuvering or hiding.

"Stop, Daddy! Just wait!"

I stopped, shocked by the tone of her voice. She sounded pissed, and she dug her little sneakers into the concrete and locked her legs.

"What's the matter with you?" Sweat rolled from my head and dripped into my eyes. Pulling her behind a white SUV, I crouched down again, this time facing her.

"I want Mommy!"

"Sshh!" I grabbed her shoulder. "Be quiet!"

Her eyes got big, then that lip came out. It shook a few times, and then there were tears.

I sighed and pulled her to me, letting her bury her face in my musty shirt.

"I'm sorry, Sweetie Peetie. Daddy didn't mean to holler at you. C'mon." I pulled the front of my shirt out my pants and tried to dry her face. "Stop crying, Hunnie. Be a big girl for Daddy."

"I'm scared, Daddy. I wanna go home!" She was crying like I'd never seen her do before. Her eyes were squinched shut, and her nose was running.

"C'mon, baby girl." I got down on one knee and planted my other foot on the ground, then lifted her onto my thigh. "Don't cry, Hunnie. Daddy's here with you and everything is gonna be okay, baby. I promise."

She stopped crying long enough to give me a look that was so sad that if I was a crying man, I'd have wept along with her. What the hell had I been thinking? What made me believe I could just take my baby away from her mother, away from everything she'd ever known, and not tell her anything? Damn straight, she was scared. I woulda been too if I was five years old and my father had thrown me into a mix like this.

"I'm sorry, Hunnie." I hugged her and kissed the tip of her nose. I noticed that one of her braids was up higher than the other, and the ends on both of them were crawling loose. "Listen," I said, trying to choose my words carefully. "I'm gonna tell you the truth, baby girl. Okay?"

She nodded, her eyes red. She looked so old for five. Too damned old.

"The reason I'm taking you home to Poppa Daddy is because I don't think you're safe here."

"What do you mean?"

"Baby, there are a lotta bad people in this world, and I'm afraid somebody might try to do something to hurt you."

"Why?"

I swallowed. "Because, baby. Because some people make decisions that hurt other people. You could get hurt even when somebody thinks they're doing something good for you."

"Is Mommy coming?"

"No, Hunnie. Not right now, but remember, we're gonna call her as soon as we get to Poppa Daddy's house."

"But I want her."

She said this as a natural fact, without whining or crying, and I felt a little better because it gave me proof that she still trusted me. I stood her up and smoothed down her shirt, then got back to my feet and took her hand.

"I know, Sweetie Peetie. I want her too."

||||||||||

I explained to Hunnie that we were trying to get out of the airport without being seen. I didn't tell her it was her grandfather's men who were looking for us, and of course I didn't tell her that I could be killed for snatching her. That woulda been way too much to expect her to suck up and swallow. We were back on the narrow ledge, and although nobody had jumped out at us, my gut was telling me that trouble was nearby.

Several cars had gone by, and one or two of them had been driving too slow to suit me. My eyes were constantly moving, sweeping from side to side for a sign of static, and I coulda sworn I smelled Banjoko's cologne. We got all the way around to the other side of the garage before Hunnie stopped me again. "I have to make pee-pee, Daddy. Real bad."

I'd forgotten. Up ahead I saw a hunter-green minivan parked beside a bright yellow Camaro. "Okay, just a second. I'll take you over by that van."

I'd seen Abeni hold Hunnie up many times when she had to go and there was no toilet available. Squatting wide-legged between the car and the minivan, I lifted Hunnie into my arms and held her with her legs sticking out. "Go ahead. Pee-pee."

I don't know why I thought she would pee straight down, 'cause when she let go her urine flew straight out, splattering the chrome wheels of the Camaro.

"Hey! That's my car! What you doing, my man?"

I spun around with Hunnie in midstream, and more pee splashed the car's door.

"Awww, no! You're letting her pee on my car!"

He was a young guy, not much more than a teenager. If it wasn't for his African accent I woulda taken him for an American, 'cause his clothes and sneakers made him look just like a brother straight out of a rap video.

"My bad," I called over my shoulder, making sure Hunnie was finished before putting her down. I stepped around her puddle, then reached into her bag and found a crumpled tissue to wipe her with.

"I'm sorry, bro'. I didn't mean to splash your ride. The baby girl had to go."

The way he was dressed was throwing me off, making me talk

to him in the common language of black men in America: all base and balls.

"Cool." He nodded, and I saw a large bag slung over his shoulder. Looking at Hunnie, he grinned. "Gotta wipe her down anyway. Been sitting here for a minute."

I wanted to ask him where he had just come from. It had to be somewhere in the States, and just looking at him made me homesick. I looked back as I led Hunnie away. Bro' had cranked up his car and turned up the sounds and was using a large towel to wipe down his ride.

Back on the ledge I moved fast but was mindful of my baby trying to keep up behind me. Her little hand felt so trusting in mine, and I prayed she wouldn't be too traumatized by any of this. We were standing beneath the exit sign, which pointed toward a down ramp. I peered as far as I could see above us to make sure no cars were coming, then picking Hunnie up again and staying close to the rail, I headed down the ramp, letting my momentum push me into a jog.

There was an exit sign on this level too, pointing toward the right, and I stayed at the foot of the ramp until a station wagon went by. I gave Hunnie a smile that was supposed to make her think everything was okay, and a moment later I was on the ground level, and looking ahead, all the way on the other end of the garage, I saw a ticket booth and then daylight. Relief ran through me as I hurried in that direction, holding my baby girl as tightly as I could.

We were about halfway there when a car came speeding into the garage heading straight toward us. I ducked between two parked cars and, holding Hunnie, crouched down into a ball between their front fenders. My heart was pounding as the car approached, and I put my hand over Hunnie's head, pushing her into my chest and doing my best to make myself look like a piece of the Toyota I was trying to become.

The car was right up on us, and I peered up as it went by. I almost cursed again when I saw it was the same taxi that had picked us up outside the restaurant. The same driver too, moving slow and sweeping his eyes from side to side as he passed. I clutched Hunnie tighter and held my breath, letting it out only after I heard the motor fading in the distance.

"You okay?" I whispered to my daughter as I eased to my feet. My back was bent and I held Hunnie low as I scooted toward the cars' trunks and looked left. The taxi was still cruising, riding his brakes, his taillights bright. Hunnie nodded but didn't speak. Her little body was trembling and her eyes were circles.

"Hold tight to Daddy's neck," I said as I stood up straight and broke out jogging toward the exit again.

"Ouch! Daddy! Ow!" Hunnie cried a few moments later, and I stopped in my tracks, breathing hard.

"What?" I peered down at her and she stuck out her tongue. A small drop of blood was on the tip.

"You made me bite my tongue," she said. "I think it's bleeding, Daddy."

I wiped at the spot of blood with my thumb and hoisted her up higher on my shoulder. "Keep your mouth closed tight. Daddy has to run, so I need you to hold your teeth together and keep your mouth closed."

I was on the move, closing the distance, jogging as fast as I dared. I had just switched Hunnie to my other hip when I heard it. The sound of an engine, at my back and moving fast. I took off running at full speed, bouncing my baby on my hip and swinging her bag from my other hand. I opened my stride and ran so fast I would have made Michael Johnson look like a scrub. Up ahead I could see the clerk in the ticket booth, could almost feel the sun that was shining in through the exit, and then I saw the second car. Coming toward us. This one a black limo just like the kind used at Omorru and Associates.

"Shit." I came to a halt, sucking wind and holding my baby as sweat ran from my body. The car behind me was close, and it took me a minute to realize what I was hearing. *"Fuck Martinez! Fuck-Fuck Martinez! Martinez's wife, you know she sucks a mean dick . . ."* An old cut by 2 Live Crew. I spun around and faced the yellow Camaro. Youngblood was bopping his head, the bass echoing off the concrete. I looked back and the limo was almost on top of us. I stepped into the Camaro's path.

"Yo!" I waved my arm as he hit his brakes, then I ran over to his driver's window.

"What's wrong?" he said, turning down his sounds, "you gotta pee too?"

I reached in and grabbed his shoulder, then glanced at the car moving toward us. "I need your help, man!" Sweat was pouring off me and I knew I looked crazy. "I gotta get my daughter someplace safe. Let us in, bro'. Let us in!"

He unlocked the doors, and cradling Hunnie, I dove in, crawling toward the other side. He was moving before I could reach over and pull the door shut. I pushed Hunnie to the floor, then stretched my body out over her.

"What the hell is going on?" he said over his shoulder as he turned down his radio.

"Drive! Just drive!"

It seemed like forever as he paid his parking fee. I hovered over Hunnie, my mouth dry, my baby shaking like a leaf. "Is anyone behind us?" I asked as he waited for the clerk to count out his change.

"Yes. A red car. Looks like a Honda." He drove out of the garage and into the sunlight. I sat up and pulled Hunnie onto the seat beside me. "What's going on?" he repeated, looking at me in his rearview mirror. "Who are you running from, and what did you do?"

He really was a kid, maybe nineteen, his face as smooth as Hunnie's. His eyes grew big in the mirror.

"Hey, hold up. That *is* your little girl, right? You didn't jump in front of my car because you stole somebody else's child, did you?"

I pulled Hunnie closer and glanced out the back window. "Yeah, she's mine. Why would I steal a kid?" Traffic was heavy, but I didn't see any suspicious-looking cars, not that I wasn't still wary.

"So where are you going? I've got things to do. Where can I drop you off?"

I thought for a moment. The heat was on. The shit had definitely hit the fan. I couldn't go back to the airport—security had our pictures, and I couldn't get us a ticket if I tried. Malcolm said he had friends in Mombasa, and that if push came to shove, we could find help at the U.S. consulate there. Well, Banjoko was shoving me all right. Damn near off a cliff. "I need to get to Mombasa," I replied. "How far is the train station from here?"

He whistled. "Everything is far in Nairobi traffic, my friend. Do you want to go to the station in Kahawa or the main terminal in the city?"

There was no way in hell I wanted to get on in the city. I couldn't avoid going through Nairobi, but I damn sure didn't want to get caught waiting on the platform.

"Kahawa," I decided.

He looked at his watch and whistled. "I don't know, man . . . I'm actually heading in the opposite direction."

I sighed, hoping I wouldn't have to break his little ass up and take his car. "I need your help, man. Now, I can pay you, but I can't get out your car in Nairobi. If you take me someplace where I can send a telegram, then take me and my daughter up to Kahawa, I'll hook you up with some dollars and owe you a solid."

He shook his head and frowned. "Damn, man. I want to help you, but I got this chick waiting for me . . . I'm sorta in the doghouse with her, and I need to patch things up."

"She like diamonds?"

"What?"

"Your girl. Does she like diamonds?"

"Yeah." He shrugged. "What woman doesn't?"

"Take me up to Kahawa," I said, pulling Hunnie's sweater from her bag and draping it across her legs. "And with what I'm gonna pay you, you can buy her a diamond that'll not only get you off her shit list, it'll keep you rolling around in her sheets for the next six months."

# TWENTY·SIX

The driver's name was John Adowa, and the fact that he was driving in Kenya should have told me he was more than just a kid. He said he'd just turned twenty-five and was returning home from London, where a British production company had hired him as an extra in a music video. He was the oldest of four kids, all boys, and he was trying to get his solo demo produced. I thought twenty-five was a little old to still be bustin' a sag and singing "oooh-oooh get it get it!" but I wasn't about to tell him.

The sun was going down and Hunnie was sleeping with her head against my arm. I'd put her seat belt on because Young-blood's gas foot was kinda heavy, and I wasn't trying to save my baby from a knife just to have her go sailing through the wind-shield of some souped-up sports car that fell in a pothole. John took us to a bank that had a telegram service, and I asked him to go inside and send Malcolm a telegram letting him know I missed my flight in Nairobi and would be heading south to Mombasa.

He met my eyes in the rearview mirror. "You're from America, right? So what's your story, man?"

I shrugged and refused to meet his eyes in the mirror. "It's a long one," I said. "Bottom line, I gotta get my daughter to the States. We were gonna fly outta Nairobi, but as you can see, that just wasn't working."

We drove through southern Nairobi, north over the Ngong River on Mombasa Road, which turned into Uhuru Highway. The landscape was green and lush, and we were passing the University of Nairobi's School of Medicine near Kenyatta National Hospital when I closed my eyes and put my head back. Seeing the signs for the medical school made Gebra Burns pop into my mind, and I wondered for a hot minute how simple my life might have been if I had chased after her and eventually caught her. *Naw,* I thought. As smart and fine as Gebra was, she couldn't braid my Satin's hair. I mean, she was great for Malcolm and I was happy they had hooked up and seemed chill together, but no matter what happened, or how this all turned out, I wouldn't have traded a minute of my life with Abeni and Hunnie for all the Gebras in the world.

The sweat had dried up on me, and my face felt tight. We had passed the main train station up from the railway museum, and I couldn't wait to get further north and out of this little ass car. Youngblood had been good enough to keep the volume low, but even still, the Tupac jam he was playing was killing my head.

My failure at the airport had put us in a bind. Abeni said her father had given her a week to have Hunnie at the homestead, so that shoulda given me a few days' lead time. Instead, Banjoko had been on my ass within seventy-two hours, and the only thing I could think of was that Abeni had given us up. Maybe she'd been so tore up behind me cutting out and taking Hunnie that she'd run crying to her parents. I could see that happening, and for a minute I regretted not leaving her a note. But then I remembered how fragile she was. The less she knew, the better for all of us.

As much as I'd needed to talk this whole thing through with her and maybe get her approval, she'd already shown me where her backbone was when it came to her father. The way she'd held her head down when I begged her to go against him and tell him Hunnie wasn't to be touched damn near killed me. That was really all I had needed to see. I still loved her, of course, but her mentality had been shot from the time she was a kid, and I knew if Banjoko really tried, he could flip her in a minute.

I musta dozed off, because one minute I was thinking about my wife, and the next minute Youngblood was calling my name. "Wake up, my man. The station is right up ahead. You taking the Lunatic Express?"

"Come again?"

"The Lunatic Express. The overnight train from Nairobi to Mombasa."

I tried to stretch my legs out, then reached for Hunnie's bag. "Yeah. That's the one. What time does it leave?"

He looked at his watch. "You just missed it," he answered, fighting his way to the curb. "I think it left around seven." There were quite a few things I was gonna miss about Kenya, but the driving wasn't one of them.

"So what time does the next train leave?" I sat Hunnie upright, bracing her head against my chest.

"Tomorrow night. Same time."

*Shit!* My brain spun as I tried to come up with a plan. There was no way I wanted to be cornered overnight in a hotel. I could see the door being kicked down in the middle of the night and Hunnie being taken. They'd probably kill my ass right there in the bed. No, I needed some wide-open spaces. Someplace where we could hide if it came down to it.

Opening the cash bag I'd taken from her backpack, I counted out the shillings and my head almost spun. "Here you go, 'blood," I said, passing him all but 100,000 shillings, the max I could take through Kenyan customs anyway. He stared at the stack of bills in my hand and shook his head.

"Damn, man. What'd you do? Hit a bank?" He shook his head again. "That's okay. I'm cool. Put that away, my friend."

"C'mon, John-boy. Either I give it to you, or I claim it and answer a whole lotta questions going through customs. I swear it's clean. Came right out of my bank account."

I left the youngblood staring at the money and lifted Hunnie out of the car. My legs were cramped and my whole body felt sore, but I knew things coulda been much worse. We coulda gotten caught at the airport and my ass coulda been dead by now. I wouldn't even let myself think where Hunnie could be, or what woulda happened to her if John hadn't come along. Yeah, we missed the train and that shit was fucked up. But I took a couple of deep breaths and reminded myself that it wasn't the end of the world. There was another train leaving tomorrow, and somehow we'd survive the night.

IIIIIIII

We wandered into Nairobi's Temero Park just past sunset. The park was large and grassy, and there was a pond and a play area nearby. I'd bought me and Hunnie some dried fruit from a street vendor, but neither one of us had much of an appetite. It had been a long, hard day of running and dodging, and we were wrung out. We walked around for a while, then I put her in a swing and pushed her back and forth until her eyes got heavy and her head fell to her chest.

I'd told Hunnie we were gonna camp out. Sleep outside like we were on a camping trip, something Abeni and I had always promised her we'd do. She'd been looking forward to it for a long time, but when I explained that it would just be me and her sleeping in the park, there hadn't been a bit of excitement in my baby's eyes. They'd grown real old in the last few days, and the message in them seemed to say, "Okay, Daddy. Whatever the fuck you gonna do, just do it and leave me out of it. I can't take too much more of this shit."

I found us a bench off a narrow bike path, and cuddling Hunnie in my arms, I laid her backpack down first, then stretched her out so her head could rest on it. There was a lamppost not far away, surrounded by moths and mosquitoes, so I grabbed one of my shirts from the bag and covered her arms and back with it, then used her sweater to cover her legs. I sat down on the bench and eased her head onto my lap, backpack and all, then put my arm around her and watched her sleep. I thought I had just blinked, but when I opened my eyes again they were standing in front of me.

One dude was tall and built almost like Malcolm, but with a soft-looking stomach that hung over his belt. He was an older guy, light-skinned, and in the light from the lamp his lips looked like somebody had chewed them red. There was a crooked scar running down his forehead, and I didn't like the way he was staring at Hunnie. The other guy was dark and skinny and had one of those deformed half-arms. He looked about my age, but he was so skinny it was hard to tell.

"Whassup?" I nodded and stood up. Using Hunnie's bag as a pillow, I lowered her head to the bench. I was careful to keep my eyes on them while making sure I didn't wake up my baby. I'd seen men like them before, and I knew the deal. The joint had been full of niggers with predatory looks in their eyes, and I decided these two wasn't gonna get no whole lotta conversation outta me tonight.

The skinny one spoke to me in Swahili. "Hey, my friend. We are hungry and there is no work." He pointed toward the knapsack nestled under Hunnie's head. "Do you have any food in there?"

I shook my head and stepped toward them. "Naw. No food."

The tall guy glanced at Hunnie again, then moved around to my right and spoke. "Any money?"

I nodded. "Yeah. I got plenty of that," I said, whirling as I slammed both my fists in his gut.

He didn't know what hit him, and I didn't know how to stop. All I heard were grunts and cries and the sounds of my knuckles connecting with his flesh and breaking his bones. When I finally came to my senses, his long ass was stretched out on the ground with blood running from his nose and mouth and those red lips were spitting out teeth.

The other guy took off running. I knew Nairobi was full of bandits and thieves, but where I came from even the lowest motherfucker knew not to fuck with a man in the presence of his child. Especially his baby girl. Their lack of respect got jumbled up with the rage I felt toward Banjoko and every other mother-fucker who was willing to try me like my love for Hunnie didn't count for shit. I caught that skinny fucker in about ten steps and didn't take a bit of mercy on him for being handicapped neither. I broke his ass up just like I'd done his friend. Little arm and all.

For the rest of the night, I kept my eyes open, ready for anything. We walked back to the station early the next morning, stopping at a roadside stand for a bite to eat. I got us a couple of breakfast sandwiches of lamb with gravy and some juice that was half warm, and we ate as we walked.

Hunnie started limping and whining about halfway there, and I knew there was nothing wrong with her feet. She was just tired. Plain tired. I picked her up, kissed her lips, and let her lay her head against my shoulder, and I carried her the rest of the way as she dozed.

Inside the station I paid for our tickets while holding her in my arms. Hunnie's fare was only half price, and because I had an American passport and visa we were considered tourists and got assigned a first-class compartment. The train wasn't leaving until seven, and we would arrive in Mombasa at just after eight the next morning, and that was cool with me.

Hunnie woke up as I was putting my wallet back into my pocket, and I saw reality crash down on her when she realized she was still living under the same crazy circumstances in yet another strange place.

"Hey, Sweetie Peetie." I gave her my best "everything is just fine" smile and kissed her on the bridge of her nose. "We're at the train station now. You okay?"

She nodded and yawned. "I want something to drink, Daddy. And I need to go to the bathroom."

There was no way I was letting my baby go to the bathroom alone, even for a minute. I found a men's room and said, "Close your eyes, Hunnie," then pushed through the door and took her right in. The bathroom was beyond filthy. There was an older man standing at a urinal, but otherwise it was empty. We went into one of the stalls, where the toilet smelled like ten years' worth of old piss and didn't look much better. I told Hunnie to keep her eyes closed, and I pulled her pants down and let her pee as I held her at least a foot above the toilet.

Back outside, I found a small stand and bought her a juice and a box of chocolate cookies and put them in her bag for lunch. The clerk said there was a dining car on the train, and we'd just have to wait for that if we wanted a real meal.

The platform was crowded with porters and bellhops and folks of all different nationalities. People were crying and carrying on like they were never gonna see each other again, when more than likely they'd be right back in Nairobi in a couple of days. I found a small wooden crate and carried it all the way down to the end of the station and out into a field near the shiny row of tracks. I was exhausted, and Hunnie's eyes were scared and flat. I lay down on my back in a level, grassy area and propped my head up on the crate. I slid Hunnie's bag beneath my neck, patted my chest, and let my baby lay down on a pillow made of Daddy. With Hunnie's head on my chest, I looked left and right so many times I caught a cramp in my neck. Finally, I just lay there and chilled, patting Hunnie's back and listening to her heartbeat. The train would be pulling up before the sun went down again, and come hell or high water, me and my baby girl were getting on it.

My black ass had been spoiled. Being driven around by an Omorru driver for six years had given me a jacked sense of reality when it came to Kenyan travel, and when I saw the old-timey condition of the train I cursed under my breath. I wasn't expecting something like Amtrak to come speeding down the line, but I thought the handwritten message boards and seating charts were taking things back a little bit too far for my tastes. Sometimes you got what you paid for.

They assigned us to a first-class sleeper, which had two narrow benches that turned into beds and a tiny sink that looked like a sandbox. We were toward the end of the train, in the last compartment in our car, and lucky for us the bathroom was right next door.

There was just as much dust in our compartment as there was outdoors, but I wasn't gonna complain. I tried to brush a coating of it off the seats, then gave up 'cause all I managed to do was smear it around. Hunnie and I were already dirtier than all get-out, and I figured a few extra ounces of dust couldn't do much damage.

I was relieved when the train finally pulled out of the station, but when I opened my curtain to peek outside I almost put my fist through the glass. A face was staring back at me, a kid, no more than ten, hanging on to the outside of my window and catching a free ride. As we rounded a curve I saw that there were others just like him hanging on to the outsides of cars ahead of us, riding out there like it was no big deal. I figured after some of the hardships these folks had lived through, it wasn't. I nodded at the kid, but he looked right through me. Like he was the one who had paid for the car and I was hitching the ride. He wouldn't be out there long. Was probably going right into Nairobi Central, and I pulled the curtain closed and sat down next to Hunnie.

The conductor came around to take our tickets, and by the time the cabin steward showed his face I was starving. "Excuse me, my man," I said, letting a stack of Kenyan shillings show in my hand. "My daughter is too tired to go to the dining car. Can we have a meal brought back here to us?" Old boy was smooth as grease.

"Of course," he said, and "shook" my hand. "The Eland game is good tonight. It's been marinated in honey and garlic. And as soon as you are finished eating, I'll convert your berths so that you can rest." I nodded as he left, my stomach growling at the thought of a real meal.

I had no idea what would be waiting for us twenty miles away at the main train station in Nairobi South, but I wasn't taking any chances. Right before we pulled in, I took Hunnie into the bathroom and warned her to be quiet. I put her behind me as we huddled behind the locked door, braced myself, and waited. The first person who opened it was gonna catch a bad one, and I just hoped it wasn't some tired old lady who just needed to pee, 'cause if she managed to get past that lock, she was gonna get straight fucked up tonight.

The crowd at the main station was even worse than where we'd gotten on in Kahawa, and you could actually feel the vibrations as a ton of luggage was loaded onto the cars. I heard footsteps that sounded like herds of wildebeests, and a combination of languages and dialects that made my head spin.

I was just about to open the bathroom door and peek outside when someone tried the doorknob, then pounded on the door until it shook in its frame.

"Get a key!" a man's voice called out in Swahili. "Open this door!"

I felt Hunnie clutching my leg, cringing at the authority in his voice. The door shook again, this time almost throwing the lock as several shoulders rammed it from the other side.

"No! Wait! No Americans here! Only a very sick old woman!" I swallowed hard. It was our cabin steward, covering for a brother, and every muscle in my body was coiled as I listened to him lead what sounded like the authorities away.

A few minutes later the conductors started screaming for peo-

ple to get on or get left, and I don't think I breathed at all until I
felt the train moving again, and even then I waited, patting Hunnie's back, until we were on the outskirts of Nairobi, heading
toward the Athi River before I decided it was probably safe to go
out. I let Hunnie use the bathroom and wash her hands, then
peeking out the door, I took her back into our compartment.

"Want Daddy to read you a story?"

She seemed shaken but not shattered. She reached into her bag
of cookies and stuck one into her mouth. "Yes," she said, chewing with her mouth open, crumbs falling off her lips. "Read me
*Isra the Butterfly Gets Caught for Show and Tell*."

I pulled the large book out of her backpack, and the zipper
caught and ripped. Setting the bag on the seat, I held up the book
that had a big butterfly on the cover. It looked like it had been
drawn with colored pencils. "Hold up, little girl," I said, tugging
one of her braids. "You're old enough to read to Daddy now!"

And she did, running her finger along the page beneath the
words and holding her head to one side just like her mommy did.

The cabin steward came back with our dinner and I gave him a
nod of thanks, then reached into my wallet and "shook" his hand
again. The food smelled good, and Hunnie ate almost as much as
I did. The steward surprised us with some Kenyan nuts and two
oranges for dessert, and I peeled the oranges with my fingers and
put the pack of nuts in Hunnie's bag in case of an emergency.

The train made nineteen stops between Nairobi and Mombasa,
and the reason I knew was because I stayed awake and counted
each one of them. We looked out the windows before it got too
dark, and I showed Hunnie herds of Thomson's gazelles, zebras,
and hartebeests. We even saw some of the Masai shepherds, decked
out in their colorful red clothes and beads as they tended their
flocks.

We were about two hundred miles outside of Nairobi, close to
the Tsavo station and Man-Eaters Junction, when Hunnie got
cranky and started missing her mommy. No matter what I said,

she wouldn't stop crying, and eventually she laid her head in my lap and fell asleep. I sat up guarding my daughter the entire night, watching her toss and turn in her sleep, sometimes crying out and opening her eyes to look around wildly. I felt the same way she did, and I cried inside as I thought of Abeni and all we'd been through. I wasn't Slim Willie by no stretch, but I'd earned the right to the blood of my father that flowed through my veins, and for me that was the long and short of it. My task was clear, and there wasn't no two ways about it.

It was either get my daughter home safe, or die trying.

# TWENTY-SEVEN

The train was supposed to get into Mombasa at 8:15. I got Hunnie up at seven and took her to the bathroom to let her brush her teeth, then changed her into her last pair of clean panties and put yesterday's shorts back on over them. I asked her to turn her back, then used the toilet myself real quick. Our cabin steward brought us some hard-boiled eggs, chicken sausage, and sliced pineapples for breakfast, and I paid him one hundred Kenyan shillings for his trouble.

I opened the curtains and saw fields that Sugar Baby woulda loved to dig her hands in. The vegetation looked thick and healthy, and much greener than any I'd seen in Nairobi or Kairami or even Alabama, for that matter. I stuck my hand out the window and into the warm breeze. The sun was high and the temperature was heating up, the smell of seawater cutting through the traces of diesel filling the air. The Malindi station was just up ahead, and I was edgy and aggravated. After being up all night I was tired, my eyes felt gritty, and the endless clicking of the track joints was working my nerves and wearing them out.

I took Hunnie back into the bathroom right before we hit the station, and when the train came to a stop and they unlocked the doors, I made sure we got off right in the thick of the crowd. I wanted to give her a piggyback ride, but I was too scared some fool might try to snatch her from behind, so I held her in my arms instead.

"Where are we now?" she asked as I moved along the platform, heading away from the interior of the station where people were lining up to wait for their luggage.

"This is Mombasa, baby," I told her, trying not to keep looking over my shoulders. "It's a big city where ships and airplanes come in. We're gonna try to get a flight out again today, okay?"

She nodded with no emotion, and I knew she was worn-out, almost at her breaking point.

I saw a sign for a shuttle bus that went to the airport, but I was leery. Not only didn't I want us being exposed to any old body, but I'd known people to get their pockets picked on a crowded bus, and I wanted to concentrate on getting my baby to the airport and not fighting off some petty thief. There were four or five *matatus* waiting outside the station, and I almost ran as I saw them filling up with whole families squeezing to get in together. I picked a bright blue one that looked like it might have room for a few more bodies and paid the driver who stood outside the van holding his hand out.

There were three rows of seats in the *matatus,* not including the driver and front passenger seats, and I slid Hunnie in first, next to a heavyset black woman wearing a colorful dress, then sat down beside her. I let Hunnie have her own seat instead of putting her on my lap, and then I slid over so at least one other person could fit in next to me.

A moment later a young, solidly built man wearing a dingy white shirt got in beside me. I saw a lot of people here who looked like him—light skin, dark, wavy hair, a mixture of Arab and African and Indian—and even though my shirt was fragrant after a couple of days on the run, I still didn't have shit on him. I didn't care how bad he smelled though. As long as me and Hunnie were sandwiched between folks and could blend in and not be seen, he could have smelled like a pig in shit and I woulda rubbed up against him and hidden in his shadow.

Finally the doors slammed shut and the *matatus* took off, lurching away from the curb and swerving onto the street so fast I had to put my arm out across Hunnie to hold her back. The traffic was bumper-to-bumper as we headed north from the station to drop off the first passengers on Hailie Selassie Road, when a shrill whistle blew and a uniformed policeman ran out in front of the van, waving like a madman.

Our driver hit the brakes and flung open his door, yelling at the cop in a mixture of Swahili and Arabic. I hugged Hunnie close to me and tried to scoot down in my seat. When that didn't work, I concentrated on keeping my head behind the guy's in front of me and out of the cop's line of sight. Everybody in the van started talking and shouting at once, and before I knew it, all eyes were on me.

"What's happening?" Hunnie cried. "Is he mad at us?"

I pressed her face into my chest, "It's okay. Everything is okay."

"What are they saying, Daddy?"

I caught a word or two in Swahili, but my Arabic was nonexistent. Didn't matter, though. I understood the universal language of it all. The cop was looking for an American and wanted the driver to pull over and let him search the *matatus*. He wanted to see our passports or travel visas. The driver was enraged. He had a schedule to keep, and besides, there were no Americans in his van.

I whispered to Hunnie in Swahili, hoping she would take the hint and switch languages. She did. "I don't know, Hunnie. I don't understand everything he's saying."

"Is the airport far?"

"No, it's not far. As soon as he lets us go, we'll be heading straight there."

"Then can we get out?"

I shook my head and peered through the window at the cop, who had his gun out and was going ballistic. Getting out was the last thing I wanted to do. I braced myself as the driver jumped from his seat and, cursing and stomping his feet, came around to the passenger side and pulled open the door. The cop was right behind him, waving his gun, his cap pulled down low over his eyes. I couldn't see much of his face, but what I saw was the same light-coffee-colored skin as the man who had slid in beside me.

"You! You!" The driver pointed dead at me. "You must get out. I am sorry, you are wanted by the Central Police and you must get out!"

"What! Why?" I yelled in Swahili.

I pressed back into my seat and felt every bone in Hunnie's body trembling in fear. "Let's get out, Daddy," she said in English.

And now the other passengers were telling me off, wanting me out so they could get on to their locations. The guy sitting next to me stepped from the van to let us out.

"C'mon, Hunnie," I whispered, rage rising in my chest. "Don't be scared, baby. Everything is gonna be all right."

Standing outside the van, I faced the cop, pissed. Pissed at Banjoko, and pissed that I had to run from him or anybody else. My baby girl had been scared for three days straight, and that pissed me off most of all.

The funky dude with the white shirt stood beside the cop. The driver slammed the door and ran back around to his side, then jumped in and took off. The cop motioned us to follow him toward the side of the building where a faded sign made me think at one time it mighta been some kinda Indian bar. It was deserted now, and the cop and the wrestler had me hemmed in between them. I wondered if they knew they were getting ready to get fucked up.

Slinging her bag over my shoulder, I pushed Hunnie behind me, and she held on tight to my leg. "So?" I barked at the cop, a storm swirling inside of me. It was fight-or-die time, and I was pumped. It was all I could do not to jump on his ass. Gun or no gun, I was ready to take him out. "I paid for that ride. What the hell you want, man?"

He raised his cap and I stared into his eyes. They were greenish gray slits, and I couldn't read a damn thing in them. He stuck his gun in its holster and took a step toward me.

"Are you Bishop Johnson?"

"Why?"

I felt the younger dude moving in close like he wanted some too, and I turned toward him, ready to put his thick ass down first. By the time their backup arrived, both of these motherfuckers were gonna be on the ground bleeding. The young guy glanced at a piece of paper he was holding in his hand, then nodded. "This is him. And that's his daughter."

I reached back and pressed Hunnie close to me with one hand, then went into a crouch.

"Malcolm sent me."

The cop had spoken, and for the first time I noticed how dirty he was. His uniform looked grimy, and the last two buttons were gone from his shirt.

"Say what?"

"I am Ari Sowotho, his friend, and this is my son, Samir." He shrugged and pointed at the sandals on his feet. "I am a farmer, not a policeman. The airport is unsafe. Malcolm sent a telegram, and I am supposed to guide you and your daughter to the American consulate on Kimathi."

I stared at him.

"You don't believe me?" he said. "I have a message from Malcolm."

I took the paper from his hand and read:

MOMBASA AIRPORT UNSECURE. AM TAKING NEXT FLIGHT INTO BOI. WILL MEET YOU AT U.S. CONSULATE. GO BY FOOT, BUT KEEP YOUR CHIN TUCKED. END

I stared at both of them and couldn't believe it.

"Come," Ari told me. "You must walk to the consulate. It is a long way, and we must keep you from being noticed. We will walk through the Makupa market on Mwembe Tayari, and there you will look like any other father out for a day of shopping with his daughter."

Nodding, I lifted Hunnie into my arms and kissed her nose. She closed her eyes and tears fell down her face.

"We're okay, Sweetie Peetie," I whispered, trying to soothe her. I felt her sigh, then tremble quietly, and it hurt me to my heart that it was me who had taught her how to cry without making a sound. "Go ahead and cry out loud if you need to, baby girl," I told her, holding her as tight as I could. "Daddy's got you, and you're safe. But you can cry if it makes you feel better."

We walked across the open market, threading through the crowd with Ari leading the way and his son bringing up the rear. Salt was in the air, and the ocean breeze was perfect as I cradled Hunnie in my arms, much the same way I'd done when she was a little baby. The sound of haggling vendors and the smell of burning incense seemed to relax her, and although her eyes stayed open, her body grew limp, her hand dangling down and hitting my leg.

And this is how I saved Hundiata, my daughter, Abeni's daughter, from a Kinaksu cutting. I carried her down the streets of Mombasa until my muscles screamed and felt like hot lead.

And when my arms grew too weary, I carried her on my back.

# Epilogue

The U.S. consulate in Mombasa was located near the corner of Duke and Kimathi, and I followed Ari as he turned south on Digo Road and cut across Kilindini. Up ahead I could see the building, the American flag waving outside. Two men stood on the steps, and from a distance, if I didn't know better, I woulda sworn that one of them was my brother and best friend, Malcolm.

I kept walking, my eyes blurry, Hunnie sitting up on my shoulders, and every fiber in my body, from my head to my feet, screaming for rest. As I watched, the white guy went inside of the building, and a moment later the other man hit the stairs and began walking toward me.

Hunnie called it first, but I was right behind her. "Uncle Malcolm!" She squirmed on my shoulders, and I eased her down to the ground. She took off running, and Malcolm caught her as her arms went around his neck.

"Hey, Funny Hunnie!" He tickled her and she wriggled down to the ground. "You okay, little one? Your daddy took good care of you, didn't he?"

"I did my best, Bro'," I said, dapping him, then reaching for a hug. I knew I was funky and dirty, but after all I'd been through in the last forty-eight hours I was so glad to see him I didn't give a damn.

"It's good, Chicken," he said, and to my surprise I believed him. "It's all good. Help is here, and your baby is safe."

He shook hands with Ari Sowotho and his son, and when I reached out to shake Ari's hand, I saw that his pants had a hole in them and didn't even match his shirt.

"Thanks." I smiled as I remembered how close he'd come to getting knocked out. "Good thing you had that gun," I said, pointing toward his holster, " 'cause I was planning on killing you."

Ari glanced at Samir and laughed. He pulled the gun out and pointed at the tip. It had been soldered closed, and the barrel was dented. "I got this from my nephew," he said. "He found it in the back of a *matatus*."

Holding Hunnie's hand, I let Malcolm take her bag off my shoulder. "Careful," I told him as we walked up the consulate steps. "My money is in there, and the zipper's busted."

"We'll get her another one."

We stepped into the building, and I coulda stuck out my tongue and tasted the air-conditioning, it felt so good. A bunch of white men stood around in a huddle, and I saw two press photographers balancing cameras on their shoulders.

"Man, what's this?" I pulled Hunnie close and touched Malcolm's arm.

"It's your traveling party, man. We had to put the eyes of the world on you, man, to make sure you got out of here alive with our baby girl. Your boy is here in Kenya too. Casper Wilson. You've got friends in low places, Bro'. His car is on the way in, so come on and let's go meet him."

We were on one of the largest aircrafts I'd ever seen. It was a Lufthansa and had two rows on each side of the plane and a long row down the middle. We sat in first-class seats that were wide and made of soft leather.

"You cool?" Malcolm asked.

I sat between him and Hunnie, who was staring out the window watching the African continent, and the home of her mother, become a memory. "Yeah, man," I said. "I'm all right." I sat back in my seat and closed my eyes. I'd found the letters. The letters Satin must have written when she figured out what I was planning to do. I'd bought Hunnie a new backpack, a pink Powerpuff Girls bag, from a gift shop in the airport. Surrounded by the press and a posse from Mombasa's Central Police, we'd rolled up in the airport and cleared security without a bit of trouble.

Trouble had come later, when I was switching the money and Hunnie's clothes from her old bag to the new one. I'd pulled back the inner zipper, and running my hand along the inside, I'd come out with Abeni's letters. She had written my name on the outside of the envelope in her big loopy script, and when I looked inside I saw Hunnie's name centered on one of the two folded sheets of paper and mine on the other.

I'd wanted to wait until I was someplace calm and private to absorb her words, and now, sitting in an airplane flying at thirty thousand feet in the air, I didn't quite have the nerve. I mean, the fact that she had written letters and stashed them in Hunnie's bag meant she'd been onto me from the beginning. All that extra money in our account had to have come from her too.

So did this mean she was down with what I'd done for our baby, and was giving me her blessings? Would her note tell me just how right I was to snatch her daughter and leave, or did she hate me, and was the letter gonna burn my fingers when I pulled it out the envelope? The whole time I'd been scheming with Malcolm on how to protect my daughter, I'd told myself that as soon as Hunnie was safe I'd come back for Abeni. With Hunnie gone, Banjoko had no power over us, and as twisted as he was, he loved Hunnie, and I knew he wouldn't keep Abeni from her daughter forever. Even now, as the airplane sped toward Amsterdam and I headed down the aisle toward the bathroom with the letter in my hand, I calculated how soon I could catch a flight back. How many days or weeks would it be until I could look into my wife's eyes and hold her in my arms again?

The flight was less than half full, and there was plenty of room for people to sprawl across the empty rows. I nodded at a stewardess as I passed, then went into one of the narrow bathrooms.

I locked the door and braced my back against it to stop my legs from shaking as I unfolded Abeni's letter. I could smell her scent as I opened it, and something stirred deep inside me as I remembered the last night we'd lain together. A wanting struck me so deep it almost made me wanna turn the airplane around and go back. Go back and deal with whatever and whoever I had to, just as long as I could have my sweet Satin by my side again.

*Bishop,*

   *Dear husband, your love has given me a joy that is simply indescribable, and even now, as you prepare to leave with our child, I am the happiest I have ever been. What a lucky daughter our Hundiata is! To have a father who is willing to risk his life for the love of his girl-child and the strength and conviction of his heart. Because of your courage, our Hunnie will never know the pain I've known, or suffer the indignities and shame that permeate the lives of countless young African girls. If I lived to see Mount Kenya crumble into dust, never could I repay you for healing my broken spirit and providing the emotional shoring that has bolstered my soul.*

   *Bishop, before you there was desolation and anguish, but with you came joy and happiness, the twin gifts of peace and Hundiata, both of which my father sought to deny me in the name of sanctity and honor. And now, although my flesh has grown cold and been returned to the earth, know that my heart will journey with you on every road you travel.*

   *I leave it at your discretion to give Hundiata her letter at an age when she can absorb it without hating me, when she is able to comprehend why I*

*left her so, and understand that my actions were motivated by my desire to
have her live as free as she was born.*

*My love, from the moment we met, each of us ceased to exist as indi-
vidual beings. Bound together by love and Spirit, this new existence,
forged by the halves of our hearts, became everlasting and enduring, and
unlike our flesh, will never die. Don't look back, and do not grieve, for I
wait for you on the other side. I am still here. In the earth that nourishes,
in the wind that caresses, and in the fire that warms, and I anticipate the
moment we meet once more, this time in spirit, to fall in love all over
again.*

*Abeni*

I read the letter twice, my stomach rolling, deep, hacking sounds
flying from my mouth. And then the tears came. Ten years' worth,
rising up from my feet, forming a river in my nuts, bubbling up
through my chest, and falling from my eyes like one of them Japanese monsoons in May.

*And now, although my flesh has grown cold and been returned to
the earth, know that my heart will journey with you on every road you
travel. . . . Don't look back, and do not grieve, for I wait for you on the
other side.*

She was gone. There was nothing of my wife left behind in
Kenya, nothing left there for me to return and reclaim. Hunnie
and I would now carry Abeni in the center of our hearts, where
we'd keep her safe forever. Holding on to the sink, I let the tears
fall for what seemed like hours, until I was completely dry. I cried
for Abeni, and for our baby girl who would grow up without
the touch of her mother, for Slim Willie, for my mother, Dimples, for my granmaw, Sugar Baby, for the lives I'd taken, and for
every little girl who had ever felt the cold blade of a knife between her legs.

And finally, for the first time, I cried for myself, for all that I'd
lost. Then out of nowhere the tears stopped and peace fell upon
me. It was like a switch had been flipped somewhere deep in my

heart, right in the spot where the wind had swept Abeni's voice. Tearing off a towel, I wiped my face and swallowed my pain, 'cause not only did I have to man up for my daughter, I had to honor my wife and keep her proud of me. A minute later I walked back to my seat, trembling but solid, and lifted our daughter into my lap as we headed for home, racing across the sky, flying above the ocean.

# Acknowledgments

As with most literary works, *A Woman's Worth* was fashioned in solitude, but its deliverance was accomplished by the efforts of many. I'd like to thank my merciful God, the Owner of the world, the Master of the Day of Judgment, the Giver of all gifts, for blessing me with literary talent while keeping my paths straight and peacefully balanced.

Thank you to my husband, Greg, for finding a million ways to make my life easier and for being a man who truly loves God and family. (YWYDSB?)

To our sons and daughters, each of whom we pray is filled with self-confidence and understands and embraces the worth of a woman: Kharim, Erica, Greg Jr., Kharel, Kharyse, and Khaliyah. What can we say? How wonderfully each of you shine! We love you and are proud of you and thank you for being well-grounded, independent thinkers who enrich our lives just by being yourselves.

To my sister, Michelle Carr, for being willing to fly fourteen hours just to visit me, and for everything else you do for my children and our nieces and nephews as well. I love you!

Thanks to my nieces and nephews and godchildren, especially Auntie's Booger, Darius Demetri, and Auntie's Poppy, Justice Samir. Auntie loves you!

Endless thanks to Mel Taylor, acclaimed author of *The Mitt Man,* for holding my hand and baby-stepping me through every word of this novel. Your expertise and guidance were invaluable, and I could not have done justice to these characters without your tutelage and support. Thank you for being both a good friend and a wise mentor.

I send my love and my thanks to my wonderfully supportive

friends. Even if unnamed here you know who you are. Special thanks to Kim and Jimmy Kendrick, Tawana Harrington, Bertha Turner (yeah, you're my girl and you are special to me and I love your crazy tail to death!), Kim Stanley, Sheryl Hinds, Tracey Williams, Pat Houser, Dawn Williams, Rhonda Tatum, Phyllis Primus, Vicki Crenshaw, Renee Shahid, Carmelia Scott-Skillern, Robin Bowman, Michelle "Shelly" Hill, Robin Oliver, Irma Royster, Army Captain Myles Cagins, Dee Gilbert, Edie Hall, Steffie Howard, Sandy Jones, Alfreada Kelley, Lauretta Pierce, Army Specialist Stephen McCray, Teresa Taylor, Latonia Parks, Sherrie L. Respass, Carlyn Hard, and Jackie Holliday, and my home girl, Gwendolyn McNeil.

Thank you to my fellow authors who are diligently striving to produce quality fiction while maintaining an atmosphere that is welcoming and edifying to new writers: Gloria Mallette, Karen E. Quinones Miller, Kimberla Lawson Roby, Lolita Files, Christine Young-Robinson, Zane, Nancey Flowers, Rita Coburn Whack, Pat G'Orge Walker, Trevy McDonald, Margaret Johnson-Hodge, RM Johnson, Travis Hunter, Jamise Dames, Carl Weber, Mary Morrison, Marcus Major, C. Kelly Robinson, Daaimah Poole, Brandon Massey, Brian Egeston, Scott Haskins, and many others. It is a pleasure to have each of you as a colleague.

Big thanks to Nakea Murray of As the Page Turns Bookclub, Tee C. Royal of RAW Sistaz, Yasmin Coleman of APOOO, Marwan Mackenzie of Black Books 2, Thomas "Teej" James and Orlanda Thompson of Busara Nayo, my girls from Jersey—Sistahs with a Vision Bookclub, Thumper (your reviews have me ROLLING), Linda Watkins, and Troy Johnson of AALBC.com, Robilyn and the Girlfriends Reading Circle, Yvette Hayward, and TaRessa Stovall, my dear friend and business partner in TnT Explosions, and the countless other book club members and libraries who support my work. Much love to my girls Jackie McGuire, Renna Wilkinson, Rena Finney, Kim Burney, and Yvette Gray, and to Malana Tucker, and all of the other wonderful sister-friends who invited me into their homes as well as into their lives. Malana, that aloha send-off you ladies gave me was simply the best. I love you all!

Thanks to all of my new friends in Hawaii, especially Linda King (my good walking buddy!), Evelyn Phillips, Fleeta Penton, Lenell Lopez, Gladys Endozo, Sandra Franklin, Lawana Russell, Michelle Vollmer, Susan Goeckner, and Sam and Ethel Smith.

Thanks and appreciation to Melody Guy and Djana Pearson Morris, and love to Emma Rodgers, Marita Golden, Shirley Johnson, Kim and Andre Kelton, Mr. and Mrs. Tills, and all of the other booksellers and libraries who have supported my works.

Greatest thanks to the readers who take the time to blow up my e-mail account and flood my mailbox with praise and feedback. It is for you that I write, it is for you that I create. As usual, you can visit my website at www.tracypricethompson.com, and I can be reached at tracythomp@aol.com. I look forward to hearing from you.

Peace and balance,
Tracy

# A WOMAN'S WORTH

## Tracy Price-Thompson

*A Reader's Guide*

# A Conversation with Tracy Price-Thompson

**Q:** *A Woman's Worth* is extraordinarily evocative of time and place. You drew Birdtown and Bull Run, Alabama, with such richness and finesse. The dusty, earthy, heat-drenched roads come alive; it feels very cinematic. What was the impetus for setting *A Woman's Worth* in the rural South?

**A:** My mother's family hails from the rural South, and re-creating that environment as the setting for *A Woman's Worth* was a tribute to my proud but humble roots, a heritage and an environment that I fear my own children will never have a chance to experience or enjoy.

Although I was born in New York, my roots are in the deep South. It has been a few years since I've spent much time there, but my memories are rich and vivid, and they enabled me to transfer my feelings about that culture onto paper.

**Q:** Your depictions of Kairami, Kenya, rural Kenya, and Abeni's Kinaksu culture are vibrant and sparkling. Is this your imagination or did you draw from real-life travels to Kenya? Is there really such a culture as Kinaksu?

**A:** I have not yet had the fortune of traveling to the Motherland, so all my depictions of Africa, in particular, of Kenya and Kenyan culture, were drawn from research and creative license. I deliberately created a fictitious tribe of Kinaksu people in an attempt to not offend or inaccurately portray an existing Kenyan tribe and its customs. I've heard it said many times that an author can only write what he or she knows, and with *A Woman's Worth* I hope to disprove that statement. I do not know Africa. I *dream* Africa, and my creative spirit does the rest.

**Q:** This is your first novel set in Africa. Were you trying to dispel any stereotypes or explore the romantic ideals people may have of Africa?

**A:** I chose Africa as a setting in an attempt to stretch myself creatively, and to convey a message that dispels the stereotypes that all Africans are running around barefoot in the bush. Many readers have written to me and said that they'd never before heard of a wealthy African, or that they had no idea that most African countries have cities of great economic importance, which offer the same luxuries and indulgences and intelligent Black [people] that we have in this country. I learned a lot about the Motherland during my intensive research for this novel, and I hope my readers learned something too.

**Q:** What other classic or contemporary novels did you have in mind when you conceived and wrote *A Woman's Worth*?

**A:** Of course Alice Walker's *Possessing the Secret of Joy* was close at hand, as was *Desert Flower* by Waris Diri. *Mama Day* by Gloria Naylor has influenced this work to a great extent as well. Among those three authors I was pretty much covered in terms of inspiration and guidance in writing a novel whose characters experience events that are outside of the norm in commercial African American fiction.

**Q:** You open the book with a letter to the reader about always staying on top of your game and writing resonant, moving, and

creative works, not a rehashing of your previous novels. We, your readers, applaud you for this and for being so mindful of our intelligence. What compelled you to write this letter?

**A:** I'm the type of writer who refuses to be put into a box. I reserve the right to explore the range of my creativity and intelligence and to write whatever type of book I feel compelled to write at any given time. I wanted my readers to know that I respect them enough to present them with fresh, innovative reading material each time they purchase one of my works. I deliberately guarantee them they will not be receiving a rehashing of my previous works, because I'd consider that short-changing them. I've read a lot of books where the author simply changes the minor details of a story—names, locations, and the like—but the basic plot remains the same book after book after book. I figure you can get away with doing that for a short while, but eventually your readers will catch on. Because I respect my readership and appreciate their support, I prefer to work hard to give them something different and compelling each time at bat.

**Q:** Was there ever an alternate ending to the book?

**A:** I always knew Abeni would die. Like you say, it was the ultimate sacrifice; and after the life that she had lived, it would have diminished her character if she allowed her daughter to experience that same kind of pain and rejection.

**Q:** Were any pivotal parts of the text cut, added, or drastically changed from earlier drafts?

**A:** We didn't make any major changes to the meat of the novel. My editor wields a velvet whip and is very respectful and mindful of the vision of her authors. She allows me to tell my story as it comes from my heart, which I believe makes our relationship, and

my novels, very successful. However, there was one pivotal part of the novel that was cut from Malcolm's section.

Initially the work was divided into three parts, Fire (Malcolm), Wind (Chicken), and Earth (Hunnie), but at the time we believed Malcolm's portion didn't deserve as much weight as the other two portions of the story. As a result, the background information the reader gets about Malcolm's early life is drizzled throughout the story and revealed mostly through a dream. In hindsight that may have been a mistake, because many readers have written me to say that they wanted to know more about Malcolm and what his early life and his dead parents were like—details that would have been more fully revealed had Fire not been cut.

**Q:** Tracy, the love scenes were phenomenal! They hit just the right note, alternating between fierce and frenzied, lustful and erotic, tender and epiphanic. Girl, you evoked waterfalls of tears when Abeni and Bishop are physically intimate for the first time! Were the sex scenes as fun to write as they were for us to read?

**A:** Oh yes. They were fun because, for the most part, they were pure. Even though Abeni had been promiscuous, when I wrote the love scenes between her and Bishop it was as if she was experiencing physical joy for the very first time. Those scenes touched me because of their tenderness.

**Q:** And not to be *too* all into your business, but did you let your husband read the love scenes as you were writing, or only when the book was done?

**A:** My husband is not a big fiction fan. He prefers books on history and religion. However, he took a copy of *A Woman's Worth* with him to Iraq, and after he read it he wrote to me that it was a book that made him laugh out loud and cry out loud. He loved it and thought the love scenes were great. He is a wonderful Black

husband and father, and much of what Chicken did for Abeni and Hunnie are character traits and behaviors that my husband exhibits with me and our own children.

**Q:** This is a technically complex novel. You write in the first person and in the third person, from the perspective of characters who are living and who have passed on, and with two different tones. And most impressive is how we learn about Chicken/Bishop's life through other people. It's not until the end that we actually hear the story from his voice, told from his first person point of view. You pull this off beautifully. What was the easiest and the most difficult part of putting all these technical, risky mechanics to use?

**A:** I simply had to listen to the characters and allow them into my head. The most difficult character to hear was Abeni, as I have had limited conversations with African women. I have many African friends and have interviewed quite a few for the novel, but the culture and the tone is not native to me, so listening to Abeni and accurately portraying her thoughts and feelings was quite a challenge. Chicken's portion was actually the easiest to write. I had a wonderful Black father and a loving Black brother. I am married to the absolute best Black man. All I had to do was imagine what any of them would do if they found themselves in Chicken's shoes, so his voice and character came easily to me. As for blending first and third person narratives and giving voice to those living and dead, I like to explore different methods of storytelling and the only rule I write by is: the method has to work.

**Q:** It almost feels like 2 different books. Chicken's part, told through Malcolm, was very immediate and visceral, while Abeni's was told in a very distant tone. Was this intentional—to mirror each person's personality, perhaps?

**A:** Absolutely. It actually felt like I was writing two different books. At the end of Chicken's section, told through Malcolm, I deliberately launched into the circumcision scene using African words and phrases to transport the reader into a different realm. Abeni's voice is first heard through the words "I was dead before I was born," which was meant to be sobering and insightful into the kind of life this woman had lived and her perspective of that life.

**Q:** You accomplish so many feats with *A Woman's Worth,* Tracy. Among the most stunning was writing from a man's point of view. You captured the cadence and male-bonding vernacular so wonderfully. Did you have a man reread the portions told from Bishop's and Malcolm's point of view? Did you worry that this wouldn't sound authentic?

**A:** Oh yes! Several times I had to ask my husband whether or not a certain passage of dialogue sounded like something a man would say. He was great at correcting me and helping me navigate around a few conversations. I believe writers have to possess an ear for dialogue, which is invaluable when writing in the voice of the opposite sex, or as characters from different countries or cultures.

**Q:** You tackle a very controversial subject: female genital mutilation (FGM). Has this always been an issue of great importance to you? Why choose to develop a book with this hot-button issue at its core?

**A:** This practice has always interested me, but I did not write *A Woman's Worth* as a vehicle to explore it. At the core of *A Woman's Worth* is a story about a regular Black man who loves his woman and child enough to lay down his life for them. So often we hear about Black men who are described in such unfavorable terms, and while these types of men do exist, there are many of our brothers out there who love the women in their lives the way that Chicken did. And using a traditionally patriarchal sexually-debasing procedure as a means of showing the protectiveness and love that Black men can and do have for their baby girls was the primary focus of the novel.

**Q:** You depict FGM in a vivid, but also fair, way. Did you take pains not to demonize your Kenyan characters who believe it *is* necessary? How much research was involved in exploring the FGM issue on medical, emotional, and physical levels?

**A:** Oh yes. Which is why I created a fictitious tribe. I respect the individual rights of all people and I also respect the customs and traditions that people choose for themselves. Mutilation gives the procedure a negative connotation. Circumcision is more widely understood and accepted. There was absolute care taken not to demonize the tradition because I am fully aware that many women embrace it, and not only in Africa. This is not an African tradition. It is a tradition practiced in many areas of the world. I conducted extensive interviews with women who had been circumcised and I was surprised to find that their opinions and views on the procedure, and its effects on their lives, varied widely.

**Q:** Who was your favorite character?

**A:** I think I loved Chicken best in this novel. He was hurt but fearless. He was larger than life. He was braver than he should have been. He did the right thing even when he knew how much it would cost him. He is my father, my husband, and my youngest son rolled into one being.

**Q:** Did you love and look forward to writing a particular subplot or piece of text more than another? Which one and why?

**A:** I actually enjoyed writing the circumcision scene because I wanted readers to be able to visualize it. There was a great challenge in putting that scene on paper in such a way that the reader would be fascinated enough to keep reading, even while they were clenching their thighs together and squirming in their seats.

**Q:** Did you dread or fear writing a particular one? Which one and why?

**A:** I think I dreaded writing Abeni's letter to Chicken at the end of the story. I have a writing mentor, Mel Taylor, author of *The Mitt Man*. Mel actually baby-stepped me through every word of this novel chapter by chapter, and after the first draft of Abeni's letter was written, Mel chastised me and sent me back to the drawing board. He said, "Oh no, baby. Now you're cheating the reader! You can do better than that!" As a result, I went back to my desk and sat down and wrote what had been too painful for me to write initially. Abeni's good-bye letter, which liberated Chicken and gave him the strength to carry on without her.

**Q:** What are you working on next?

**A:** I just finished writing my next novel, *Knockin' Boots,* which is light and very, very sexy!

**Q:** Will we be reunited with Bishop and Malcolm in a future novel?

**A:** I won't totally discount the possibility, but it's highly unlikely. Once I'm finished with a set of characters I generally don't feel moved to write a sequel. But who knows?

## READING GROUP QUESTIONS AND TOPICS FOR DISCUSSION

1. At its heart, this is a love story; and part of love is the sharing of rituals. Poppa Daddy paints Sugar Baby's toenails, and Bishop does the same to Abeni. It is the men's ultimate expression of tender loving care. What rituals have you and your former or current loves relished? What kinds of loving rituals did you witness or experience in your childhood homes?

2. Revenge is a central theme in *A Woman's Worth*. In Chicken's and his parents' lives, in Malcolm's world, and in Abeni and her parents' experience, discuss how revenge is enacted.

3. Black nationalism is a strong theme. Gebra schools Malcolm about the unique power and beauty of Black women; Chicken has devoted himself to having a relationship with Black women and no other ethnic group; and Malcolm and Chicken go "back to Africa." What commentary, if any, do you think author Price-Thompson is making about blackness and Africa? What are your memories and experiences with "Black is Beautiful" or connecting with Africa in some way?

4. A dying Slim Willie urges Chicken to "be a man." Poppa Daddy and Chicken urge Malcolm to do the same. Even Abeni's father Banjoko has his own idea of masculinity. What does being a man mean to Chicken, Malcolm and Abeni, and their families? How do the characters accomplish or fail, given these varying viewpoints?

5. In your life, what do you identify as "being a good strong Black man?" How and when do you teach this to our growing Black boys?

6. What is a woman's worth to Malcolm and to Chicken? How do their perspectives on the feminine change over time?

7. Mizani's father, Dr. Hamid, says, "The virtue of a woman lies in her heart. Not between her legs." Does Abeni ever believe this? How does Abeni's worth and the value of being a woman change over time? Who or what is responsible for this evolution?

8. Bishop believes Abeni's "mentality was shot" as a child—that her female circumcision was so traumatic, and the effects left untreated and unexplored for so long, that they left permanent emotional scars. What were all the effects of Abeni's circumcision?

9. In what physical and emotional ways was Abeni healed? In what ways was she not?

10. Abeni makes a life-altering decision: she sacrifices herself—literally, ultimately—for her child's and her husband's lives and safety. Did you anticipate this or was it a total surprise? Was her family better off with her dead?

11. Abeni and her father Banjoko have a very complex relationship with each other, both in the business and personal realms. In what ways do they express their feelings for each other?

12. Malcolm has features that resemble those of the Kinaksu people. Have you tried to trace your ancestry back to Africa? Have you been told you resemble a particular African cultural group?

13. Jalisa, Abeni's close friend states: "Ain't nothing like a black man. No other man on the face of the earth can hold a light up to

him . . . when a brothah loves you, he loves you right." How is this statement true in the novel and in real life?

14. In the novel, in your own life, and in popular culture, discuss some of the stereotypes African Americans have of Africans? What are some stereotypes Africans have of African Americans?

15. Even though Chicken and Malcolm are not biologically related, they truly are family. Discuss this familial love as it appears in both Chicken/Bishop and Abeni's worlds.

# Tracy Price-Thompson's Recommended Reading

THE HOLY QURAN

THE HOLY BIBLE

MAMA DAY
*by Gloria Naylor*

BAILEY'S CAFÉ
*by Gloria Naylor*

BEFORE THE MAYFLOWER
*by Lerone Bennett*

POSSESSING THE SECRET OF JOY
*by Alice Walker*

THE THIRD LIFE OF GRANGE COPELAND
*by Alice Walker*

THEIR EYES WERE WATCHING GOD
*by Zora Neale Hurston*

HOT JOHNNY AND THE WOMEN WHO LOVED HIM
*by Sandra Jackson Opoku*

ROSA LEE
*by Leon Dash*

## About the Author

TRACY PRICE-THOMPSON is the nationally bestselling author of *Black Coffee, Chocolate Sangria* (a Main Selection of the Black Expressions Book Club), and *A Woman's Worth*. She is a highly decorated Desert Storm veteran who graduated from Army Officer Candidate School after ten years as an enlisted soldier.

A Brooklyn, New York, native and retired army engineer officer, Price-Thompson is a Ralph Bunche Graduate Fellow of Rutgers University who holds an undergraduate degree in business and a master's degree in social work. She lives with her husband and their children in Hawaii, where she is currently at work on her next novel. She can be reached at tracythomp@aol.com.

Tracy is happily and healthily addicted to her husband, Gregory Thompson.

## About the Type

This book was set in Bembo, a typeface based on an old-style Roman face that was used for Cardinal Bembo's tract *De Aetna* in 1495. Bembo was cut by Francisco Griffo in the early sixteenth century. The Lanston Monotype Company of Philadelphia brought the well-proportioned letterforms of Bembo to the United States in the 1930s.